The Captain's Men

The Prayer and her crew have been lost in space for four years. Thomas is lonely and homesick; Zachery is angry and mutinous; Rick is just terrified. And all of them are *really* in need of some hands-on time with their captain.

The only thing holding them together is their captain, whose methods are unconventional but extremely effective. But now the captain has a choice to make: do they continue their fruitless search for a way home or try to start a new life in this strange galaxy?

The Captain's Encounter

The captain's luck is finally changing. They've found an inhabitable planet to land on. The whole crew—and his lovers—are happy to set foot on terra firma again. But the fertile landscape hides a secret. When the captain finds himself abducted by an alien life form, he's got limited time to get back to his crew before they succumb to infighting. Only the alien is so very attractive...

The Captain's Calamity

Having welcomed an alien into his crew and his bed, the captain has more than enough to worry about without the looming threat of a birthday he'd rather forget.

When his ship develops a catastrophic malfunction and crash lands, he and his men follow Rux to an abandoned city in search of replacement parts, one disaster follows another. Worse yet, Zachery, is developing a crush on the one member of the crew he really shouldn't...

The Captain's Promise

Now that the crew of *The Prayer* have settled down on an alien world, their captain intends for them to forge a new life for themselves. But his plans are interrupted when the ship receives a distress call from a nearby planet. While most of his lovers are excited, First Officer Antoine argues that responding might endanger the crew. As it turns out, his fears are well placed...

This is a work of fiction. All characters, places and events are from the author's imagination and should not be confused with fact. Any resemblance to persons, living or dead, events or places is purely coincidental.

Published by
NineStar Press
PO Box 91792
Albuquerque, New Mexico, 87199
www.ninestarpress.com

Warning: This book contains sexually explicit content which is only suitable for mature readers.

Print ISBN #978-1-945952-09-8
Cover by Natasha Snow
Edited by Raevyn

ADRIFT: THE COLLECTION

Volume One

T.J. Land

Dedication

To Kim, Layla and Bianca, with my love. Also to Mark, with something else.

THE CAPTAIN'S MEN

CHAPTER ONE

The captain hated masturbating.

Although, that statement needed a few qualifiers. He didn't hate touching himself. Sliding his hand down his shaft the way he liked it—slow and tight—feeling himself thicken, knowing he had complete control over how long his pleasure lasted—no, he didn't hate *that* at all. And God knew he didn't hate coming. In the last few years, those perfect seconds—when his grip tightened, his body shook, and he didn't have to think about anything at all—had become the best part of each long, tedious day.

No, what he hated were the moments afterward, when the haze of orgasm was just starting to fade, and he needed a lover to give him a deep kiss to ease the transition back to reality, but no one was there.

"Ah, God," he grunted as he thrust into his hand one last time, finding release. His body had been uncooperative today, and he'd almost given up halfway through. But his erections always took ages to subside, and they expected him on the bridge in ten minutes. Moreover, to start the day without at least one orgasm was, for him, worse than foregoing breakfast. He'd have been in a filthy mood for hours. As it was, the white streak now staining his sheets brought him, if not pleasure, then at least a workmanlike sense of satisfaction. *That's over with, then.*

With quick, efficient movements, the captain cleaned up and finished dressing. To his irritation, one of his boot laces snapped when he pulled it tight, and as he looked around for a replacement, his eye fell on the calendar.

Oh. I almost forgot.

It wasn't a proper calendar. He'd finished that one off years ago, although the twelve glossy portraits of shirtless firemen remained in the drawer beside his bed. This one was far simpler—a broad sheet of paper

1

with the days numbered and ticked off in a manner not dissimilar to the sort of thing one would expect to find on the walls of a prison cell. Beneath it, there was a small desk, on which lay a copy of *Lysistrata* bearing the battle wounds of a text that had weathered seventeen re-readings over the course of four years. There was also a pen and a framed photograph of himself and a thin, dark-skinned man with the words *Mon Bien-Aimé* scribbled in the corner. With movements made mechanical by habit, he picked up the former, and on the calendar, he drew a little line next to the one thousand, four hundred, and fifty-three other little lines he'd drawn so far.

He then made the mistake of staring at it for a bit too long. A lump formed in his throat. Swallowing it down, he scolded himself. *Come now. If you're feeling this battered, imagine how the others must be struggling.*

As always, it felt grubby to use the unhappiness of the crew to distract himself from his own encroaching despair, but it worked. While he scanned the room once more for replacement bootlaces, his mind returned to the list of ways he could improve morale he'd been compiling.

One idea occurred to him. It made him smirk and then chuckle, and he dismissed it as ridiculous. But it wouldn't quite go away, instead hovering in a corner at the back of his mind as though waiting patiently for the next opportunity to spring forward.

At last, he abandoned his quest for laces and thought, *Oh, to hell with it.* He kicked both boots off, and then, thrilled to be doing something uncharacteristic for once, he tugged off his socks as well. It wasn't as though it made any difference in the long run.

Barefoot, the captain made his way out of his private quarters and towards the bridge.

☆☆☆

The captain isn't wearing any shoes.

Thomas had developed a crick in his neck from craning his head back for glimpses. As luck would have it, his chair was positioned farthest from the captain's because God hated Thomas and didn't want him to have even one thing in his life that didn't suck.

But Thomas didn't care, not today, because he could see the captain's *feet*. They were long, with high arches and short toes. His toenails were impeccable and even, as if he'd filed them with a ruler and a magnifying glass. Just below his left ankle, there was a scar, like an old burn, and Thomas wondered where it had come from. On the whole, they were much better-looking feet than should have belonged to anyone who'd spent the last four years of their life stranded in deep space, trapped on a ship with twelve crewmembers and one shower.

What made it even weirder was that this was *the captain*. Not quite a month ago, he'd raked Rick over the coals for arriving at his station without having shaved. If Rick, or any of them, had showed up without their shoes on, Thomas had little doubt the captain would have had them shot.

"Thomas!"

Thomas jumped and knocked over the mug of synthesised nutrients that were supposed to be his breakfast. *Shit. Fuck.* He'd been so focused on the captain's feet he hadn't noticed the captain's head swivelling in his direction, like a periscope on a nuclear submarine.

"Yes, sir," he said, swallowing.

Anyone who looked at the captain for long enough would eventually realise they were staring at one of the most handsome men they'd ever seen. However, if they only eyeballed him for a few seconds, the dominant impression would be one of severe austerity. With slightly sunken cheeks and a thin, prominent nose, the captain's face was almost sinister in its sternness, particularly given that the expression most habitual to it was a dark scowl. He had a small, impeccably neat beard, more grey than black, and when you fucked up—and you *would* fuck up—he'd rest his chin in his palm and tilt his head in a way that made you feel like the worst human being alive.

Not only was he doing it right now, the captain was also giving Thomas that rare look he wore when he'd had to say someone's name three times to get them to answer a question. *Shit.* "Tell me, Mister Meléndez; did you, by any chance, have a catastrophic aneurism before arriving at your post this morning?"

"Uh...no. No, sir, I did not."

3

His liquid breakfast had now spread across his station and was beginning to drip onto the floor, each wet *plink* louder and more embarrassing than the last.

"Truly? Is there, then, some problem in your personal life you're working through at the moment?"

"No, sir."

"No, I didn't think there would be. Because you don't have a personal life; do you, Thomas? You barely have a life, in all but the most purely biological sense of the word."

The captain had been born in Cairo—one of the only things anyone knew about him—and his first language was Arabic. When he was pissed, he got a bit of an accent, which Thomas thought was supposed to sound menacing, but it just sounded sexy. He shifted in his seat, hoping the captain wouldn't notice how turned on he was.

Everyone had swivelled around to stare at him with either pity or amusement. *Assholes.* Like they hadn't all been gawking at the captain's feet right along with him a moment ago. Because, of course, no one had any real work to do. Every single screen on the deck was saying the same thing it had been saying for the last one thousand, four hundred, and fifty-three days, which amounted to a big, fat *You're all fucked, boys.*

The captain was now leaning on his chair's left arm, his chin still in his palm. "So what could be the problem, then? After all, no one else seems to be having any difficulty demonstrating a basic level of workplace competence. Let me consult the crew to make sure. Ricardo?"

"Yes, Captain?" said Rick, smirking like the little asshole he was.

"Are you finding your duties particularly onerous today?"

"No, Captain."

"Excellent. Echo? What about you?"

Echo didn't speak—whether he *could* speak was something none of them had yet figured out—so he replied with a languid headshake.

The captain sat back in his chair. "It seems the only person unable to avoid *fucking up my morning* is you, Thomas."

Thomas hung his head. "I'm sorry, sir. Won't happen again."

"If I throw you out the airlock, it won't," agreed the captain. Not for the first time, Thomas reflected that the captain was sort of a massive prima donna. "Now that you've rejoined our ranks, would you be so good as to check whether we've had any communications in the last twelve hours?"

The captain, of course, knew what the answer to that would be. Thomas knew, without even looking. Every single person in the room knew. But they still did this every single day, every single morning, because as long as they did, it meant they hadn't completely given up. So, dutifully, Thomas turned to his screen, ran his fingers over it, and said, "There are no messages today, sir."

Except, perhaps, some tiny stupid part of them was still intent on deluding itself, because as Thomas spoke, he watched disappointment flicker over every face in the room. Even his own shoulders had slumped just a fraction when he turned away from the screen.

The captain's expression, of course, hadn't changed one iota.

"Thank you, Thomas," he said with a touch of sarcasm and then ordered Rick to read out his report on the status of their oxygen garden.

Consumed by embarrassment, Thomas forgot to wonder where the captain's shoes had gone.

☆☆☆

They still didn't know what had happened.

Four years ago, *The Prayer* had been a licensed merchant ship transporting a cargo of building equipment and food to a new settlement on Pluto. The problem was, by the time they got to Pluto, it was a war zone. The enemy—yeah, they had a real name, but you needed mandibles to pronounce it—had arrived. Thomas was one of only one hundred or so humans alive who had seen the enemy close up, and he knew three things about them: they were smarter than humans, meaner than humans, and some could teleport.

He didn't know for sure, but he suspected that last fact had something to do with *The Prayer*'s current predicament.

Long story short, *The Prayer* had found herself surrounded. If it wasn't for the captain, they'd probably all be dead. He'd known what to do, and for a few moments, Thomas had thought they were winning. But the enemy ships had done...something. There'd been a flash of blue light and a noise that almost burst his eardrums, and then everything had gone quiet. A second later, with his ears ringing and spots dancing across his field of vision, Thomas had looked around the bridge, where everyone had the same "did that just happen" expression.

Then, the navigator had said, "Er...captain?"

It had turned out that whatever the enemy had done had transported *The Prayer* to a part of the universe so remote that, even after four years of trying, they had no idea where the Milky Way was. All their attempts to contact Earth, Pluto, or another vessel had failed. If there were any other life forms in this galaxy, they hadn't seen them yet. And so, barring a miracle, none of them were ever going to set foot on Earth again.

Considering that mind-numbing horror, the captain's absent boots shouldn't have been a big deal. But Thomas couldn't stop thinking about them or about the captain's beautiful ankles. He felt like a dork, but it wasn't as though he'd had any fresh fantasies to fuck his fist to in four years.

And, by lucky chance, today it was his turn in the shower.

The Prayer had been an ancient monster when first they'd set out on what was supposed to be her last voyage before being consigned to the scrapheap, but she'd been good to them. All twelve crewmembers had everything they needed to survive however many more years they were alive. The antimatter generator was working fine, so they weren't going to run out of fuel. The medical pod was fully functional. The garden kept them supplied with oxygen and fresh food, although to get sufficient protein they had to supplement their diets with the nutrient shakes and chewable bars that had originally been intended for the settlement on Pluto. Her water recycling systems were still operational, but the plumbing needed work in a few places. The showers were the most prominent example; there were three stalls, but they could only use one at a time. Repairing the problem wasn't difficult in the technical sense—three members of the crew had advanced engineering degrees—but it would require cannibalising parts from elsewhere on the ship, and the captain hadn't authorised that yet. So they had a roster, and the stream cut off after two minutes.

Thomas learned years ago how to get himself off in one minute and thirty seconds.

On the way in, he bumped into Echo, whose upper half was obscured by a stack of towels—washed, ironed, and folded with meticulous care. All Thomas could see was the top of his wispy blond hair.

"Thanks, man," Thomas said awkwardly, taking one. After all, taking care of his laundry wasn't Echo's job. Though, to be honest, Thomas didn't know what Echo's official job was, and neither did anyone else; he seemed to do all the chores the rest of them couldn't be fucked to do themselves.

Echo hung the rest of the towels on a rail and left without saying goodbye. Once he was sure Echo was gone, Thomas stripped, dumping his clothes in a heap to one side. As he did so, he caught a glimpse of his body in the mirror and flinched. He'd been pale and freckled when they'd set off, but four years without sunlight had turned him into a fucking ghost. It had also stripped all the fat off him. Most days, he had his nutrient cup for breakfast, a strip of chewable nutrients for lunch, and for dinner, a bowl of something fresh from the garden—usually beets, cabbage, or spinach. All of which he hated—his palate was still tuned in to burgers and beer—so he didn't eat much. *Enough moping.* Sighing, he made his way over to the shower. He really wanted to jerk off.

So he was *really* pissed when he found someone was already showering. In his time slot.

"Rick, if that's you, I am going to break your fucking..." he began, kicking open the door, and then froze.

"I'm almost done," said the captain, without turning around.

Every curse word Thomas had had lined up on his tongue withered and died because...*Jesus Christ.*

The water in the showers never got hot, so there was almost no steam. He could make out just about every inch of the captain's body, and *fuck.* Thomas *knew* he should look away. He didn't. Instead, his brain started soaking in as many random details as it could. For example, the captain cleaned himself with the same brisk, efficient

7

movements they all did, but he managed to make it look elegant and—*fuck it*—sensuous, like he was in a gay shampoo commercial. Also, wow, he was *tall*. Had he always been so tall? And broad? He'd always loomed over Thomas on the bridge, but now he looked huge, filling every inch of Thomas's vision. Ooh, and then there was his hair. Thomas already had a salt-and-pepper fetish, but now it was soaked and plastered to his scalp, and... His *feet*. His motherfucking *feet*. They were right there, and they were clean and wet, and...and...

Thomas's brain did a record scratch as the water stopped flowing.

"Your turn," said the captain, turning to face him.

Fuck. The thing was, he said it in the same commanding voice he used on the bridge, and he had on the same permanent light scowl Thomas had spent four years crushing on. And...*ah, hell*. Had he caught him staring at his feet? Again?

"Th-thank you, Captain," Thomas said, averting his eyes. Hell if he was going to ask why the captain was showering in his slot. Not after the fiasco that morning.

But the captain didn't step forward to retrieve a towel. Instead, eyes narrowed, he said, "Mister Meléndez, are you a fetishist?"

"Sir?"

"You've been bestowing an inordinate amount of attention on my feet recently," said the captain. "Both of which are, to my mind, unremarkable—unless there's some particular peculiarity about them that you've noted?"

"Um."

"A growth?" the captain pressed. "Or a fungus? Or..."

"You've got nice-looking feet, Captain," Thomas blurted and then wanted to die.

The problem—the real problem here—wasn't just that Thomas was, at heart, a gibbering moron. Nor was it the fact that the captain was gorgeous, brilliant, well read, ruthlessly efficient, and had a sexy, sexy accent. The real problem was that Thomas *liked* him. A lot.

Thomas wasn't much of a rebel, but he didn't usually like the guys he worked for. He did as he was told and kept his opinions to himself. But from the moment he'd been introduced to the captain, he'd been impressed. For all that the captain was a sarcastic prick and would pretty much rip out your liver if you fucked up in front of him, he was the most decent employer Thomas had ever had. Sure, he was *mean*, but he treated them like they were a pack of prized hunting dogs he'd hand-reared from birth—who, every now and then, needed a kick to keep them in line—instead of just a bunch of random assholes thrown together by bad luck. So, yeah, somewhere along the line, Thomas had gotten himself a touch smitten.

The captain's response to his latest idiotic statement was as bad as it could have been. He did that thing with his eyebrows, the thing where they somehow managed to arch and knit simultaneously, and all Thomas could think was that if he'd looked at the enemy like that, they'd have all teleported themselves back to wherever the fuck they'd come from.

"Do you think so?" the captain said, looking down at his own feet.

The captain was *still naked* and...oh, Thomas realised, so was he. He'd already had his clothes off by the time he opened the door, and now he was standing there without a damn thing on, with a body much less defensible than the captain's, and what was becoming an obvious erection.

That was probably why the captain hadn't left yet. Thomas was in his way. So, shoulders hunched, Thomas stepped to one side. As he did, he looked down to see just how bad the situation was and cringed upon remembering that, in addition to his dick being hard as a rock, there was also the god-awful tattoo of a red-tailed hawk adorning the right side of his chest to worry about. He'd got it while drunk off his ass and celebrating his last night on Earth. While it wasn't the worst decision he'd ever made (that award went to the misquoted Yeats poem tattooed on his scalp that his hair thankfully concealed from view), it wasn't the sort of thing the captain would approve of. Thomas suspected that his views on the matter would align with Thomas's uncle, who'd often announced, "The only decorations on a man's body should be scars or medals."

The captain, meanwhile, had reached for a towel and was applying it to his hair. Then he said, "Given that they meet with your approval, perhaps you could save us both time by drying them for me."

Speechless, Thomas could only blink at him. Looking quickly at his face, the captain added, "Otherwise, give me another moment to finish up myself."

At that, Thomas's body gave up on waiting for his brain to unfreeze. Before he knew what he was doing, he'd crossed the floor, stepped into the stall, and knelt at the captain's feet.

The captain's *feet*. Dappled with droplets. Larger than his own, with those ridiculously clean, even toenails. Fuck, he wanted to kiss them.

Thomas's heart sank when he realised he'd forgotten to bring a towel in with him.

"Here," said the captain, offering him one. This close, Thomas could see water clinging to the hair on his chest and that he had a small scar on his upper lip. His expression was, as per usual, sternly authoritative, but his grey eyes had a weird light in them, almost as if he was just a bit drunk. Thomas doubted he was, as the captain only drank brandy, of which they had exactly one bottle on board, and he saved it for special occasions.

Staring up at his face, a pulse of raw fondness went through Thomas's body, and he knew what to do. Taking the towel, he returned his attention to the captain's feet and made his hand into a cup. The captain caught on, lifting his foot and sliding his heel into Thomas's palm. For a bizarre moment, Thomas felt like he was Cinderella's prince, holding up the glass slipper. The lapse into fairy-tale romantic shit made him feel like a pervert, because while his brain was flooding with mushy nonsense, the rest of him just wanted the captain to press his heel against Thomas's hard, aching dick.

Thomas dried the foot slowly, trying not to make it seem like he was caressing it—even though he totally was. The whole time, he was conscious of the captain's dick just beside his head.

"Need to..." Thomas cleared his throat. "I need to do the back of your heels, sir. Can you turn round?"

"I suppose I can," said the captain, and Thomas could hear the smirk in his voice. As he turned, Thomas couldn't resist the chance to sneak a quick peek, now that he wasn't being watched.

Holy fuck. The captain's ass was *amazing.* And Thomas wasn't just speaking as some guy who hadn't had sex in four years. Once upon a time, Thomas was something of an ass *connoisseur.* In college, he'd whored his way through fifteen lecturers and an eighth of the student body. But not one of them held a candle. Sure, Thomas had known the captain was scarily fit. When they'd left Earth, he'd looked athletic, like an Olympic diver, even with his clothes on, and he hadn't lost an inch of musculature in four years. God knew how—they had a gym, but no one had ever seen the captain in it, unless he timed his visits to make sure they wouldn't. The view of his ass offered by his smart, snug pants had already been promising, but the reality was just...wow.

I want to touch him everywhere. Thomas thought he might want that more than anything in the world. More than getting home, even.

"You can touch me, if you'd like."

The captain was peering back at him over his shoulder, his eyelids hooded.

Oh. He... All right, then.

Thomas dropped the towel and slid his hands up the captain's thighs. On the left, he found yet another old scar, like a nasty burn, and on the right, only smooth, warm skin. As Thomas moved his hands over the captain's ass, which felt as perfect as it looked, the captain gave an appreciative rumble. Thomas leaned forward and pressed his lips into the small of the captain's back.

He smells like soap, Thomas thought, which was a dumb thing to focus on at a time like this—*of course* he did, he'd just finished showering—but he'd always thought the captain would smell like the sort of rich-guy cologne his dad used to wear. Not honeysuckle.

Meanwhile, his other hand slid round to brush against the captain's cock, tentatively, in the hopes that maybe—*please, God, please*—the captain would let him give him a handjob. Not to brag, but Thomas gave the best handjobs ever. So he was nothing short of fucking delighted upon finding that the captain was already hard.

This is the best day of my life.

When Thomas wrapped his hand around the captain's cock, while simultaneously applying his teeth, very gently, to the curve of his ass, the result was everything he could have hoped for. The captain bucked, his hips jerking forward and sending his cock into Thomas's grip, and he made a gorgeous noise. Glancing up, Thomas saw that his arms were now braced against the tiles, and his shoulders were heaving with deep, steady pants.

By this point, Thomas was desperate to jerk off, but that would have meant removing one of his hands from the captain's body. Something he was not even remotely inclined to do. So he shuffled forward on his knees until he was able to press himself against the back of the captain's leg.

"What long fingers you have," the captain said, and one of his hands came down to enfold the hand Thomas had wrapped around his cock. "Like a pianist."

The compliment made his heart flutter like a lovesick teenager's. "Thank you, sir. Actually, in school I used to play the flute."

He gave the captain's cock a gentle squeeze and rubbed his thumb over the tip. The captain hissed and replied, "Yes, I'm sure you did. May I fellate you?"

"Sir?" Thomas squeaked, freezing in place.

The captain sighed. "Would you object to my sucking your cock, Mister Meléndez?"

"Um. No, sir."

Thomas's legs shook as he stood—with lust or fear, he wasn't sure which—and he was worried they'd give way. But the captain took hold of him and, in one smooth motion, had him up against the wall, giving one of his nipples a pinch before sliding to his knees. If there was anything in this world that could rival the sight of the captain naked in the shower, it was the sight of the captain naked and kneeling in the shower, his hair still damp and his shoulders even more densely packed with muscle when viewed from above.

I am the luckiest motherfucker alive, Thomas told himself.

"Lovely," the captain murmured as he inspected Thomas's erection, like it was a fucking *objet d'art*. Then he took Thomas into his mouth and his throat.

Thomas swore and regretted it because he knew the captain didn't like cursing. But Jesus H., the captain sucked cock like a specialist. He gave Thomas the most generous tongue bath he'd ever had, and when Thomas came in his mouth, he swallowed every last drop and licked him clean.

Content, Thomas relaxed against the shower wall as the captain rose to his feet and bracketed his face with his hands. He was sort of flushed, and his thin lips were pinker than usual.

"Say, Captain?" Thomas asked, reaching down to finish the handjob. "What *did* happen to your shoes, exactly?"

The captain wrapped one arm around his waist and pulled him tight against his chest. Peppering his neck and jaw with kisses, he mumbled, "One of the laces snapped. I didn't have a spare pair on hand. And I prefer to arrive on the bridge punctually. *Ah!*"

Thomas grinned in victory as the captain's hips snapped forward. "Maybe you tie 'em too tight, sir. That can wear them out."

The captain gave him a sharp-toothed grin. It made him look a lot younger and sexy as hell. "It's true, I do prefer *tight* things."

Oh, I am way too into you, Thomas thought.

He wanted to watch the captain's face while he made him come, but the captain was a fucking excellent kisser, and Thomas contented himself with hearing him give a muffled groan. For a while afterwards, they just stayed like that, Thomas leaning against the wall with the captain's hands on his ass.

Thomas licked his lips. "I can lend you some laces, sir. I've got spares. They're in my quarters. Under my bunk, I think."

"How very kind of you, Thomas. We'd best retrieve them."

"Um...actually, sir, how about I go and get them myself?" said Thomas, wincing as he remembered the state of his room. He couldn't let the captain think he was a fucking animal. "Then maybe I could meet you in your quarters, and...and help you lace them up?"

"All right. I'll meet you there in ten minutes. After all—" He glanced down at Thomas's abdomen, stained with a thick streak of come. "—you do still need to shower."

☆☆☆

13

"Fuck me," Thomas rasped an hour later, rolling onto his back.

"Again, Thomas?" asked the captain with some amusement. "I'm afraid you'll have to wait a while before that's possible. Maybe in the meantime you could have another go at me?"

It was stupid, but Thomas giggled anyway, cuddling up to his chest. This had been the best day he'd had in four years. Actually, if he was honest, it was probably the best day he'd had in about ten. He wanted to run a victory lap around the ship. He wanted to get a picture of the captain's face and the words "Guess who just tapped that" tattooed right next to the stupid hawk. He wanted to show up on the bridge bare-ass naked tomorrow, so everyone could see all the teeth marks (damn, the captain sure was *bitey*. He also wanted a cigarette, but he pushed the craving aside. When Fate was being this good to you, it didn't pay to push your luck.

"There's come trickling out of you. Would you mind if I licked it up?" the captain asked, in the same polite, inquiring tones he'd asked for everything else so far. Thomas knew it was an affectation—the captain was many things, but politely restrained, he fucking well was *not*. But it was still hot, and Thomas swallowed as he nodded and rolled over.

The captain's tongue was warm, and it tickled. Thomas bit his lip, and as he did, his gaze happened to fall on the captain's desk. When Thomas had come in with the laces, the captain had been standing at it, looking at a framed picture which he'd quickly put face down before drawing Thomas in for a kiss. Thomas only got a glimpse of it—two figures, one of whom looked like the captain.

Thomas had known better than to ask. They all had people they missed.

"Sir?" he said as the captain's manicured nails dug into his thighs. "Can we do this again sometime?"

"We can do it again in half an hour, Thomas, if you'll just be patient."

"I mean—"

"And we can do it tomorrow," the captain confirmed, licking a stripe across his ass. "And the next day, too, if you like."

"S-sounds good, Captain."

☆☆☆

On the bridge the next morning, it was like it had never happened. "Mister Meléndez," barked the captain. "Any messages?"

His boots were back on, laced up good and tight. Thomas spared them a glance before checking his screen and answering, "No, sir. Not today."

But today it seemed as though the barb of disappointment was less sharp than it had been yesterday. After all, life on *The Prayer* wasn't that bad. Not so long as they still had running water... and the captain.

☆☆☆

As experiments go, that one was a winner, thought the captain. He'd known since Thomas had first joined the crew that the younger man had been attracted to him, but he'd had no idea he was such a passionate lover. Once the shyness started to fade, Mister Meléndez also proved a lively conversationalist—particularly on the subjects of conspiracy theories and bird watching, oddly enough—and willing to indulge the captain's propensity to ramble about Aristophanes. Over the next few days, they came to a very agreeable arrangement made up of casual but regular liaisons in the shower or the captain's quarters.

But the captain slowly became aware of an unforeseen snag.

His body seemed to have come alive again. It was as though someone had flipped a switch; it not only wanted sex all the time, it needed it, keened for it. It didn't seem to matter where he was or what he was doing. On the bridge while issuing orders, in the cargo bay while inspecting their supplies, at the dinner table surrounded by the crew—without warning, his cock would stir and his lips would start to tingle. He'd taken to resting a holo-tablet in his lap to disguise the problem.

Constant arousal was not, he acknowledged, a dilemma with which he was unfamiliar. His libido had always been high. On Earth, before *The Prayer* had embarked on her fateful voyage, he'd been part of a tetrad, and all of his lovers had teased him for being the most shameless slut they'd ever met. Even so, he was taken aback by how...*vigorous* he felt. In another life, he'd always found that after fasting for a lengthy enough period, he simply lost interest in food. He'd somehow assumed his four-year abstinence would have reduced his appetite for sex in much the same way.

Ah, well. Nothing to be done about it. It would hardly do for him to go about seducing every member of his crew. No, he wouldn't be greedy.

Chapter Two

One of the first things Rick had learned upon boarding *The Prayer* was that the captain and his first officer didn't always get on.

"Why are we even arguing about this, you witless geriatric?" shrieked First Officer Antoine, who had one of those nasally, high-pitched voices that made every word sound like you were being stabbed in the ear.

"We are not 'arguing.' I am issuing an *order*, and you are being *insubordinate*," the captain hissed. They'd been at it for twenty minutes, and he'd started sporting what Rick thought of as the "scary, bug-eyed, axe-murderer" look. It wasn't that Antoine wasn't good at his job. It was just that somewhere along the line, he seemed to have decided that one of the most important duties of his job entailed turning the captain into a crazy person.

Operations on the bridge ground to a halt as everyone took a break from work to observe the unfolding spectacle. Since the holodeck had broken down, arguments between the captain and his second-in-command were by far the most novel source of entertainment available. Across the room, Thomas was miming eating popcorn.

Today's cabaret came down to the fact that there was a system with three rocky planets in the Goldilocks Zone—not too hot, not too cold, just the right distance from the sun for liquid water—not far from where they were currently drifting. For months now, Antoine had been saying they should check them out, maybe attempt a landing. Every time he brought it up, the captain refused point-blank. It was the most common source of their shouting matches, and today, just like every day, it had started as a perfectly reasonable conversation between two intelligent authority figures. But like a snowball rolling downhill, it had gained speed and momentum, and now they were snarling at each other like angry dogs, hackles up and fists balled.

In essence, the captain's argument was that there was, for the moment, no reason for them to land. They weren't in any danger of running low on food or fuel, and they had no idea how hostile any of the three worlds was to life. More to the point, landing on an uncharted world without permission from the powers that be was one of the most illegal things a commercial vessel could do. Antoine's argument was much simpler and, so far as Rick was concerned, a lot more compelling; they were bored, and who would know?

Rick didn't have a horse in this race—not that he didn't want to get off the ship—because he wasn't eager to go hunting for signs of life in unknown and, quite possibly, dangerous territory. No, what drew his attention was the rare spectacle of the captain losing his temper. For all that he was naturally impatient and liked to bark out orders left and right, he hardly ever lost it as bad as he was losing it right now. Untidiness might turn him into a bitch, incompetence might turn him into an autocrat, but only Antoine could make him go all-out Vice Admiral Bligh. And today, Antoine was goading him because Antoine was a motherfucker. A *French* motherfucker, no less. (Well, French-Senegalese, whatever.)

Antoine slapped one of his skinny girl-hands down on the report he'd brought in to try to prove his case. "This data indicates that two of those worlds register an eight on the Ons-Cabet Planetary Habitability Scale. They have water. They have *oceans*, for fuck's sake!"

"Why do you need an ocean?!" the captain roared. "How will an ocean improve our situation? Unless one of those worlds happens to be host to an alien species so technologically advanced they can reverse time and prevent us from ever having left Earth in the first place, they are of no practical use to us!"

"So you'd have us spend the rest of our lives floating aimlessly through space, trapped in this ancient crate, waiting for the life support systems to fail?"

"Our navigators are working tirelessly to—" began the captain, preparing to launch into a speech they'd all heard at least five times now.

But this time, Antoine cut him off. "To do what? Even if we knew where the Milky Way was, what good would that do us? It's impossible for us to get there, scientifically impossible. *We are never, ever going home!* How long is it going to take you to wake up to that fact?"

Oh, shit just got real, thought Rick. Everyone in the room stopped breathing, watching them. It wasn't like Antoine was saying something they didn't already know. They knew. They knew damn well. But they didn't talk about it, not like that. Certainly not in front of the captain.

The captain, whose face had drained of colour, opened his mouth, shut it, and opened it again.

"Get out of my sight," he said, a strange rattling sound coming from his throat.

Even Antoine looked spooked. He took a step back, eyes narrowed, like something feral caught in a trap. Then, all at once, he turned on his heel and stormed out of the room.

No one said anything. The captain just stood there, fists clenched, with that terrible look on his face. Then he got a hold of himself and grunted, "Get back to work."

For the next half hour, the bridge was as quiet as the grave.

☆☆☆

After that complete shitstorm, Rick felt entitled to a little "him" time, so he went to the garden.

The garden was Rick's favourite part of the ship. Actually, it was one of his favourite places to be, full stop. If someone gave him a choice between being at home lying on the beach watching girls oil themselves up and being in the garden? No contest. The garden was all his. It was the one place on the ship where no one was more competent than he was.

At twenty-one, Rick was the youngest member of the crew, and the others loved to give him shit for it. The only one who didn't was Echo, but he didn't give anyone shit because he was basically a robot. Everyone else treated him like a brat, as though he didn't know a damned thing. But in here? In here, he was God. His dad had owned the best flower shop in Salvador, and when Rick was a kid, he'd planned to be a horticulturalist. He knew plants, he liked plants, and plants liked him.

19

The Prayer's garden had flourished under his touch—the cabbage, the radishes, the broccoli, and the spinach. The crew ate damn well considering their circumstances, and it was all thanks to him. He liked knowing that—and that everyone else knew it too.

So the garden was understood to be his turf. No one questioned what he got up to in here, even though everyone was aware of the patch, just at the garden's leftmost edge, where Rick had been growing excellent weed for the last four years. Right now, he was curled up by the spinach with a joint at his side, and as was customary on occasions like this, he'd just finished jerking off.

When Rick heard the doors slide open and close again, he rolled his eyes and bit back a curse. Typical. The assholes he lived with always had to come wandering in when he was trying to have a little privacy. Maybe they wouldn't notice him if he stayed down, because as much as he hated being reminded of the fact, he was short.

He heard footsteps somewhere in the vicinity of the broccoli. They were too heavy to belong to Thomas and too slow for Echo. In fact, they sounded a lot like...

Carefully, Rick craned his neck up over the spinach leaves.

Goddamn it all to hell. The captain, of all people, had decided to pay the garden a visit. He was standing at the edge of the broccoli patch, his hands clasped behind his back.

What the fuck was the captain doing in the garden? Did he also come here to jerk off?

Not likely, Rick thought. The captain hardly needed to resort to his own hand for companionship. Everyone knew he was fucking Thomas, ever since Thomas—the smug asshole—had started wearing short sleeves so everyone could see the hickeys. And even if Thomas wasn't available, pretty much every other guy on the ship would hump the captain's leg if given half the chance. There were a lot of theories as to why, in the year 2195, heterosexual men were a distinct minority on commercial space vessels. Rick's mom had been a sociologist, and she'd written a long book about extraplanetary same-sex relationship dynamics, which he'd gotten two pages into before all the long words had him throwing it into a corner. Rick, for his part, hadn't ever dipped his toe in those particular waters, and he doubted he ever would. He liked women, worse luck for him. Of the four on board, Irene was old enough to be his mom, Khali was a lesbian, Cecelia hated him, and Yanmei was way, way out of his league (and probably sleeping with Khali).

Maybe, now and then, he'd notice that Zachery had impressive biceps, or that Thomas had this one thick, curling lock of hair that looked cute when it fell across his eyes. It didn't mean anything.

He craned his head up and looked again. The captain wasn't doing any of the things people usually came down here to do—which was either smoke weed with Rick or lay on the soil and pretend they were back home having a picnic at the park. The captain was just standing there, back straight, posture perfect. Rick couldn't see his face, but his head was tilted downwards, as though he was trying to establish a psychic connection with the broccoli.

Why is everyone I work with so fucking weird?

Then Rick's eyes widened. He'd heard a sound, a sound he thought he knew, but it couldn't be...

Holy shit. Was the captain *crying*?

The quiet noise came again, like a tiny gasp. There wasn't anyone else in the room but the two of them, and watching very, very closely, Rick detected an almost imperceptible tremble in the captain's shoulders.

It scared him more than anything he'd seen in his life (and Rick had seen *some shit*). Because the captain, *their* captain, didn't get upset. Not *crying* upset. Even when they'd first tried to contact Earth—after the encounter with the enemy had left them drifting who the fuck knew where—and got no response. Or when they'd first looked out the porthole and seen that all the constellations were unfamiliar. And not even when they'd woken up to the fact that not one of them was ever going home, had the captain seemed distressed about it. He'd been angry, scarily angry, but crying? No. Not the captain. Rick had been the one crying—like a bitch—because even though he didn't have many friends left on Earth, he hadn't been able to deal with the idea of never seeing his mom again.

What the hell had happened? Was it just Antoine and his crap? No way. They fought all the time. Rick sometimes thought they enjoyed it. No way was that enough to make the captain cry.

Maybe he's had some bad news, Rick thought suddenly. What, though? One of the very few advantages of being lost in space was that they never got bad news. Space was boring as fuck.

Oh, shit. Maybe he's sick. Maybe he's just found a giant tumour in his gut. Or maybe there's something wrong with the ship, something we can't repair, and we're all going to be dead in hours. Or maybe he's finally run out of brandy.

The longer Rick crouched there, spying on him, the worse he felt. The smart thing to do would be to stay hidden until the captain left. If he'd come here hoping no one would see him having his nervous breakdown—or whatever the hell this was—chances were he'd be *pissed* to find out Rick had been watching. So he should probably just...

Then the captain gave another of those quiet, barely perceptible gasping noises, like someone who was trying as hard as they could not to sob, and something in Rick's chest twisted.

Fuck it.

He stood up and said, "Captain?"

The captain froze and then turned, as if in slow motion, to look at him. His eyes were red and wet, but he hadn't let a single drop out onto his face. *Thank God.* Maybe Rick could pretend he hadn't heard anything.

"Ricardo," said the captain. He didn't sound pissed—well, yes, he did, but that was just the captain's normal way of speaking. As casually as he could, Rick crossed over to the broccoli patch.

"Whadya doing here, sir?" he asked, as though he hadn't noticed. Most of the crew already thought he was stupid—he was the only one among them who hadn't finished school—and playing dumb worked pretty well for him.

Suddenly, it dawned on Rick that even though he'd finished the joint an hour ago, the smell was probably still clinging to his clothes. *Fuck.* It wasn't like the captain didn't know about his hobby, but Rick had always tried to be discreet about it. The captain was so picture-perfect, with his square jaw, clean fingernails, and flawless speech; just being near him made you ashamed of your bad habits.

The captain didn't reply, and an awkward silence settled. Rick rubbed the back of his head, trying to think of something to say, but everything he came up with sounded stupid.

Eventually, when he couldn't stand it anymore, he blurted out, "Has something bad happened, sir?"

The way the captain's stony expression flickered, and the tiny wince that went through him, told Rick he'd fucked up. Should have kept his stupid mouth shut because the captain's eyes were still wet and...and that looked so *wrong*, so unnatural. *Stupid, Rick. Stupid!*

"No," said the captain, looking away. "Nothing has happened."

And Rick just kept right on talking, like the filter on his mouth was broken. "If...if something *has* happened, sir, can I...help? Like, at all?"

Even as he said it, all he could think of was how little he could do, how the others treated him like the most useless member of the crew, and he wasn't always sure they were wrong. If their captain had a problem even *he* couldn't solve, what use could Rick possibly be?

Once again the captain fell silent, but this time Rick watched him closely and saw his jaw was locked and his brow creased in concentration. It was very similar to the way Rick's mom had looked the day he'd told her he was joining *The Prayer*'s crew and he'd be gone for at least three years—like she was summoning every inch of her will not to break apart in front of him. Rick panicked and did the only thing he could think of doing. He took a step forward, raised himself onto the tips of his toes, and gave the captain the tiniest bird peck on the cheek, just like he'd given his mom.

"Quit crying, sir. Please?"

As noted, Rick was short, and when they were this close, he had to tilt his head up to meet the captain's gaze. As he did, he found the captain staring at him as though the kiss had surprised him as much as it had surprised Rick. Then he cupped Rick's jaw and, bending down, pressed his mouth over Rick's.

Fuck. Fuck. Fuck. What the hell is he...
Oh.

...

Ooooh...

When he drew back, Rick just gaped at him, slack-jawed, his thoughts scattered about his brain like shrapnel. What the hell had just happened? What the hell had he done? Men weren't his thing. Yeah, he could admit, the captain was hot. So what? Didn't mean he liked him. Okay, yes, he liked the captain. The captain was the biggest badass ever. But he was, like, a billion years old—or forty, whatever — and he was a guy. Rick didn't go in for guys.

Even if they did smell nice, and their hands were big and warm, and their faces were right there...

Ah, hell.

The captain's beard was scratchy, and his teeth seemed kind of sharp as he dragged them over Rick's lower lip. Maybe all guys had sharp teeth. Rick wouldn't know.

What he did know was that one of the captain's hands was now pressing into the small of his back, making him arch up and...*oh, fuck*, press his dick against the captain's thigh, which was firm and strong and...and...*fuck*. When the hell had he gotten hard? He'd already gotten off just a half hour ago.

The captain pulled him closer, and Rick whimpered at the reminder of how strong he was. *He could pick me up in one hand*, he thought, unable to account for why the prospect made him horny as fuck and a bit dizzy to boot.

By the time their lips broke apart, allowing them a moment to pant and regard one another, Rick had pretty much finished his personal crisis. He didn't do guys. But this wasn't just some guy, this was the captain. The captain was special. And tall, and handsome, and sexy in an old-guy kind of way.

Maybe I can cheer him up, Rick thought suddenly. *Maybe that's one thing I can do.*

He buried his face in the captain's chest, which was as warm as a furnace. His heartbeat was steady and strong, and Rick moaned as he felt the captain's hand slide down the back of his pants to squeeze his bare ass.

"Do you wanna…sir, do you wanna…"

He didn't know exactly what he was offering, other than whatever the captain needed to pep himself up. He knew what guys did together; he wasn't *that* young, but just the thought of it scared him to death. On the other hand, he was feeling really good right now, and he sort of wanted to let the captain pick him up and just…use him, however he wanted. Also, there was the little fact that the captain's erection was now pressing against his own, and yikes, he was fucking huge.

"May I remove your shirt?" the captain rumbled in his ear.

"What? Oh. Uh, sure, Captain."

Rick knew he was hot—he worked out every day, and he didn't have any embarrassing tattoos, unlike certain people he could name—but he still felt self-conscious as the captain tugged off his vest. Anyone would. The captain was *cut*.

"Hold on," said the captain, and Rick realised he meant it literally when the captain hoisted him off the ground and held him high enough that his eyes were level with Rick's collarbone. He didn't show any sign of exertion at all; it was as though Rick was a puppy instead of a five-foot grown man.

"Captain…?" Rick ventured. Then, he yelped as the captain licked one of his nipples.

"You make the most appealing noises," the captain observed. "Out of interest, have you ever been with a man?"

Oh, God. This was the part where Rick admitted his experience was limited to a spectacularly bad blowjob from the only girlfriend he'd ever had. After she'd dumped him, he'd been too fucking miserable to do anything besides look around for any off-planet work that would have him. He'd have to admit he was just a dumb fucking *kid*.

"Not really, Captain." Rick had wrapped his arms around the captain's shoulders, clinging in a way that made him feel childish but helped keep his nerves in check.

"Oh? Then should I be flattered to be your exception?" the captain asked, as Rick squirmed in his arms. "Or am I your last resort? Perhaps you've already tried out the rest of the crew…"

"Captain!" Rick cried, aware he was being teased. In retaliation, he

25

wrapped his legs around the captain's waist and landed a kiss on the tip of his nose. "Quit being mean. Only just now found out I've got a thing for hot old guys."

The captain barked a laugh and gave his ass a swat. And oh, hey, *that* was surprisingly nice. Hell of a day for untimely revelations.

"Insolent brat," the captain said before kissing him again. By this point, Rick was damn near ready to go off, having been stiff as a board for the last five minutes. But he didn't want to come before the captain did or for the captain to think he was only interested in his own enjoyment, or that he lacked self-control. The captain, he knew, put a lot of store in self-control. So he willed his body to behave and said, "Captain, you... Whatcha want, Captain?"

He could feel the other man's cock underneath his ass, pressing against his crack. And yeah, Rick was nervous. He was man enough to admit that.

"Mm," the captain mused, nuzzling his neck. "Why don't you fuck me?"

The captain was really bad for the shock absorbers in Rick's brain. But Rick wasn't a quitter. "Okay, Captain. Sure. Ah...here?"

"I was thinking of your quarters, actually," said the captain.

Ah, hell. Rick winced as he envisioned the catastrophic mess that was his floor, and his bed, and his cupboard, and how the captain would react to his posters of naked ladies in cowboy hats.

Maybe if the sex is good enough, he won't notice.

☆☆☆

As it turned out, Rick was awesome at this whole "fucking men" thing.

Unless the captain was just a good actor. But even so, Rick had made him come; he could see it drying on the sheets as they lay beside one another, panting. So there was concrete proof he'd done something right. And wow, the captain was *pretty* when he came, his skin glistening and his eyes dark as coals, and he made this really hot moan too. Rick wished he'd recorded it, so he could play it back every night before he went to sleep.

"Good work, Ricardo," the captain said, rolling over and pinning him to the mattress. It smelt like weed, but he hadn't said anything. "Ten out of ten."

"Thanks, sir," Rick said, both arms around the captain's waist. The captain, it turned out, was a cuddler. Who knew?

Rick wanted to ask him again what had been wrong, why he'd been crying, but at the same time, he didn't want to remind him about whatever it was. So he kept his mouth shut and instead, wondered how long he would need to wait to suggest a second round. He didn't want the captain to think he was a giant whore or anything.

"In future, I'd appreciate it if you avoided masturbating in the garden," said the captain. "I like to maintain a certain standard of hygiene on this ship."

"Sorry, Captain. Won't happen again."

The captain made a sceptical noise. "So you say. Even so, I think we'll do this once a day for the foreseeable future, to ensure you aren't tempted."

"Sounds good to me, sir."

☆☆☆

Damn.

The captain soothed his conscience with the reminder that it had been an accident. It wasn't as though he'd scripted that pointless, ugly argument with Antoine, or he'd wanted Rick to catch him snivelling like a schoolboy, or that he'd ever even considered Rick as a potential romantic companion.

But he couldn't say he regretted it in the least. Rick had been perfect, responsive and eager and surprisingly intuitive for a man his age. And, yes, the captain could admit the experience had been a boost to his ego. He'd had several bisexual partners in the course of his life, but there was something deeply flattering about being another man's first.

However, enough was enough. He had Thomas and Rick now, two warm, skilled lovers, and a quiet discussion at breakfast the morning after his tryst with Rick had confirmed that neither of them objected to the other's presence in his bed. At some point, he'd need to get all of them in the same room so they could have "the conversation," the one that would end with drinks and a threesome with any luck.

Two lovers. More than enough. From now on, he would control himself.

CHAPTER THREE

It was easy to lose one's sense of time on *The Prayer*. No day, no night, no weather. No browning leaves, no spring buds, no snow. No relatives whose birthdays they had to remember.

Not that Echo had any relatives. It pleased him to allow Thomas and the others to believe the reason he had no last name was because he'd been manufactured in a secret government laboratory. The reality was far more mundane; Echo had been born on the moon, shortly after a series of economic catastrophes had left the satellite's infrastructure and public services in tatters. As a result of this spectacularly bad luck, he'd spent the first fifteen years of his life being circulated through a foster care system so inept and badly managed that he'd never been given a legal surname.

Which had never bothered him much. No, what had bothered him was not having a birthday. Not because he liked cake, balloons, and presents. (Although he did occasionally wonder whether he might have enjoyed such things if he had ever experienced them.) No, what he found perturbing was never being exactly sure how old he was. He was, in all likelihood, twenty-seven. But twenty-seven and *what*? How many days, how many weeks, how many months until he was twenty-eight? Such questions ate at Echo. Seven different foster parents had observed that he had an unchildlike fondness for precision. "Creepy," they'd called it.

Still, one played with the hand one was given. He dealt with it and *The Prayer*'s current predicament by maintaining a rigorous daily schedule, carefully timing all his activities.

Getting up, getting dressed, completing his ablutions—because, contrary to speculation, he was not a robot—took him seven minutes. Walking to the mess hall, preparing himself a nutrient cup, and drinking it—ten minutes. Preparing breakfast for Moxie, the ship's cat—three minutes. Filling up the captain's cup with something that tasted like coffee and putting it on a tray with a bowl of something that tasted like oatmeal—eight minutes. Carrying the tray to the captain's quarters and knocking on the door—four minutes.

That was where his schedule became fuzzy. Recently, the time it took the captain to respond would vary depending on whether he had someone in his bed with him, and what sort of thing they'd been doing when he knocked. Today, however, the door opened promptly.

"Echo. Good morning," the captain greeted. He was wearing only white cotton briefs that were, Echo thought, a size too small. Perhaps Thomas had left them behind and he'd put them on by mistake. Or perhaps he just enjoyed the constriction.

Echo responded with a nod, carrying the tray into the room and ascertaining with a glance that the bed was empty. What wasn't empty was the captain's desk. Three holo-tablets lay open upon it, each one projecting a different three-dimensional light show. After putting down the captain's breakfast, Echo went over to tidy up, as he did every morning. It was because of his willingness to tend to such chores that the rest of the crew thought his relationship with the captain was sycophantic. In all honesty, Echo had no idea whether or not they were right. There had been few people in his life who'd hung around for any extended period of time, a fact he had attributed to his alleged "creepiness." The number of actual relationships he'd had—sycophantic, romantic, companionable or otherwise—was in the low single digits.

But if he was a sycophant, then it couldn't be such a bad thing for a man to be. After all, the captain valued and liked him, and the captain was the finest judge of character Echo knew.

"Leave those," said the captain, taking his not-coffee, just as Echo was about to clear away the tablets. "I promised Antoine I'd look over them."

Echo very much doubted the exchange had been quite so civil.

"He's still trying to convince me to authorise an exploratory mission to the Holy Trinity," the captain continued, crossing over to the desk and brushing his fingertips over the tablets. The lightshow changed to three spherical objects, each a different size, hovering in space. "That's what he's calling them now."

Echo made a face.

"Yes, I quite agree," said the captain. Moxie, who had slunk in after Echo, twined about the captain's ankles and received a rough stroke.

As the captain gazed at Antoine's models, Echo, in turn, gazed at his briefs. He couldn't decide whether or not they were doing anything for him—which wasn't an uncommon problem for Echo.

The rumor he was a robot had begun when the rest of the crew had learned he didn't like porn. Not the sort of thing his coworkers would have been aware of under ordinary circumstances, but in the last four years, porn had become one of their primary means of entertaining themselves. As a result, Echo's preference for filling up the empty hours with laundry and cooking had been noted and remarked upon. No one had been all that surprised; Echo disliked conversation, music, gambling, and sports, so it made sense to them that he'd dislike sex too.

In truth, Echo didn't dislike sex. Nor was he entirely disinterested in it, like Antoine. He'd had sex three times in his life, with men and women, and liked it very much. But the fact was—perhaps as a result of his apparent "creepiness"—he often felt disconnected from other people, even those he loved. He could register that a treasured friend was sexually attractive but still find the idea of having sex with them strange and unnerving. And watching the strangers in Rick's film collection copulate made him ill.

So, although he admired the way the captain's briefs clung to his buttocks and drew attention to his powerful thighs, Echo wasn't sure whether today was one of those days when his body wanted to do more than just look.

"This one here—" The captain pointed to the central sphere, the largest. "—is apparently the likeliest candidate for conditions compatible with sustaining life."

The captain's expression took on that deep bleakness he never wore when any of the other crewmembers were present. "Which hardly makes the decision any easier. The whole point of landing on a viable world would be to terraform it so we could consider settling there in the long term. If the planet is already host to life—any life, even bacteria—we

31

ADRIFT: THE COLLECTION | T.J. LAND

can't contemplate such an action without violating the Planetary Preservation Convention. Do you remember when they first started terraforming Ganymede? Decades upon decades of red tape and environmental protests, and there's nothing *on* Ganymede but rocks and ice."

Echo didn't proffer an opinion. He never did, which was, he suspected, one of the main reasons the captain confided in him so readily. He did, however, reach out and briefly lay a hand on the captain's arm, his cheeks heating at the sensation of warm skin and solid muscle. It seemed as though today was one of those days after all.

The planets disappeared as the captain deactivated all three tablets and put them in a neat stack on the edge of his desk. "I received a message from Zachery a few minutes ago. No specifics, but apparently it's 'urgent.' Do you know anything about it?"

Echo shook his head.

"That man is impossible to deal with," the captain muttered, in a tone of voice bordering on sulky. "Why did I hire him in the first place?"

Impatient now, Echo took a step forward and pressed his fingertips lightly against the captain's lower lip.

"Oh," said the captain, catching on. "You...?"

Echo nodded and tapped his wrist. Much as he wanted to linger now that he knew what he wanted, he'd been here for eight minutes. He was falling behind schedule.

He lay a hand against the captain's jaw, feeling the faintest trace of stubble, and their lips met, tentative at first, then hungry. The kisses they shared were always a comforting reminder of how well they knew one another. Understanding there were several places on Echo's body where he preferred not to be touched, the captain's hands folded around the back of his scalp, never once straying below Echo's shoulders. Echo appreciated his consideration and returned the gesture with a soft hum, a noise only the captain had ever heard him make.

And then, he'd had enough. Content, as though he'd eaten a pleasant but filling meal, he drew back and bowed his head in thanks.

"No, thank *you*, my friend," said the captain with courtly politeness, his brief smile bright and fond.

After collecting the captain's laundry, Echo left him to finish his breakfast. There was, after all, much to be done.

☆☆☆

Well, that didn't really count, did it?

After all, Echo had been with him from the start. Long before his recent return to sexual activeness and their encounter with the aliens, Echo had been arriving at his door every morning with breakfast and, now and then, a kiss. Just a kiss, usually, and months could go by without his asking for more. The captain had never pushed him, understanding that for some, an occasional kiss was enough.

Still, a kiss was just a kiss. Echo didn't count as a *lover* by any reasonable metric. A romantic friend, perhaps. Unless the word "lover" referred more to being in love than to making love, in which case, fine, he probably did count as a lover. But a platonic lover. Well, nearly platonic—that kiss did sometimes turn rather ardent.

Two sexual lovers and one nearly platonic lover wasn't being greedy. Surely.

No more, the captain told himself, eating his oatmeal. *This has gone quite far enough.*

Chapter Four

As far as Zachery was concerned, the captain was just a bossy bitch.

"When did you first notice the problem?" the captain asked in his bossy-bitch voice while Zachery fantasised about punching him in the face.

"Yesterday afternoon, sir," he said, loading up the *sir* with as much derision as possible.

"You mean to tell me our engines have been malfunctioning for twenty-four hours, and you only bothered to notify me *now*?"

Gritting his teeth, Zachery said, "Thought it was something I could take care of myself, sir. Our engines are old; they throw a shitfit every other month. Usually, I can fix it without bothering anyone."

"Watch your language," snapped the captain.

Asshole. Thinks he's so high and mighty.

Zachery didn't even know what the captain was doing down in the engine room. It wasn't as though he knew the first damn thing about how *The Prayer* worked, or how much effort it took Zachery just to keep her running from day to day. And without a scrap of help from anyone, as there were only two other people on board who had the education to do what he did. One was Echo (who was just too fucking creepy for words), and the other was Antoine (who was, if anything, even more of a bossy bitch than the captain). Zachery didn't want either of them on his turf. He'd only gone to the captain to ask if he could cannibalise some parts from the ship's artillery, which was basically useless now, seeing as how the enemy was an entire galaxy away. The last thing he'd expected or wanted had been for the captain to demand to see the problem for himself. Playing tour guide first thing in the morning to a man he despised was not Zachery's idea of fun.

"Regardless of your personal opinion on the significance of any one mechanical failure, it's your duty to report all discrepancies to me," the captain was saying. Whenever he got to lecturing, he would clasp his hands behind his back and lean forward a little, so it seemed as though he was looming over you. It didn't work on Zachery, seeing how Zachery was one of the only people on board tall enough to look down on him.

You don't scare me, you bossy bitch.

What really bit Zachery's ass was the way everyone else fell over themselves trying to suck up to him. Thomas was the worst of them—the memory of the way his eyes had popped out of his head at the sight of the captain's bare feet was downright embarrassing. But the others were almost as bad. Rick turned into a blushing schoolgirl in his presence, and Echo was basically his *pet*. And rumour had it all three of them were taking it morning, noon, and night from their mighty leader.

Zachery just didn't get what all the fuss was about. It wasn't like there was anything special about the guy. Zachery had been in this business for a long time, and he'd seen a hundred just like him. Unappeasable, petty, arrogant fucks who thought they were God's best gift to man.

"Are you listening to me, Mister Halberstam?" growled the captain. His brow was damp with perspiration; the engine room was usually the warmest place on the ship, and right now, the air conditioning system was offline to save power.

"Sure am, sir," Zachery drawled, flicking his hair out of his eyes. He'd been growing it out, along with a scrappy, half-assed goatee. And wasn't that just the sort of thing old stick-up-his-ass would hate, with his neat beard and his tidily cropped salt-and-pepper?

The captain's lips thinned, but he didn't take the bait. Instead, he told Zachery to show him exactly where the problem was. Which, Zachery knew damn well would mean he'd have to break down the complicated workings of *The Prayer*'s fuel system into baby talk. Except, to his annoyance, the captain didn't seem to have any trouble understanding what he was talking about, didn't once ask him to repeat or clarify anything.

"And to fix this, you want to take parts from our artillery, am I correct?"

36

"That's right. Only way."

The captain shook his head. The gesture got on Zachery's nerves, just like everything else the man did. They'd disliked one another more or less from the moment they met, but it hadn't been a problem so far given they hardly ever saw each other. Zachery stayed down in the engine room, the captain stayed on the bridge, and they'd never actually been alone together before.

"Given that we are as yet uncertain as to whether or not there are any hostile life forms within this sector, I'm disinclined to start dismantling our only means of defence. Are you sure you have investigated all alternatives?"

"I know how to do my fucking job, sir," Zachery spat out before he could stop himself.

He saw the other man's jaw lock and knew he'd gone too far. But fuck it. What could the captain do? He *needed* Zachery. There wasn't anyone else within however many millions of light years who could keep *The Prayer* going.

You can't do anything to me. So Zachery smirked and folded his arms, letting the silence stretch. Watching the captain's face, he could practically see his fuse burning down, inch by inch, his lips getting thinner and thinner. He had, Zachery noticed for the first time, a small scar just at the edge of his mouth.

Then he noticed the captain's eyes gliding from his boots to his brows. They were, he realised, sizing one another up.

Okay, Captain Cunt, if that's how you want it.

Zachery made one or two tiny adjustments to his stance, preparing himself. The old man had no idea what he was in for. Zachery had been born in one of the shittier Martian colonies, and he'd been fighting since he could walk. First, the mean kids who'd tried to steal his lunch money and then the gangs who'd tried to scare his mom out of her shop because they didn't like immigrants. To pay for his engineering degree, he'd fought in the Pit, an underground arena host to some of the most illegal blood sports on the planet. Guys would inject themselves with any number of unhealthy substances and then go at each other until one of them was crippled or dead. By age twenty-five, when the captain had found and hired him, Zachery had made a name for himself on his home world by surviving eighteen tournaments, three more than his closest rival.

As for the captain? No one knew anything about him. Not even basic shit. Zachery had done some surreptitious snooping, and he'd found out exactly three things: he'd been born in Cairo, had doctorates in Philosophy and Astrophysics, and had never married. That was it. But if Zachery had to guess? He'd wager "His Majesty" hadn't done much *real* fighting in his time. He probably wasn't nearly as tough as he made out to be. With big biceps, a pinched waist, and a regal nose that clearly hadn't been broken even once, he looked like a bodybuilder, like the sort of airhead who spent his life in the gym making himself *look* like a badass.

Vain, bossy little bitch.

As far as Zachery was concerned, he had the captain all figured out. What he liked, what he *really* liked, wasn't just being in command and ordering them around. What the captain really liked was being looked at. That was the reason for the body, for the immaculate fingernails and shiny boots. For all his pretences toward gruff military professionalism, the man was a filthy fucking exhibitionist.

"Apologise immediately," the captain said in that commanding voice everyone was so afraid of.

Zachery wanted nothing more than to throw him down and...he didn't know. Strangle him. Crush his windpipe. Crush his skull. Make him whimper, and beg, and moan, and...

"Go to hell," he said instead.

He was expecting the punch. What surprised him was how fast it was; he ducked it, but only just.

He didn't duck the next one.

Mother of FUCK. Zachery had taken a lot of hits in his day. Less than three had been able to knock him on his ass.

"We don't have an official medical officer on board," said the captain, shaking out his fist. "So I can't break as much of you as I would like to. Nevertheless..."

Zachery hooked his foot around the captain's knee and took him down.

Things happened fast after that. Zachery was on him the second he hit the floor, driving a knee into his gut. The next second the captain had him by the throat, which was actually kind of terrifying until Zachery headbutted him. They broke apart, and he saw blood spewing out of the captain's pretty nose.

"Whoops," Zachery said with a grin.

When the captain tackled him at waist height, Zachery realised he was enjoying the hell out of himself. It had been years since he'd had a good punch-up. All the other guys on board were too weedy for him to really cut loose.

Zachery yelped as the captain got a hold of a handful of his hair and almost ripped it out of his scalp. In retaliation, he put his fist in the captain's diaphragm and smirked at the breathless choking sound the captain made from all the air driven out of his lungs.

But something was bugging him. He kept trying to get a fix on the asshole's style and couldn't. There was a little boxer in there, and a little taekwondo, and whole lot of dirty bastard fuckery. Like when he sank his *teeth* into Zachery's arm, as though he was one of those cyborg Rottweilers rich Martian businessmen kept to guard their homes. Eclectic, but when it all came together, it rang a bell in Zachery's brain.

He was distracted from speculating when the captain did some freaky judo nonsense and knocked him back several paces. As the back of his head connected with the opposite wall, making stars burst into his vision, Zachery realised he wasn't entirely sure he was going to win.

That was when he worked out what was bugging him. Damned if the captain didn't fight like he'd come from the Pit. More than that, he fought like one of the guys who'd known how the Pit worked. It wasn't just about survival; if you wanted to actually make money, you needed the crowd to like you, and that meant being a good showman as well as a good fighter. It was a hard line to walk. The sort of flashy, unnecessary moves the crowd lapped up were exactly the sort of moves that tended to get new guys killed.

"Out of interest, sir," Zachery said, licking at his split lower lip and savouring the sting, "you ever been to Mars, by any chance?"

Instead of answering, the captain jumped to one side to avoid Zachery's next lunge and dealt his face a swift, sharp slap as he passed.

"Mind your own business, criminal."

Okay, so he's got good reflexes.

The skin on his cheek stung, though not half so much as being called a crook. He'd paid his debt to society, and getting off-planet work had been a tall glass of pure hell with three years of hard time to his name. He knew it was goading, knew he shouldn't let it get to him, but *fuck, he hated this guy so much.* So he went for him again, and the next few minutes were a blur of violence and swearing. Who'd have thought Mister Perfect had such a dirty tongue in his head?

Zachery finally got the upper hand. He pinned the captain to the floor, sitting on his thighs to keep his legs immobilised, and just in time because Zachery was about done. He had bruises in places he couldn't name, one eye he couldn't open, and what felt like a sprained wrist. His only consolation was that the captain looked worse, lying on his back with both his arms pinned in place, grunting underneath Zachery's weight, twisting this way and that in a failing attempt to free himself. His nose was still bleeding.

Got you, fucker, thought Zachery, feeling drunk on victory. *Gonna make you pay. Gonna make you beg for mercy, you arrogant prick.*

It was the first time since leaving Earth, the first time in four years of being stuck in his fucking space coffin, he'd felt alive.

"Surrender, sir?" he asked.

The captain had stopped struggling. Weirdly, he didn't look angry. He looked sort of...smug. "That depends."

"On what?"

"On what sort of man you are. I've always held that one can deduce all one needs to about a person's character from the way they treat those who are at their mercy. Do you have mercy, criminal?"

As he spoke, his eyes slid down from Zachery's face to his crotch. Following his gaze, Zachery noticed for the first time that both of them were hard.

"Well?" said the captain, smirking.

Thunderstruck, Zachery realised the bossy bitch was flirting with him. Tilting his head like that, arching his back, showing himself off. Fucking exhibitionist.

Still keeping his arms pinned to the floor, Zachery kissed him. It hurt; Zachery's lip had been split open in the course of their tussle. And the captain's mouth tasted like the blood still trickling from his nose. But Zachery had to give it to him; he kissed pretty good.

Neither of them closed their eyes, their gazes remaining locked, challenging the other to break the kiss first. Zachery was increasingly conscious of the way their dicks were now grinding together through their clothes.

"You know what I think, sir?" he said, drawing back. "I think you're kind of a whore."

"Watch your *fucking* language," the captain hissed, his pupils blown wide.

"Apologies, sir. Now, how about you roll over so I can fuck your brains out?"

He took a calculated risk in releasing the captain's arms, but at this point, he was too horny to care. The room smelled like sweat and blood and reminded him of the cell where he'd fucked a man for the first time. The second the captain rolled onto his front, Zachery pulled down his pants, noting the old burn scar on his left thigh.

"So, those rumours true, by any chance? That you let every single man on board have a taste of you?" he asked, getting his dick out. "I know you've been messing around with Thomas—not that he's really a man—and I heard someone mention Rick..."

"Get on with it," the captain snarled, bucking beneath him like an unbroken horse.

Fuck, he's beautiful. The thought came out of nowhere. It didn't feel like something he'd think. But he didn't have another word for it, for the way the captain's broad shoulders rose and fell as he panted, and all of a sudden, Zachery wanted to see what he looked like naked.

"Take your shirt and jacket off," he said, thrilled to be the one giving orders for once. His breath caught in his throat as the captain stripped, exposing his muscles and golden skin. Zachery spat into his palm and wet his cock, which throbbed as the captain arched his back and showed

41

off the gorgeous curve of his ass.

"You don't have any diseases, I trust?" said the captain. "How many men did you offer yourself to *in prison*?"

"You keep that up and I'll fucking gag you," Zachery muttered. He didn't bother being gentle. The bossy bitch deserved everything coming to him.

Wow, that is a beautiful ass. There it went again, the voice in his head. And, yeah, okay, it was a better ass than Zachery would have expected to find attached to a man of forty-something. And he was tight, tight and perfect as Zachery thrust in.

"I'll bet poor Thomas never got to do *this* to you, sir," he whispered in his ear.

"Do I detect a hint of jealousy?"

The captain's accent was starting to show. Zachery thrust in again, hard, and watched as the captain's whole body rocked forward. His fingers dug into the skin on the captain's hips so hard he suspected there'd be bruises. But when the captain shuddered, almost like he was in pain, Zachery stopped. He became conscious of the fact that—for some fucking reason—he actually wanted both of them to enjoy this.

"You all right down there, Cap?" he asked.

The captain looked up at him with a sneer. "Is that the best you've got, reprobate?"

Well, to hell with you, then, Zachery thought and gave up on civility entirely. The next few minutes were unlike any sex he'd ever had. They rutted like animals, snarling and cursing, and at some point, Zachery wrenched the other man's hips off the floor and took his rock-hard cock in hand.

"Well, ain't that a nice surprise?" he mocked. "Thought maybe you'd have run out of Viagra by now..."

"Do you ever not talk?"

Actually, talking was becoming difficult; Zachery was getting out of breath. Where the hell did the captain get this much stamina? The floor was covered in their sweat, which would have been gross if Zachery had given a fuck about anything but getting off.

As he came, he shouted a curse word. And even though the captain pretended he didn't like swearing, it must have done something for him because he spilled barely a second later.

"*Hnng.* Ah. Not...not bad, Zachery," panted the captain as Zachery collapsed on top of him. It was the first compliment he'd ever received from the bossy, sexy bitch. And, much as he hated to admit it, he fucking loved the way his name sounded with the captain's luscious accent wrapped around it.

"Th'n'ya, sir," Zachery mumbled, exhausted, pressing his nose into the captain's neck.

After a long while, they began to pull themselves back together, compiling inventories of their injuries.

"Ooh, here's a nasty one," said Zachery, showing the captain a blossoming bruise on his shoulder. "Think I came off worse than—fuck, is that a bite mark? Did I bite you?"

The captain inspected the red crescent on his lower arm. "Apparently so. I should have known you'd be a dirty fighter."

Zachery laughed. "That's rich, you asshole."

Burying a hand in the captain's hair, Zachery kissed him, feeling more upbeat than he had in months, years even. A good fight, a great fuck—give him a beer and a big dinner and today would rank in his top ten.

"Well, well, *well*," came a voice from behind him. "What *do* we have here?"

Leaning against the wall of the engine room with his hips cocked like a bored hooker, *The Prayer*'s first officer pushed his glasses up his nose and ran his eyes over them both.

"Antoine," said the captain in a monotone, adopting his commanding, chest-out, hands-clasped-behind-his-back pose. It was less effective than it might have been, due to the noticeable damp spot on the front of his pants. "Mister Halberstam was just informing me of a mechanical error in our engines. He's put in a request to strip parts from our weapons system in order to correct it, which I have authorised."

"Oh, I see. So you've been inspecting the machinery, have you?" said Antoine, turning his gaze on Zachery.

"That's my job," Zachery grunted.

"Hmm. Of course it is. And I imagine it's quite a difficult job, isn't it, Zachery? After all, the machinery *is* prone to failure. Which is to be expected, given how *very old* it is," said Antoine, smirking at the captain.

"She's a good ship," said Zachery, not liking the way the other two men were looking at each other one bit. In all honesty, he liked Antoine well enough, but he sure as hell didn't want to get caught in the middle of one of *their* spats. The way those two fought made the dust-up he'd just enjoyed look like a tea party.

"Good, but indisputably run down these days. Past its best. Practically an antique, really," said Antoine, still looking directly at the captain with a wicked gleam in his eye. "Honestly, it's a miracle anyone can get it going. You are a talented man, Zachery."

The last thing Zachery expected was the wave of protectiveness rising up within him. He'd no idea why—he knew damn well the captain could take care of himself. But he'd always been inclined to act on his instincts, so he folded his arms and said, "Old or not, she's the best damned ship I've ever served on. Reliable as hell. Wouldn't mind riding on her for the rest of my life."

The captain cleared his throat, and...holy fuck, was he blushing?

"Right," said Antoine, arching one of his aristocratic eyebrows. "Well, given our captain's refusal to even entertain the notion of an exploratory mission to the Holy Trinity, you'll probably get your wish. On that note, captain, I've left my latest report in your office. It indicates the average surface temperature of two of the worlds under scrutiny is within five degrees of Earth's."

That said, he turned and sauntered off.

"You okay, captain?" Zachery asked, as the older man shook his head. He looked...weary.

Instead of answering, the captain said, "You may begin dismantling the artillery. Send me a detailed account of the parts you need, and the amount of time it will take you to complete repairs."

"Yes, sir," Zachery mumbled, feeling a twinge of disappointment.

Then the captain spun round, fast as a viper, and had him up against the wall. "And *then* you can report to my quarters, and we will continue

44

our discussion of your insubordinate tendencies. I feel you may be in need of further correction."

Bare inches from his, the captain's lips twisted into a hungry smile, and suddenly, Zachery had an idea what all the fuss was about.

"Sounds good to me, sir."

☆☆☆

Goddamnit all to hell.

The captain lay on his back, staring up at the ceiling while Zachery snored beside him.

Four lovers. What had he been thinking? Quintets were damned *difficult* to make work. On Earth, it had taken him years to find just three other people whose relationships were strong and equitable enough to keep everyone happy. And that wasn't even taking into account the fact that he was his new lovers' employer—a hideous can of worms all by itself. So many ways everything could go wrong.

To clear his head, he got out of bed and went to sit at his desk. After staring up at his calendar for a while, he turned his attention to Antoine's holo-tablets.

CHAPTER FIVE

It was their anniversary. Four years to the day since they'd left Earth, and the captain had given them all the day off. They'd decided to have a party because—why the fuck not? So now, with the aid of a miniature hologram projector, the mess hall looked like a sunny beach bordered with dense vegetation and crawling with crabs and shrimp. It was purely visual; Thomas couldn't smell the sea air or hear the albatross circling overhead, but it was great just to see some trees again.

What he *could* smell was the new batch of weed Rick had brought along; bless his filthy heart. He was sharing a joint with Zachery, who'd stripped down to his boxers, like they really were at the beach. In between taking drags, their chief engineer was trying out a new song he'd composed on his guitar, and to Thomas's surprise, he had a really nice singing voice. Most of the crew was sprawled nearby listening to him, with the exception of Khali and the other girls, who were playing poker under the shade of a coconut tree.

As for Thomas, he lay spreadeagled on the illusionary sand, trying to avoid thinking about anything. If he got nostalgic, he'd get weepy, and then Zachery would give him shit for it.

The only crew members not in attendance were the captain, Antoine, and Echo. The latter was busy in the kitchen, putting the finishing touches on an apple pie. You wouldn't have thought the creepy fuck knew how to cook, but it wasn't the first time. Thomas was actually looking forward to it. Sure, the filling would be bland synthetic shit, but Echo was so good at mixing spices you could almost believe you were chewing on real apples. As for Antoine, he was cooped up in his lab, assembling more data on his precious Holy Trinity. And as for...

"Whaddya think the captain's doing?" Rick said suddenly.

"Trimming his nose hair, watering his pot plants, yelling at inanimate objects—who gives a fuck?" Zachery muttered, preoccupied with tuning his guitar.

Frowning, Rick said, "He should be here. He came to the last party, didn't he?"

"Fuck, you're such a whiny brat. Yeah, he did, and he spent the whole time sitting in a corner not talking to anyone and being a buzz kill. Remember? It's a blessing he's not here."

Listening to Zachery talk, Thomas thought he was trying to convince himself as much as Rick. Rolling onto his belly, Thomas observed that both of them now looked a touch hangdog. Trying to help, he said, "The captain's probably busy with his paperwork or something. You know he—"

"Is a pathetic workaholic, yeah," Zachery interrupted. "If anyone in the history of mankind ever had an excuse not to do their goddamned paperwork, it's him. Not like anyone's ever going to read it."

But Rick looked even more troubled. "What's he do for fun, anyway?"

That was a good question. Obviously, Thomas knew *one* thing the captain did for fun. But as for what he did at those moments when he was neither working nor giving out excellent free blowjobs, Thomas didn't have a damned clue. He couldn't imagine the captain fucking around in his room watching porn or stupid movies, the way Rick spent his free time, or playing cards and complaining about bands he didn't like, the way Zachery spent his. He couldn't imagine the captain chilling.

"Think he's in the gym," Irene called to them without looking up from her cards.

Thomas watched Zachery's ears prick up. "The gym? He doesn't use the gym."

"No, he just doesn't use it when you're there," Irene retorted. "No offence, baby, but when you work out you grunt like a fucking musk-ox giving birth. It's gross."

"Why don't we go get him?" said Rick.

Everyone stared at him.

"'Get him'?" Thomas said. "You mean like..."

"Like we bring him here. Or just bring him some of Echo's pie and some weed."

"That uptight asshole doesn't like pie. Probably only eats bark and broken glass," said Zachery.

Rick looked to Thomas for support, making his eyes big and appealing. "C'mon, man, it's not right that we're having fun and he's all on his own. I mean, it's not like his life doesn't suck just as much as ours do. He's stuck in this coffin with us."

"Aaw, sweet. Rick's all concerned," Irene teased.

Thomas got to his feet. "Yeah, and he's right."

"What?" said Rick. Thomas figured he probably wasn't used to people agreeing with him.

"I'm going to see what he's up to," said Thomas. "Any of you want to come?"

Rick hopped up and followed him. To his surprise, Zachery did the same, muttering something about "Goddamn *fanboys*."

"You guys mind if I finish the weed?" Irene called after them.

☆☆☆

The Prayer's gym was pretty crummy, at least compared to other vessels Thomas had worked on (and even as he thought that, he could hear his grandfather, who'd been a naval officer and spent large chunks of his life on a submarine, calling him a pussy from beyond the grave). It was small, and there was only one bike, so Thomas didn't use it much. He took a run around the ship twice each day and lifted weights in his quarters. He knew he was probably the least badass member of the crew, but frankly, he didn't give much of a fuck; he was good at his job, and he was a better shot than any of them.

When they got there and peered through the window on the door, they found that Irene hadn't been fucking with them. The captain was, indeed, in the gym. And he was...

"What the fuck is he doing?" said Zachery, coming up behind Thomas and tilting his head to one side.

What the captain *appeared* to be doing was a handstand. On one hand.

Which hadn't been the first thing Thomas had noticed. No, that would have to be the fact that all the captain was wearing were loose pants, and his ass looked just as nice when it was upside down.

"That is so cool," Rick said in a hushed voice.

"Stupid old prick's gonna topple over and hurt himself," Zachery mumbled.

What struck Thomas was how *weird* it looked. He'd always pictured acrobats as skinny elf people, like Antoine; the captain was a large, large man.

It's also kind of hot, said a voice in Thomas's brain. It sounded like something his dick would say.

Through unspoken agreement, they all kept quiet as mice while the captain slowly lowered himself to the ground and rolled up into a sitting position. He stood, and stretched, giving them all an amazing view of his back, shining with sweat.

Thomas glanced sideways and saw that Rick and Zachery both had on the same glazed, slack expression.

When the captain finished stretching, he went back down again and started doing push-ups, and of course, Thomas counted. Eighty-five in two minutes. By the time he was done, Thomas realised that all three of them were panting openly.

For all that he'd whored around in college, Thomas had had two or three serious relationships with people he really cared about, and in each one, he'd struggled with jealousy. So watching the other two, he sort of expected to feel all *fuck off, I saw him first*, but he didn't. He knew the captain wasn't his. He belonged to all of them.

After standing and stretching again, the captain went over to the bench where a towel and a water bottle were waiting. A soft sigh swept through his audience as he upended the bottle over his head, letting the water splash over his face and down his chest.

"Mary, mother of God," said Thomas.

"Shouldn't be fucking legal," Zachery rasped.

Rick made a whimpering noise.

It took all three of them a while to notice Echo, standing just five feet away, a steaming apple pie in his hands. When they did, Thomas actually jumped back, and Zachery swore.

The captain's head snapped round to where they stood at the door of the gym. "What are you three doing?"

"Er," said Rick, seizing up like a deer in headlights.

Thomas looked from the captain to Echo to the pie and back to Echo again. Echo, meanwhile, looked downwards, pointedly, at all three of their erections.

"We were just thinking maybe you'd like some pie, sir," Thomas said, hearing exactly how stupid it sounded as he spoke.

The captain—still holding the empty water bottle—looked at them with steely eyes.

"Pie," he repeated.

"Yeah, C'pn," said Rick, shifting his weight from foot to foot like he always did when he was embarrassed. "We were all just at the party, and we noticed that you were, uh, not there, and so we...thought we'd come and find you."

"I see," said the captain.

Putting the water bottle aside, he walked up to Echo, who gave him the same solemn nod with which he greeted him on the bridge and then proffered the pie.

"For me? How kind of you, Echo. I shouldn't, though. All that pastry..." the captain said, sliding a hand down over his abs.

Echo made a small pout, which was easily the most emotion Thomas had ever seen him display.

"Oh, if you insist." The captain raised a hand and pressed two fingers against the crust, and goddamn it, all Thomas could think of was the way those same two fingers had split him open just yesterday. When the crust gave way, exposing the pie's piping hot insides, he saw Zachery surreptitiously slide a hand down over his own dick.

The captain withdrew both fingers, coated in apple filling. He raised them to his lips and licked some of it off, before saying, "Well done, Echo. As ever, you excel yourself."

"Don't you think so, gentlemen?" he added, turning to the three of them and holding out his fingers.

For a moment, none of them moved. Then Rick inched forward and gave his fingers a kittenish lick.

"Good?" the captain asked.

His throat clicking, Rick said, "Y-yeah, sir. Real good."

With a smirk, the captain turned his gaze to Thomas and Zachery. "What about you two? Wouldn't you like a taste? After all, Echo has put in so much effort. I think we should all show our appreciation."

Echo sighed and flicked his eyes to heaven.

"Oh, fuck this," Zachery grunted. Striding forward, he took hold of the captain's wrist and plunged both fingers deep into his mouth. When they were drawn back, every inch of sauce had been cleaned off. Thomas almost wept with disappointment.

"Greedy," the captain admonished, running his thumb over Zachery's lips. "You've left none for poor Thomas."

"Fuck him," Zachery said and kissed him. Rick, meanwhile, had attached himself to the captain's side like a limpet and was basically humping his leg.

Like the dumbass he was, Thomas stood there, wanting to join in but unsure of whether it was what the captain wanted of him. After all, he'd just been exercising—maybe he only had enough energy left for two of them.

But then, the captain said, "Thomas—aren't you hungry?"

No matter how much he flirted, Thomas reflected, the captain hardly ever sounded like he was being a flirt. He kept his face perfectly blank, his tone perfectly even; he'd invite a guy to an orgy with as much sultriness in his voice as he would if he was asking him to pass the salt. It fucked with Thomas's head.

"Yeah, Captain," he said cautiously. "Guess so."

Rick was now pressed against the captain's bare chest, while Zachery had moved to stand behind him, with his arms wrapped around the older man's waist and his groin against his ass. One of Zachery's hands had begun to tug down his pants, exposing a generous slice of thigh.

"Take some, then," the captain ordered, gesturing to the pie.

Feeling like even more of a dumbass, Thomas dipped his index finger into the mangled pastry, trying not to blush under the scrutiny of Echo's cool, frank gaze. Was he getting off on this too? Was getting off something Echo even did?

Before Thomas could taste it, the captain seized hold of his wrist and took his finger into his mouth. He licked it clean, all the while maintaining eye contact, and that was about all Thomas was willing to put up with. Taking a step forward, he cupped a possessive hand over the captain's dick, earning a grunt of approval.

"Captain," he said, "if you don't want to come to the party, maybe we could have our own party. In your quarters?"

Honestly, right then, Thomas would have had no problem getting down to business in the corridor.

"Hmm," said the captain, rubbing his chin and eyeing them all. "I suppose my bed *is* the only one big enough to accommodate all three of you..."

Behind his back, Zachery pumped his fist.

"...or possibly four of you," the captain continued. "Echo—would you like to join us?"

Rick took a break from the love bite he was busy carving into the captain's chest to whine, "Him? He's creepy."

"Don't be an asshole, asshole," Zachery scolded, slapping the back of his head.

But Echo declined with a graceful gesture and went off in the direction of the mess hall, bearing with him what remained of the pie. The captain sighed. "Ah, well. Gentlemen?"

Rick seized hold of his right arm, Zachery his left, and Thomas trailed behind, replaying the captain's weirdly hot handstand in his mind and wondering if he'd let him try giving him a blowjob upside-down.

☆☆☆

"So," Thomas asked, several very enjoyable hours later. "Does anyone want to talk about this? This...*us* thing?"

"Nope," said Zachery sprawled over the captain's legs.

"We prob'ly should," sighed Rick, curled at his side. "It'd be...like, the adult thing to do, I guess."

Rousing himself, Zachery cleared his throat and said, "Okay, here we go: This was fun. If you guys want to, we should do it again sometime."

"Sounds good to me," said the captain, from somewhere beneath a mound of pillows and limbs.

CHAPTER SIX

The ship was quiet. The crew slept.

All except two.

First Officer Antoine Mbaye sat alone in his quarters, trying to contend with a cramp in his wrist. The cause of his affliction sat on the desk beside him; notebooks, dozens of them stacked on top of one another. The captain had his calendar, Echo had his schedule, but Antoine had found no better way for dealing with their endless voyage than keeping exhaustive diaries. Every evening, he filled pages upon pages with whatever had occupied his mind that day—an old song he'd remembered, a new grey hair on the captain's head, findings from his latest research.

He always wrote more when he was homesick or lonely, and today he'd reached twenty-three pages before his wrist had failed him.

As he rubbed it gingerly, his attention wandered to the opposite wall. It was mostly bare; no calendar, no dirty posters. There was only a small framed picture featuring himself and a taller, bearded man standing in front of the entrance to the Tuileries Garden. A bad picture; one side was out of focus and both their eyes were red. Nonetheless, it made Antoine smile involuntarily.

Abandoning his wrist, he stood and stretched.

Enough, he thought. *This has gone quite far enough.*

☆☆☆

The captain sat alone on the bridge, staring out through the nearest porthole into an endless ocean of stars, as Moxie sat purring in his lap. His jacket hung over the back of his chair, and a glass of brandy waited nearby.

He wasn't going to drink it, not when he only had five glasses left to last him the rest of his life. But he did like to pour one out now and then, just to have it on hand, so he could look at it if he wanted to. When he was done brooding, he'd pour it straight back into the bottle and put the bottle back in his safe.

So distracted with his thoughts, he didn't notice Antoine's approach until his first officer's scowling face blocked his view.

"What are you doing?" Antoine demanded.

"Thinking," he replied. "It's one of my hobbies. It's quite enjoyable, actually; one does it with one's brain. Happy anniversary, by the way."

He watched Antoine's eyes move down to his brandy glass and quickly drew it out of his reach.

"You've done the rounds, then?" his first officer said, stepping forward and perching neatly on the arm of his chair. "Gone from room to room offering your cock to anyone in need of it, like some kind of fucked up Florence Nightingale?"

"As you ask, I just had a very enjoyable liaison with Thomas..."

Antoine sneered.

"...and Rick..."

Antoine winced.

"...and Zachery."

At that, even the cornea of Antoine's eyes seemed to wrinkle. "Zachery? God only knows what you've picked up."

"He's actually very sweet."

"You really have no standards whatsoever, do you?" Antoine sighed, taking off his glasses and rubbing his temples. "If I went down to G deck and drilled a small hole in our ship's reactor core, you'd probably spend the last few minutes before we exploded fucking it."

The captain glared at him and then returned his gaze to the porthole. For a few minutes, they sat in silence disturbed only by the ubiquitous hum of the ship's engines. Moxie woke up and nudged at Antoine's hand until he stroked behind her ears.

Ever since the quarrel on the bridge, the captain and his first officer hadn't been on speaking terms. It wasn't a state of affairs the captain was at all comfortable with. While shouting matches had always been a core component of their relationship, they usually forgot whatever it was they'd been angry about within a few hours. This drawn-out bitterness was new, and he hated it. Even so, he'd stubbornly resisted apologising. In all the years they'd known one another, they'd only exchanged apologies once, and the captain had no desire to conjure up memories of that awful afternoon in Paris and the engagement ring that still lurked in the back of his desk drawer.

"There she is," said Antoine, pointing. As was usual on those occasions when they were alone together, he'd switched to French, the only language they'd had in common when they'd first met. "The host star. Seventy-three percent hydrogen, four billion years old, eight hundred and seventy-two thousand miles across...uncannily like the Sun. You know, we should give it a proper name. Actually, we should start giving all of them names. You see that constellation there? I've named it 'the Goldfish.'"

The captain squinted. "It looks more like a crab."

"Yes, I know, but there's already a constellation called 'the Crab' back at home. We should try to be original."

"There's a Chinese constellation called 'the Goldfish.'"

Antoine cursed. "Really? Damn. I'll have to think of something else, then."

Then, tentatively, he continued, "So, have you read..."

"Yes, yes, I've read through your reports. Exhaustively."

"The largest one is our best bet. I thought we could call her 'Leia.'"

The captain rubbed his beard, frowning. "After the nymph? The one with the swan...?"

"No, that was Leda. Leia, Princess Leia, you idiot. From *Star Wars*?"

Of course. While they had both studied Ovid in college, Antoine had been the one to cultivate a fetish for obscure speculative fiction. "And your reasoning?"

Grinning now, as though he'd been building up to it, Antoine declared, "Because she offers us a new hope."

The captain stared at him blankly, until Antoine added, "It was the name of the first movie?"

"I thought the movie was called *Star Wars*."

"No, no—God, you're ignorant—that's the franchise. The first movie is called *A New Hope*. It's my favourite. I saw it when I was ten, and it was the first time I realised I wanted to live on a spaceship."

"I wanted to be Captain Nemo when I was ten," the captain imparted, bracing himself for a "long, hard, and full of seamen" quip.

Antoine smirked. "Oh, so you could abduct handsome Frenchmen, or so you could wage an aquatic war on an evil empire?"

"I think I was drawn to the prospect of spending my life exploring the ocean."

Waving a hand at the window, Antoine said, "Well, there it is! Three whole worlds full of ocean, all for you."

Gracefully, he slid from the arm of the chair into the captain's lap, dislodging Moxie with a yowl of complaint. "Because that's why we really went into this business, isn't it? We wanted to explore the universe. That's the only reason anyone really does what we do; it's dangerous, and the pay is shit. All your men, they're here because they wanted to go 'where no man has gone before.' They deserve better than to live out their days in this miserable coffin, with nothing to hope for. And so do I. And so do you, Khurshed."

The captain couldn't remember the last time anyone had called him by his first name. He didn't even think the rest of the crew knew what it was.

He took a deep breath. "These men—my men—they trust me with their lives. Trust me to get them home—"

"Which you cannot do. No matter how determined or clever or brave you are, you *can't* get them home. But you might be able to give them a new home. Isn't it worth trying, at least?"

After a lengthy pause, the captain muttered, "Get off. I'm getting an erection, and I don't want to have to wake anyone up."

He hadn't been exaggerating, but he regretted speaking the moment Antoine's warmth left his lap. Despite the fact that their sex drives were radically dichotomous, they were both tactile men. The captain's strongest memories of their time together before Paris were of Antoine's fingers clutching his while they waited for the train, and the sensation of working massage oil into Antoine's ankles and calves when they'd returned home after walking in the rain.

For what felt like the thousandth time, he wondered whether sex would have made their relationship simpler or even more complicated. But of course, the question was a fatuous one. Antoine was what he was, and the captain wouldn't have had him otherwise. And his asexuality had been far less a factor in their eventual disintegration underneath the Arc de Triomphe than the captain's natural tendency toward polyamory.

"You fall in love with half the people you meet, Khurshed," Antoine had told him after he'd put the ring back in his pocket. "And I've never been any good at sharing. Eventually, you'll meet someone else, you'll be smitten, and you'll ask me if they can join us. I'll say yes to make you happy, but I'll secretly hate them, and you'll spend all your time playing peacemaker. You don't want that. I don't want that."

Angry and hurt, he'd said a handful of despicable things in response, which Antoine had returned in short order. Although they'd never exactly broken up, their relationship had entered a sort of limbo, from which it hadn't yet emerged. When the captain had purchased *The Prayer*, Antoine had been his first recruit, and they'd agreed not to disclose their history to the crew so as to avoid accusations of favouritism. In that, at least, they'd succeeded; Thomas and the others seemed convinced they despised one another.

Rubbing his eyes, he tried to organise his thoughts. His half-hard cock didn't make the task any easier.

"We will enter the planet's orbit," he said. "We will undergo a *lengthy* process of risk assessment. We will learn everything we can without setting one foot on her. And *if* I judge the data we have collected to be sufficient, and *if* that data indicates the danger is minimal, I will authorise an exploratory mission."

Antoine jumped back into his lap and cradled his face with his hands. Switching to English, the language that—so long ago now—he had learned specifically so the two of them would have a second tongue in common, he said, "Thank you, Captain. You'll not regret this."

"Get *off*," the captain moaned, feeling his cock thicken under Antoine's pert rear.

Placing one chaste kiss on his cheek, Antoine whispered, "I'd like to celebrate."

"In what fashion, pray?"

"How about we go back to your quarters and finish off your brandy? Then I'll read *Lysistrata* to you while you fuck your fist. Sound good?"

It did. Antoine's Greek was the auditory equivalent of bathing in warm honey. With reluctance, the captain cleared his throat. "My quarters are occupied at the moment. Very occupied."

Antoine rolled his eyes. "Of course they are. We'll use mine then, *mon bien-aimé*."

As Antoine took his hand and pulled him away from the bridge, the captain looked out through the porthole once more, at their new hope, shining in an ocean of stars.

THE CAPTAIN'S ENCOUNTER

CHAPTER ONE

The captain's bed wasn't big enough for an orgy, not that Rick was much of an authority on orgy-related logistics.

This was only the third time they had come together like this. But he couldn't help but feel that he'd have been able to get into it a whole lot more if Zachary's giant elbows didn't dig into his gut, and Thomas's gangly antelope legs didn't sprawl over his knees. That shit was distracting. And he was already plenty distracted by the pervading sense of *Holy Mary, I'm sleeping with the captain* that still hadn't worn off, even after several months of doing exactly that.

"Oh, that's perfect," the captain moaned as Rick struggled to fit all of his cock into his mouth. It would have been challenging enough even if Rick's concentration hadn't been split two ways; while he was busy trying to repress his gag reflex, his arm was outstretched giving Thomas a handjob.

Admittedly, they'd have had even more difficulty getting down to business in Rick's or Thomas's quarters, both of which were filthy pigsties that stank of old socks, or Zachery's, which didn't even have a bed. Being a bona fide weirdo, their engineer slept in a hammock. At least the captain's room was tidy. That said, Rick still thought they would have been better served doing this in the cargo hold or the mess hall, provided they could have pushed something heavy in front of the doors.

"Hey, easy, little man. Slower, yeah?" said Thomas, shooting Rick a grin.

A cute grin. A cute, friendly, gorgeous grin. And there was the real reason Rick was so on edge when he should have been having the time of his life, surrounded by three sexy men he liked. He'd already been sleeping with the captain for weeks when Thomas and Zachary entered the picture. He hadn't been alone with either of them yet. They were his friends, sure—or at least, Thomas seemed to like him, and Zachary didn't hate his guts. The thing was, Rick had never anticipated jumping into bed with them, and apparently, he was enough of a prude that getting naked with people he hadn't taken out for dinner was an issue.

Of course, the fact that they were going to attempt a landing on an alien planet in the next few hours might also have contributed to his stress levels.

"Hey, Rick, you better not make him come before I do," said Zachary, whose cock was buried in the captain's ass.

"Please feel free to ignore him, Ricardo," said the captain, winking at Rick as his back arched. Damn if that wasn't all the motivation Rick needed. He redoubled his efforts, and a moment later the captain's cock slid down his throat like it had been made for it.

Multitasking was a bitch, and he almost forgot about Thomas, until he moaned and came in Rick's hand, which had been moving on autopilot. He must have done a decent job, because a second after the captain peaked—a moment before Zachary, and all over Rick's face—Thomas clambered over to kiss him gratefully.

"My turn," Thomas told him and took hold of his cock.

On the whole, Rick reflected, there were worse problems to have than wanting to know if all three of your sexy fuckbuddies wanted to go steady.

CHAPTER TWO

Of all the planet's inhabitants, most of whom were ocean-dwelling invertebrates and only a few inches long, there was only one who took notice of *The Prayer*'s entry into the planet's atmosphere.

He had been sitting in his cave, discussing current events with the pictures he had drawn on the rock walls. These events consisted of the weather, the last meal he had eaten, and a new strain of moss growing in the dank corner where he slept. The distant sound of a spaceship descending was the most interesting thing that had happened in years, and he was about to tell his pictures about it, before reminding himself that they couldn't hear him.

He was proud of himself for remembering that. He often didn't.

Emerging from his cave, he spotted the vessel some miles away, setting down by the shoreline. He knew what it was, though it had been centuries since he had seen anything like it. Excitement and fear overcame him, and he slunk back down into the dark and curled up on the cave floor.

What if it isn't real?

Well, he told himself, so what if it wasn't? What was there to be lost by believing that it was? At the very least, it would be a distraction from the crushing tedium.

If it *was* real...

What if they are hostile? What if they see me as a threat and exterminate me?

Would that be such a bad way to go, all things considered? Certainly, it would be a more impressive death than slamming his cranium into the rock wall until he succumbed to a brain hemorrhage, a notion with which he had been toying for the last decade or so. Murdered by alien interlopers while making first contact—that would make him a martyr to the cause of scientific inquiry. His name would go down in his planet's history... Except it wouldn't, he reminded himself, because there was no one else left alive to learn about his planet's history.

The aliens might care to learn about it. They might be explorers, not conquerors.

How to be sure, though? He would have to study them from a safe distance.

Having made this decision, he emerged from the cave once more. Several bipeds had come from the vessel and were milling about in front of it, expressions of wonder on their faces. Their bodies were awkward and clumsy, and their equipment laughably primitive. Two of them were carrying weapons that wouldn't have passed muster as children's toys among his own people.

It was with particular fascination that he observed the one he assumed to be their leader. This singular creature was clearly the oldest, and it moved and spoke with a commanding air. It also smelt strongly of sex. In fact, when he sniffed again, picking up their scents despite the considerable distance separating him from the vessel, he observed that three members of the pack seemed to be mated to the leader.

They don't appear hostile. Perhaps they are explorers. Perhaps...perhaps they will want to be friends.

Unseen by any of his guests, he continued to watch.

☆☆☆

Thomas tilted his head back and closed his eyes in bliss.

A *breeze*. An honest-to-God, one hundred percent authentic breeze. And ground, real ground underneath his feet. And the sky, miles upon miles of perfect duck-egg blue. It was so beautiful he wanted to sob.

The captain had them assembled outside *The Prayer*, which had entered the planet's atmosphere ten minutes ago and made a soft landing on a sandy beach. He drew their attention with a whistle; most of them, like Thomas, were still bowled over by how big the sky was and the novelty of standing on something that wasn't metal.

"All right, everyone," the captain said, "I'm sure I don't need to remind you all of protocol..."

He didn't. Before landing, they'd sat through a two-hour lecture on the proper procedure for ensuring the safety of the crew and the surrounding environment during first-time landings on unknown terra. There had been diagrams and pie charts and a test.

"...but just so we're clear; if I see anyone touching anything you haven't been authorized to touch, or diverting from our route, or attempting to re-board the ship without going through the appropriate sterilization procedures, I will have you marooned."

"Yes, sir," they replied in one voice.

Zachary stuck up his hand and waved it around. "Hey, captain, what if we need to go to the bathroom?"

Thomas hoped it spoke more to the general air of excitement than to the overall maturity level of his crewmates that it got a few snickers. Not from the captain, of course, who replied, "You should have gone before we disembarked, Mister Halberstam. But if you must, Antoine assures me that the atmosphere is sufficiently Earth-like to permit temporary removal of your suit. Just try not to hit anything that looks as though it might object."

After spending the last two months in orbit, collecting data and assessing risk, they'd learned the planet's ocean and southern ice sheet covered eighty-six percent of her surface, and that her two irregularly shaped moons exerted a weaker pull on her tides than the moon did on Earth's. While there were things swimming in the ocean, none of them displayed any signs of intelligence. Antoine, naturally, had given his own lecture on "the definitional challenges posed by such categories as 'intelligent'," which, so far as Thomas could ascertain, boiled down to: "Don't screw with shit, because the shit you're screwing with may be smarter than it looks." As far as the land was concerned, they hadn't spotted anything big enough to be a threat, inferring a lack of large carnivores from the lack of large herbivorous herds.

Regardless, the captain had told Thomas and Irene to bring the laser rifles, the two of them being the only trained marksmen in the crew. When he'd first signed on, Thomas's official job title had been "security officer." Although, like most of them, he'd ended up doing whatever needed to be done. The one other weapon they'd brought with them was Antoine's stun gun; he never left the ship without it. It was strapped to his suit somewhere in the vicinity of his waist, though Thomas couldn't see it underneath all the other gear he had on. Their first officer was carrying more equipment than the rest of them put together, including hundreds of test tubes so he could collect samples. Even laden down, he'd been skipping around like a kid at Disneyworld ever since they'd disembarked.

"Look at him," Zachery said, coming to stand next to Thomas. "You know he's going to find some freaky alien dog and bring it back to the ship to be our new pet."

"I'm excited too. Always loved exploring new places. Back home, I used to be a birder," Thomas volunteered.

Zachery blinked. "A what, now?"

Thomas felt himself blush. He didn't know all that much about Zachery Halberstam. He'd barely spoken to the guy in four years—not deliberately, but they worked in different parts of the ship, and he'd never thought they had a lot in common. Since the captain had dragged them all into bed with him, they'd started having these strange, stilted conversations. Thomas *thought* they were becoming friends.

"A birder. Bird-watching? It's a hobby where you go looking for different types of birds, and if you see one you haven't seen before, you tick it off the list."

"Sounds weird."

"It's a lot cooler than I'm making it out to be. There's ten thousand species on Earth, and no single human being alive has ever seen all of them. I was pretty good at spotting..."

Thomas trailed off. It had occurred to him that Zachery wasn't from Earth; he'd been born on Mars. Had he ever seen a bird? Did he think Thomas was being an asshat, showing off about the fact that he'd been born on the most ecologically diverse planet in the solar system?

Before Thomas could figure out what to say next, Antoine passed by, clattering as he walked, eyes locked on the ground in search of specimens. He made a funny sight, with his weird, skinny body loping through the grass like a stick insect hunting for its dinner.

Zachery nudged Thomas. "Is it just me, or is he whistling?"

"Think so. I heard that he's got a doctorate in astrobiology. This planet's like cocaine for him."

Zachery chuckled, and Thomas found that he liked the scruffy dark stubble that covered the lower half of his face. That he could see Zachery's face at all was thanks to Antoine, who had spent the last two months examining the planet's atmosphere. He'd determined that it was safe for them to disembark with only their lightweight breathing equipment, which consisted of a strip of plastic going from their nose to the suit. The suit itself was a lot less bulky than he'd feared; as the captain had said, the planet was so Earth-like they could make do with form-fitting Kevlar and a ton of protective cream. Even the suits weren't strictly necessary, but the captain wasn't taking any chances.

They'd planned a straight route from the beach to a small mountain one mile away. It looked easy enough. The terrain was flat, and while there were trees—fat trunks, skinny branches, not unlike baobabs—they didn't clump together very much. They'd be in sight of the ship the whole time, so the guys they'd left to guard it could come to their rescue if need be. The other reason the captain had picked this route was that it would take them past a small lake Antoine had said might be a watering hole for any hither-to unnoticed wildlife.

As they started walking, Thomas couldn't help but notice that the captain cut a fine figure in his suit. It clung to him, showing off the sleek lines of his muscles and his long, powerful legs. Then Thomas saw Zachery following his gaze and smirking.

"Don't give me that look, Halberstam. You're just as dopey as I am where he's concerned."

"At least I'm less fucking obvious about it."

"You're not, man. You're really not."

The ground they were walking on was covered in a grey, grainy soil and dotted with shrub-like plants, and the footprints they left on it were shallow, the planet's gravity being slightly lower than Earth's. Thomas glanced up again at the sky, across which a few white clouds were drifting, and he smiled.

"Wow, someone's cute when he's happy," Zachery teased him.

They'd been walking for half an hour when the captain called for a halt. Antoine had found something that looked like a beehive attached to one of the fat trees, except it was purple and covered in a white foam. As he sketched it and took samples, the rest of them shared water and wandered around. The novelty of fresh air and open space put everyone in a good mood, including the captain, who was leaning over Antoine's shoulder watching him work. Weird to see them getting along like that. Not for the first time, Thomas wondered if there was something going on there that he couldn't quite make out.

Thomas was considering taking his suit off and doing some sunbathing—never thought he'd get to say that again—when he felt someone tugging at his elbow.

"Hey, man?" said Rick. "You got a minute?"

The kid had a furtive expression, shoulders hunched, eyes flickering this way and that. Confused, Thomas shrugged. "What's up?"

"You think we could talk? Alone, I mean?"

"Uh...sure. No problem."

He allowed Rick to lead him a little distance from the group, toward one of the trees, careful to watch where he stepped, not wanting to put a foot wrong and squish a bug. Antoine would lose his shit. When they reached the tree, Rick led him around to the other side until the trunk was effectively concealing them from the others.

"Whaddya want, shrimp?" Thomas asked, folding his arms.

Thomas had never known what to make of their youngest crewmate. Sure, Rick was a kid and a brat and everything Thomas was sure he'd been at that age. (*Jesus, I'm thirty now*, he thought. *Ugh.*) But there was something off about him, a sharp, cynical edge that stuck out sometimes and made him seem decades older. He came from a good family, but he never spoke about them or anyone he'd known back home.

Rick shifted from foot to foot. "Um...okay, don't be mad, all right?"

"What are you..."

Thomas's eyes widened as Rick stepped forward and pressed a clumsy peck against his lips. It lasted a few seconds, and then Rick jumped back, as if he expected Thomas to slug him.

"Okay. That was all kinds of bizarre," said Thomas.

Seeing Rick's crestfallen look, he hastily added, "Not in a bad way! Good weird. You..."

"I was straight," Rick blurted out. "I mean, I thought I was straight. I haven't...don't be an asshole, but I haven't had a lot of sex. I've had one real girlfriend in my whole life. And..."

He quit babbling and took a deep breath. "The captain is the only guy I've ever fucked, or wanted to. After the first time I was with him, I...for a while, I wasn't certain if I was into guys as well as girls, or if I was still straight and the captain was my one exception. I never thought about dudes at all until him."

Thinking he knew where this was going, and a touch pissed about it, Thomas said, "You want a control experiment to make sure? I'm not going to be one of your variables, man."

"No! No, I don't want that. That wasn't what I meant. I'm bi. I'm okay with it now; that's not what I'm worried about. Screw it. I'm messing this up. What I'm trying to say is that I didn't know I'd like it at first. Hell, I didn't have a clue what I was doing that first time. But it turned out to be great, and then you and Zachery came along, and you were great too. When we were all together, all four of us, it blew my mind. I want to do it again. I want to do it better next time."

"Better?"

Rick looked at his feet. "All three of you guys...you know a lot more than I do. I never even got the hang of hetero sex, and now there's all this...other stuff."

Thomas chuckled. "It's not all that different, Rick."

"Hear me out. If we're going to be doing it again, us four, I don't want to make an ass of myself. I want you to show me how to do all the...the stuff properly. I'm a fast learner; all I need is coaching. And there's one more thing. When we're not having sex, could we get together and do other things? Talk, play cards, watch movies, normal things? Except not in a friendly way, more in a romantic way. Not lovey-dovey, I don't mean that, I..."

Words failing him, Rick shrugged. "D'you get what I'm saying?"

"Yeah...think so. Sounds like you're asking if I wanna be your boyfriend."

71

By this point, Rick looked so shy and flustered that Thomas felt like a prick for getting snotty with him. In all honesty, he didn't know what to say. Rick was nice and funny, and for a guy of twenty-one, he was surprisingly generous in bed—far from the self-obsessed horndog Thomas had been expecting. He'd offered them all his mouth, and he kept stopping to check that they were still enjoying it. The problem was that he was nine years older than Rick.

Thomas's first boyfriend had been much older than he was, old enough to have known better than to seduce a lonely sixteen-year-old. Ever since Thomas had taken a good hard look at his first relationship in retrospect and realized how fucked-up it had been, he'd been on his guard. He'd slept around for years, but he never embarked on long-term relationships, the sort of relationships where feelings and shit got involved. And he never, ever broke his two golden rules: no virgins and no one more than five years younger. *I'm a slut*, he told himself with some degree of pride, *but at least I'm a goddamn ethical slut.*

He liked the picture Rick was painting—card games and whatever—and the sex had been awesome, but boyfriends? What if he screwed up and scarred the kid for life?

To keep the silence from stretching any longer, Thomas said in a light, joking voice, "Hey, kid, I don't know how much I could teach you. As far as I could tell, you weren't having any problems working all the 'stuff' out for yourself. I mean, that thing you did with your tongue, that was..."

He trailed off. Rick's throat was working, and his eyes were big and wet.

Thomas, you asshat.

"It's okay if you don't want to be my..." Rick swallowed. "Really, it's okay. I'm not a kid. If you want to leave it at being fuckbuddies, that's cool. Or if you just want me to be there when the captain wants both of us there, that's also..."

With an impatient huff, Thomas grabbed a handful of Rick's shirt and dragged him in for a bruising kiss. When they broke apart, he said, "Listen to me. I like you, asshole. I like you a lot. I don't know if I want to be your boyfriend, or anyone's boyfriend. I'm not good boyfriend material. But I do like you, and I'd like to get a chance to sleep with you again, whether or not the captain's there with us. If you want to do other things now and then, we can do that."

Inch by inch, a grin made its way onto Rick's face. *Shit*, Thomas thought. The tiny bastard was cute as a button.

"Thanks, man," Rick said. Then he launched himself forward and gave Thomas's ribs a squeeze.

"Don't mention it," Thomas said, gruffly, feeling his insides go gooey. "And any questions you want to ask about sex, you can ask me. I don't know everything, but..."

"Can I practice blowjobs on you?" Rick asked, his eyes bright and eager.

Thomas's eyebrow arched. "Wow, way to ruin the moment."

"Please, Thomas? You've seen the captain, he's huge. It took me a hundred years to get him down, and Zachery's is *worse*. You're...um, you're normal-sized. I think I could handle it."

Thomas snorted. "Great, so my cock is your version of training wheels. Look, we don't have much time before the others notice we're gone. How about this; I give you the fastest blowjob of your life, and you pay attention to what I'm doing so you can do it to me later when we're back on the ship."

Thoughtfully, Rick said, "Fastest of my life? I don't know about that. My girlfriend used to get me off in, like, two minutes."

"Challenge accepted," said Thomas, and he slid to his knees.

The suits were easy to unzip, and it was exhilarating knowing everyone else was a few hundred metres away, that they were hidden from view by the tree's thick trunk and nothing else. Thomas made Rick lean back against the smooth bark and set to work.

"Heh. Hope Antoine doesn't see us," Rick said. "He'd give us a lecture on...oh, *fuck*...on contaminating the natural ecosystem, or something...*ah!*"

"'S a good point," said Thomas, drawing back and lapping up a bead of precome. "Maybe we should stop."

The kid tried to kick him. "I will fuck you up, Meléndez. I swear to God..."

73

Chuckling, Thomas took him back in again. He was a nice size, filling up Thomas's mouth without it being uncomfortable, and he didn't try to pull on Thomas's hair, which was a plus. Thomas was proud of his hair.

"Oh...oh, wow," Rick gasped, his breath hitching.

Thomas didn't usually swallow, but he could imagine the face Antoine would make if he found out they'd left come all over his pristine new planet. So, he did his best, although a couple of droplets ended up running down his chin.

Rick wriggled happily as Thomas licked him clean and zipped his suit up. "You are amazing at that. Seriously, did you take lessons?"

"All down to practice," Thomas said, rising to his feet and tweaking Rick's nose. His own hard-on could wait until later, when they had time enough for him to judge how much Rick had remembered.

"Thomas! Ricardo!"

The captain's voice, echoing like a foghorn across the plains, made them both jump. Exchanging a look, they scampered out from behind the tree and joined the rest of the crew as they continued on their way.

CHAPTER THREE

Echo had never liked nature.

He'd ended up working on *The Prayer* for one simple reason; the captain worked on *The Prayer*, and within five minutes of becoming acquainted with the captain, Echo had decided that he would follow him into hell. He had, however, come to love his work on a long-haul merchant space vessel in large part because it prevented him from ever having to go outdoors. Outdoors, as far as Echo was concerned, was a place you went when you had no alternative.

He could have chosen to remain behind with the ship. His decision to do otherwise had been motivated by concern that the captain might need any number of small chores attended to in the course of the expedition. Who, for instance, would offer him water if he grew thirsty, or massage his temples if he got a headache, if Echo were not there?

"What are you moping about?"

For someone so fond of the sound of his own shrill voice, Antoine was remarkably good at sneaking up on people. When last Echo had checked, their first officer had been at the front, walking alongside the captain. Evidently, he had slowed his tread to fall into step with Echo, who had been bringing up the rear, and was now regarding him with his habitual critical squint.

"You're dragging your heels as though we're en route to a pillory," Antoine continued. "I wish you'd cheer up. You do realize that this is the most important thing that any of us has ever done, yes? We're the first human beings to set foot on solid ground in this entire galaxy. If anyone on Earth knew about this, they'd name universities after us. In one stroke, we've pushed the human frontier farther than anyone in history. Aren't you excited about that?"

Echo made an apathetic gesture. He was hot and wished he'd

thought to bring a hat to keep the sun out of his eyes.

Antoine huffed, pulling him into a tight and rather clinical hug.

"Is this helping?" he asked, a moment later.

It was a peculiar trait for an extrovert, Echo reflected, but Antoine interacted with other human beings as though he'd read about friendship in a textbook and expected to have to a write an exam on the subject. In answer to his question, Echo nodded and gave his shoulder a pat.

"Here," Antoine said, proffering a bottle of water. "Stay hydrated. It's warmer than I expected."

Grateful, Echo swallowed two mouthfuls, increasing his stride as his did so to catch up with the rest of the crew. He was aware that Antoine's awkward concern was rooted in the fact that Echo was the least physically fit member of the crew. Perhaps their beautiful first officer was wondering why Echo had come, if he was going to hold everyone up.

"I'm glad you're here, by the way," Antoine said, oddly intuitive creature that he was. "You're the only one of these clowns I can rely on. Half of them should be on a leash, the other half are too busy staring at our mighty leader's rear to concentrate on where they're going."

Echo's lips twitched.

Cocking his head and gazing ahead of them, Antoine added, "It's not a bad rear, I suppose. The vain old idiot keeps it in good condition."

A small smile marred Echo's blank expression. Antoine returned his attention to the surrounding landscape seemingly satisfied. Then he squealed like a ten-year-old. "Look! Look! Over there!"

What had drawn his attention was a tree, no different from any of the surrounding trees. However, when Echo looked closer, he saw that it had one distinguishing feature; from its lower branches hung several swollen geoids, red-brown in color.

"Fruit," Antoine said, although his tone of voice would have been more appropriate for an utterance along the lines of "Hark! The grail!" He went up to one, peered at it, prodded it, and plucked it. "Four years of synthetic garbage and now we have fruit."

Echo sniffed it and found that it smelled a bit like pineapple and a bit like paint.

"Obviously, we'll have to run tests to determine whether they're edible. But there you are. That's something to be cheerful about, isn't it?"

He placed it in Echo's hands, and they continued their march in peace.

☆☆☆

Thomas. Zachery. Khali. Irene. Rick. Echo. Mehtab. Antoine... Wait, where is Antoine? Ah. There.

The captain exhaled. Everyone accounted for. No casualties. Not yet, anyway.

They'd made it to the mountain by midday, and the crew had settled down to exchange water canisters and eat some protein strips. A light breeze had picked up, and the sunlight was muted by threads of cloud. He wasn't unduly concerned. While this region of the planet was host to ferocious storms two or three times a year, they'd timed their landing meticulously. The window of good weather would hold up for another week at least.

While Antoine made contact with *The Prayer* and reported that all was well, Echo checked everyone's breathing apparatus. It was a task the captain had assigned him in a fit of exasperation. Perhaps it was his way of apologizing for lagging behind the rest of the crew on their march, but Echo had been fussing over him ever since they'd stopped walking. Most of the time the captain was all too glad to have the younger man following in his shadow. But throughout the weeks they'd spent in the planet's orbit, the captain had endured a bout of claustrophobia, stuck on his vessel with all those miles of ocean and grassland stretched out below him. Now that they were here, he wanted to savor the open space without anyone breathing over his shoulder.

So, naturally, that was when Thomas wandered up. "Hey, Captain. Whatcha doing?"

Oh, well, the captain sighed to himself. Discoursing with Thomas was never taxing. Of all the members of the captain's newly fledged quintet, he was the most easygoing conversationalist.

"Admiring the view," he said, beckoning the younger man closer.

"Tell me, Mister Meléndez, what do you see?"

As Thomas came to stand beside him, the captain slid an arm around his waist. He liked to maintain a certain level of formality in front of the rest of the crew, but the memory of their recent tryst was in the forefront of his mind, and besides, Thomas smelled nice.

"Not a lot. Nothing moving, at any rate," Thomas replied, squinting into the distance. The mountain loomed overhead, its sides covered with the same grass and shrub that covered the plains, although higher up the slope the captain could discern a field of tangled vine-like things. The wildlife they'd encountered so far had been limited to tiny invertebrates moving through the soil, and a range of winged bugs, none larger than a fingernail.

"Does that strike you as odd?" the captain asked him. "We've determined that the oceans are home to an abundance of life. That the land should be so starkly depleted seems incongruous."

Thomas scratched his head. "I'm not a biologist, but yeah, I guess it's weird. Maybe the critters are all hiding."

"Maybe," said the captain, rubbing his beard. Taking another look at Thomas, he added, "By the way, whose semen is that on your chin?"

"What? Oh, Jesus," Thomas mumbled, wiping it away. "That...that's Rick's."

"Honestly, Thomas. What would Antoine say?"

"Sorry, captain." Glancing over his shoulder, Thomas said in a quieter voice, "Maybe I could make it up to you?"

His hand glided up the captain's thigh to brush against his groin. With some difficulty, and much regret, the captain shook his head. "Later. I need to remain alert."

He ducked his head and licked up a spot of cum Thomas had missed. "To atone, you can go see if Antoine needs help with his samples."

Watching Thomas depart, the captain willed his erection to subside. Then he stepped up onto one of the smooth, white boulders dotting the plain at the base of the mountain. One hand shielding his eyes from the sunlight, he gazed out over the landscape and attempted once again to discern any moving shapes. After a few minutes of fruitless scrutiny, he

78

moved to step back down, and as he did, a short but intense burst of pain issued forth from the middle of his back. He nearly screamed. Clapping a hand over his mouth, he kept still—dead still—until it had subsided, and then he carefully stepped down from the rock.

Damn. Damn! Not now.

Despite his crew's apparent belief that he'd been formed in the primordial ooze and had spent his youth hunting the mammoth, the captain didn't look a day older than forty—forty-five at most. Hardly ancient, given that the average lifespan of a human being living on a developed, well-governed planet was now two or three centuries. Like most people, when he'd hit thirty he'd started taking rejuvenation pills (a misnomer; they slowed, rather than reversed the ageing process), and had barely noticed any decline in his physical or mental prowess in all the decades since. Most of his men had no idea, though he would have told them if they'd asked him directly. As it stood, his true age was known only to Antoine, who had known him since long before he'd started the pills, and Echo, who used to regularly purchase them as one of the many hundreds of sundry chores he performed for the captain. He'd presented him with a new bottle on the day they'd set out for Pluto, four and a half years ago.

Ever since their encounter with the enemy that had flung them countless light years from Earth, the captain had been rationing the pills. One a month instead of one every week, and even with such austerity he now had enough to last him another year at most. He was dreading life without them. Already, he'd begun to notice a range of ominous aches and pains—sometimes in his fingers, sometimes in his wrists. His eyesight was worse than it had been one year ago. But all those were minor irritants compared to his fucking back. For six months now, it had been betraying him on a regular basis, although not to the point of impeding his mobility.

Not until now, anyway. Damn. He was still standing, but he wasn't sure he could walk.

With a growl of annoyance, he considered his options. He had two emergency pills in his suit. They'd allow him to get back to the ship without a stretcher. But he'd no desire for the crew to see their captain swallowing medication in the middle of a dangerous expedition. He wasn't ashamed; he simply valued a degree of privacy in these matters. An unusual trait for a—to use Antoine's charming terminology—"brazen whore," but there it was.

Surreptitiously, he glanced around. No one was looking his way at that moment. And...ah. There was a pile of boulders at the foot of the mountain, not twenty metres from where he now stood. If he could just get to it unaided, he could take the pills without being seen.

Cautiously, he took a step forward, wincing as the pain flared again. It was bad—as bad as it had ever been—but it wasn't insurmountable. A few more steps...

When he was in the shade of the boulders, fully hidden from view, he relaxed a fraction. Cursing his body under his breath, he dug into his suit until he had located the tube containing his pills. He tipped one of them out into his hand, bracing himself for the taste.

Both the tube and the pills flew out of his hands as something hand-like, but as strong as a steel cord, wrapped around his ankle. The ground gave way beneath his feet, and before he could even cry out, he plunged into darkness.

CHAPTER FOUR

"Hey, Zachery? You got a minute?"

Zachery sat on the ground, watching a tiny ten-legged bug he'd coaxed onto the end of a finger scurry downward into his palm. Looking up, he found himself faced with another freakish-yet-cute thing, in the form of Rick.

"Probably not. Why?" he drawled.

"I sort of...um...wanted to talk." The kid was hopping from foot to foot like he needed to go to the bathroom.

Not so much a "kid," really, Zachery corrected himself, liking the way Rick's suit clung lovingly to every inch of his body. When they'd first met four and a half years ago, Rick had been the most dorky pipsqueak he'd ever laid eyes on. Zachary, being a natural born asshole, had had trouble taking him seriously, even when said pipsqueak had dealt him a vicious kick to the shin after being referred to as "the ship's mascot." Since then, Zachery had built up a decent reservoir of respect for the younger man; he was good at his job, and he didn't stand for any bullshit, character traits Zachary valued above all others.

Of course, taking Rick seriously had been made easier by the fact that the intervening half decade had prettied him up some. His shoulders had broadened, and the last of the puppy fat had melted away, leaving behind a cheeky elfin face with big, liquid brown eyes. If it wasn't for the god-awful fucking haircut and a pronounced tendency to fidget, he'd have been a walking wet dream.

"About what?" Zachery asked.

"Er...about...stuff. Private stuff. Um. I spoke t-to Thomas earlier, and now I wanted to speak to you too, and..."

"Mm?" Zachery said, half listening as he admired the curve of Rick's ass. Not that he wasn't interested in what the kid had to say; Rick was

81

fun to talk to, most of the time. Right then, though, Zachery's lizard brain had higher priorities.

"Could we maybe go somewhere? Somewhere private, where we can talk about...about private things?" Rick squeaked, like he was about to throw up with nervousness.

Shark-like, Zachery smiled.

Three minutes later, he had Rick pressing his pretty elf face into the bark of one of the huge trees, his legs spread wide open.

"This your first time taking it in the ass, right?" Zachery asked.

"Uh... Uh-huh..."

Smirking, Zachery thrust in again, and Rick whimpered. "Thought so. You know, shrimp, I bet Thomas and the captain would be pissed if they saw me doing this to you. They probably wanted your virgin ass all to themselves. Thomas would have wanted to have you on a bed of rose petals, with lube and oysters and all that crap. 'Cause he thinks you're a delicate flower, and he's got a thing about being a gentleman. Me? I'm no gentleman at all."

Rick gave a sharp cry as Zachery took hold of his cock.

"Keep it down, stupid. Wouldn't want the captain to come over here and see what a fucking whore you are, would we?"

Obediently, Rick bit down on his sleeve. Very nice, that instant compliance. Very gratifying.

"Good boy," Zachery purred and picked up the pace. There was almost two feet of difference in height between them, and in order to get Rick where he wanted him, he had to wrap an arm around the kid's middle and all but haul him off his feet. Judging by the way he mewled, being manhandled wasn't something Rick objected to.

He actually managed to stay quiet when he came. Zachery was relieved and kind of miffed.

"Next time, puppy, I'm going to make you scream my name so hard you'll lose your voice," he told him, biting on his earlobe.

Eyes twinkling—fuck, he was so pretty—Rick said, "Challenge accepted."

Both their smiles disappeared when they heard Thomas shout, "Where's the captain gone?"

After tidying up as quickly as possible, they emerged to see Thomas standing in the centre of their makeshift camp, a worried look on his face. Well, more worried than usual, at any rate. So far as Zachery could tell, Thomas was always worried about something.

"Has anyone seen him?" Thomas said as the others looked around in confusion.

A chill came over Zachery as he realized he hadn't heard the captain's voice for at least half an hour. Scanning the surrounding terrain, he couldn't see much for the bossy bitch to hide behind. Apart from the mountain, the landscape was more or less flat in every direction. As the others began to call the captain's name, Zachery assembled a list of likeliest options. The captain was a big man, but the grass was tall, and if he was lying down in it (for whatever horrible reason), they'd have a hard time spotting him. Or he could have gone up the mountain slope, but it was sheer, and why would he set off alone without telling them?

"Who saw him last?" Thomas said.

"I did," Antoine called. "Twenty minutes ago, or thereabouts. He was over by that pile of rocks."

Zachery made his way to the sun-bleached boulders Antoine was pointing at. They sat in another patch of tall grass, but he saw no sign of the captain's boots having trampled it underfoot. As he made his way slowly around the rocks, he spotted two red things about the size of sunflower seeds lying in the dirt.

"What're these?" Zachery muttered to himself, bending down to retrieve them.

All of a sudden, Antoine was there, his skinny hand darting down with wasp-like speed, plucking both red dots from the ground. "Those are headache pills. The captain carries them around everywhere. He gets migraines."

"Really?" Zachery said, observing the clandestine way Antoine slid both of them into one of the pouches on his suit. "First I've heard of it."

"Why would he tell you?" Antoine said in his best asshole voice, looking around. "The grass appears to be untrampled. If he was attacked by something, I would have expected to see signs of a struggle."

"Have you tried contacting him on his comm?"

"Of course, you fool, that was the first thing I did," Antoine snapped.

Zachery felt his hackles rising, but kept his temper in check. *More important things to focus on.*

They circled the boulders three more times, while the others spread out, moving into the grass. After a full two hours of searching, they'd ascertained that he wasn't lying out of sight anywhere within twenty minutes walking time from their camp.

"I contacted the ship. They haven't seen him," Khali said.

"There's no way the captain would leave us alone out here voluntarily," Thomas said. "Not a chance in hell. Something's happened to him."

"You mean like aliens?" said Rick, eyes wide.

"Ain't nothing around here big enough to take him down and drag him off. Besides, we'd have heard something," Irene retorted.

Looking upward, Thomas said, "Maybe not. The wind's picked up. If a big flying thing came at him from overhead and picked him up, he could have been out of earshot before he could shout for help."

"Supremely unlikely," Antoine replied. "In two months of painstaking orbital observation, we have seen no sign that any such life forms exist on this planet."

"Unless it's got a way of hiding from our equipment," said Khali.

"There's another option," said Zachery, speaking up for the first time in two hours. "One of us did it."

Khali was the first to break the silence. "The fuck, Zachery?"

"There aren't many other options that make sense to me. There's no corpse, no blood, no sign of a fight, none of us heard anything. So something took him out quickly, silently, and then either kidnapped him or incinerated his body, all in the space of twenty minutes. Whatever did that would need to be damn smart. But there's no intelligent life on this planet; we spent months making sure of that. No intelligent life, apart from us."

"Why the hell would any of us want to hurt the captain?" Thomas asked, gaping at him.

"Interesting question, isn't it? I suppose, if we were playing detectives, we'd first have to work out which one of us had the most to gain."

"That's ridiculous!" spat Antoine.

"Um, guys?" said Rick, moving to defuse the situation. "Occam's razor, yeah? Maybe he had a heart attack, and he's lying unconscious in a place we haven't looked yet. I mean, he is kind of old."

Zachery had been trying to block out that possibility for two hours. Sure, he knew the bossy old bitch was, in fact, old. But Zachery couldn't picture him getting sick, or dying. The captain was like Stonehenge—simultaneously timeworn and ageless. You never imagined one day you'd turn around and it would be gone.

For the first time, Zachery was afraid.

"We've looked everywhere, though," muttered Thomas, who obviously didn't like contemplating the captain's mortality any more than Zachery did.

"Then we'll look again," said Antoine, pushing his glasses up his nose. "Here's what we do. Khali, contact the ship again and tell Cecelia to bring it here. We'll have an easier time searching from the air. Meanwhile, we'll divide into teams. Zachery, Rick, you two continue to search the grass. Thomas, Mehtab, you search the base of the mountain. Echo and I will go up the slope. We will check in every three minutes. If any of you see or hear anything, press the alarm on your suit belt. Understood?"

All at once, he's in charge, thought Zachery. He said, "Ant, Echo's the worst climber we've got. Why should he go up the mountain with you?"

Glaring, Antoine said, "Echo is observant and has the best eyesight."

"Yeah, but I think—"

"I do not care what you think," Antoine hissed. "Do as you're told. We've wasted enough time as it is."

Zachery raised himself to his full height and balled his fists, wanting, if nothing else, to intimidate the prissy fucker.

It didn't work. Of course, it didn't; Antoine appeared to be as tough and resilient as a ballerina, but he went toe-to-toe with the captain on a regular basis. His self-preservation instincts worked about as well as *The*

Prayer's plumbing.

"Do as you're told," he repeated coldly.

Rick tugged at Zachery's sleeve and whispered in his ear, "We don't have time for this shit, man."

Reluctantly, he conceded that the pipsqueak was right, and without another word, he set off to scour the grass again.

After an hour, worry gave way to dread. After three more, dread gave way to hatred for whoever or whatever had done this to them. By the time the sun began to set, a deep bleakness had begun to spread through Zachery's heart. *The Prayer* arrived, and they turned on the lights, continuing to search as night drew in. They looked up the mountain. They looked down the mountain. They found several new types of nocturnal fauna, but nothing that seemed interested in posing a threat to them. Everything they stumbled upon slithered or scuttled out of their way as fast as it could.

As dawn broke the following morning, Antoine ordered them all back to the ship.

"We're not leaving him!" Thomas snarled. He looked like shit, like the rest of them, huge bags under his eyes and his shoulders stooped with exhaustion.

"No, we're not," Antoine said. "We've now inspected every possible inch of ground he could have reached unaided within the twenty minutes it took us to realize he'd disappeared. We've found no hidden pitfalls or crannies into which he could have fallen. We're not achieving anything. The one remaining option is that an unknown entity ate or abducted him and carried him away at speed. We don't know where they took him, or why. If we're going to have any hope of finding him, we need to devise a plan. We're going back to the ship, we're going to eat, we're going to rest, and then we will recommence searching with a proper strategy."

"He's right, Thomas," sighed Irene. "I don't like it any more than you do, but..."

"Does anyone else think this is all a bit too convenient?" Zachery said.

Khali scowled at him. "Fuck are you taking about, Halberstam?"

86

Zachery pointed a finger at Antoine, whose posture had become rigid. "Think about it. We're fine, totally fine, for four years. Then *he* decides we should land on one of his precious worlds. The captain doesn't want to, but Antoine bullies him into it. We land, the captain goes missing, and suddenly he's throwing around orders. I said it once, and I'll say it again; the most likely culprit is one of..."

"Jesus Christ, Zach!" Thomas exploded. "You can't start accusing..."

Whatever he said next, Zachery didn't hear it. Awful, awful pain exploded across his chest from out of nowhere, shaking him to his core before throwing him back onto his ass.

As he lay on the ground, groaning, he became aware of a shadow stretching over him. Antoine. Antoine, with his stun gun. The next second, Zachery's view was obscured as Antoine's boot planted itself in his face.

"Allow me to define the term 'second-in-command' for you, Mister Halberstam," Antoine said, in the same calm, amiable voice that the captain used when he was angry beyond all reason.

To Zachery's relief—because *ow, fuck*, his chest felt like it was on fire, and the edge of Antoine's boot was digging into his eye socket— Echo appeared at their first officer's side. He didn't do anything but stand there, and when Antoine looked his way he gave a respectful nod and made a dismissive gesture in Zachery's direction. No translation needed... *He's not worth it.*

Grunting in agreement, Antoine withdrew his boot. Turning on his heel, he started back towards the ship, and the rest of them followed in his wake.

All except Rick, who hung back and crouched down next to Zachery. "Hey, man, are you okay?"

"No, I'm not okay. Nothing's okay," Zachery said, getting to his feet. Rick offered his shoulder, and he accepted. "Shit. How did this happen? Everything was looking up for once."

CHAPTER FIVE

He dreamed.

In his dream, he was in a warm room, and someone beautiful was sucking his cock. He couldn't make out their features, nor their hair color, but somehow he knew they were lovely.

He was aware, on some level, that none of it was real. It had been *so long* since he'd had an excellent blowjob, though. Thomas preferred to use his skillful hands; Rick, bless his heart, was enthusiastic, but he lacked artistry; Zachery had some peculiar idea that any sex he had that didn't involve penetrating his partner would endanger his masculinity; and Echo was averse to germs and would, the captain suspected, approach the task as he would any other mildly objectionable chore. And while the captain's tastes were nigh-infinite in scope, he had never in his life entertained the prospect of having any kind of sex that his partner didn't enjoy as much as he did.

Blowjobs had always had a special place in his heart—the intimacy and trust implied by having oneself vulnerable to one's lover's teeth. He had more often been the giver than the receiver, not least because he was happiest on his knees. But this... Had he ever known anything like this? His phantom lover's technique was faultless. They set a steady but unhurried rhythm, drawing back to lap at his crown before taking him all the way to the hilt—a notable feat in and of itself, as the dimensions of his cock proved too great a challenge for most men to overcome.

"Mm," he murmured approvingly.

They gently cupped his scrotum, and he bit his lip. Wanting to show his appreciation without breaking the tranquil silence, he reached down to run his fingers through his mysterious partner's hair. When he did, he found that it was like touching smoke.

The dream was falling apart. The sweet, wet comfort of the mouth

89

tight around him was interrupted by a severe ache in his head. With extreme reluctance, he woke up.

The warm, clean room was now a warm, damp cavern. For a moment, he didn't understand how he was able to see anything, before realizing that his suit had automatically activated the lights on his gloves and his torso, shining three beams into the darkness. The memory of how he had arrived here returned to him—a grasping hand and a long fall down a slippery incline. He was underground, then. How long had he been unconscious? Oh, good God. The suit indicated that it had been at least six hours. He tried to stand, but when he did, the world spun dizzily around him, forcing him to sit back down. Inspection revealed a large welt on his forehead. To make matters worse, his comm wasn't working, damaged by the fall.

Where was his crew? Were they searching for him? He was about to begin calling for help, when it occurred to him that he was unarmed and trapped in hitherto unexplored territory. They had some notion of what lived in this planet's oceans, and what roamed her plains, but they'd no idea at all of what lived beneath her surface. Perhaps it would be advisable to remain silent until he had a better idea of where he was.

Turning his attention to the cavern ceiling, he tried to determine if he could climb back up. While he could see the point at which he'd entered the cavern—a circular opening through which a weak beam of sunlight shone—it was ten metres up. The rock face was too slimy for him to climb, even if he hadn't been suffering back pain and a head injury.

As the captain was reviewing his options, something in his peripheral vision moved. He remained motionless, although the hair rose on the back of his neck. By inches, he turned his head toward the source of the movement.

There, sitting against the cavern wall adjacent to his current position, was a man.

He was incredibly tall, taller than Zachery, with arms large enough to snap the captain in two. He was naked, bereft of a stitch of clothing, and green—his skin, his eyes, his thick, mane-like hair, all a shade reminiscent of algae. Moreover, the captain was not so afraid that he failed to notice that his new companion was good-looking.

He was contemplating the captain with an air of mild curiosity.

"Good morning," said the captain, in a neutral voice. "Or afternoon, as the case may be."

The green man didn't move or speak. After a while, the captain cleared his throat and said, "You'll forgive me if I take it for granted that you aren't real."

In a deep, booming voice that echoed off the cavern walls, the man replied, "Not real? Why?"

Concealing his surprise, the captain said, "Because if you were real, you would be an alien. I am disinclined to believe that any aliens we encounter in this galaxy would look exactly like we do and speak English. More to the point, I'm probably concussed, and you're a likely sort of thing for me to hallucinate."

"Hmph. How so?"

"You're handsome," the captain explained. "When people get lost in deserts, they hallucinate oases. In circumstances such as these and knowing myself as I do, I would expect my hallucinations to take the form of handsome men."

"Why is that?"

A curious feature of a hallucination, that it should speak solely in questions. With some impatience, the captain replied, "Because I like sex. Specifically, sex with handsome men."

"You want me," said the alien, in meditative tones. It looked down at its body, running a hand down its chest towards a thick nest of hair and a mouth-watering cock. Then, abruptly, it returned its attention to him. "Do you like my lair, foreigner? You are the first visitor in many years."

"Given that you're almost certainly a hallucination, I would contest the assertion that this place is 'yours'," the captain retorted. "In the unlikely event that you are real, why did you bring me here? What are your intentions?"

"I saw your ship land. I saw your crew disembark. I wanted to get a closer look at you. As stated, it has been a long time since I last had company."

"We were unaware this world was inhabited by...by beings such as yourself."

"It isn't. I am the last," said the green man. "And this is not my real body. In the hopes of facilitating our conversation, I adjusted my form to match yours. Quite good, is it not? I crafted it by taking traits from each of your mates."

Yes, now that he looked, he could see that the man had Zachery's strong jaw, Thomas's Cupid's bow mouth, Rick's snub nose, Echo's high forehead, and Antoine's bright, clever eyes.

"I see. How do you explain your grasp of English?"

The alien tossed its head arrogantly. "Picking up your primitive tongue was the work of an hour or so of eavesdropping."

As they spoke, the captain recognized the effect the alien's unwavering attention was beginning to have on him. His psyche was host to a pronounced strain of exhibitionism and responded eagerly to scrutiny, to being looked at, appreciated, lusted after. Despite having no idea whether the alien was capable of sexual attraction, he felt his cock—which had never entirely softened after his dream—begin to thicken.

"Where did you come from, foreigner?" asked the alien.

"A distant world, to which I cannot return. My crew and I had hoped to make a new life for ourselves on this one. May I ask a question? Why did you call yourself 'the last'?"

The alien lowered his eyes and replied in sorrowful tones, "All the others are dead. We were mighty; for millennia, we were mighty. Now we are nothing. Our cities are dust. Our culture has been dead for two thousand years."

"Yet you remain. How?"

"How what, foreigner?"

"How are you still here if the rest of your species is dead?"

"Because I am not dead yet."

Huffing, the captain sat back, folding his arms. "I am in no mood to be teased. Today has presented me more than enough aggravations as it is."

"You are injured," the alien noted, looking at his bloodied forehead.

"I fell from a great height. Thanks to you."

"Not so great. We are a mere handful of metres below ground. Your species must be exceedingly fragile. Or perhaps it is you who is fragile? I saw the way you were suffering earlier. Are you sickly?"

"Among my kind, such questions are considered ill-mannered."

"I apologize," the alien sighed. "My aptitude for polite conversation has withered with the years. Sickly or otherwise, your physical form is superb."

"Hmph. Are we flirting now, then?" Though the captain feigned nonchalance, he had, for the last few minutes, observed that the alien was stiffening, although whether this was any sure indicator of arousal was uncertain. It was, it claimed, a shapeshifter; perhaps it was imitating him.

Instead of responding, the alien got to its feet, revealing itself to be about eight feet tall. The captain's eyes widened fractionally as his new companion stretched, shamelessly displaying a body that combined Zachery's musculature with Antoine's effortless grace.

"My senses are more acute than yours. Would it be 'ill-mannered' if I were to ask you why your heart rate has increased, and why small protrusions have appeared on your chest?" asked the alien.

Hunching down in a feeble effort to hide his pebbled nipples, which his skintight suit did nothing to curtail, the captain growled, "It's cold."

"Is it? I had not noticed. Is vulnerability to mild temperature changes another symptom of your illness?"

The alien had moved to stand over him. His weight rested on his left leg while the other tilted inward, the contrapposto drawing the captain's gaze inexorably towards his cock.

"You...you say you crafted your current body by observing my men. How did you achieve such, er...anatomical accuracy? My men are fully clothed."

"Not all the time."

Ah. Thomas and Rick.

"I take care to pay attention to detail when creating new shapes for myself," the alien continued, obviously proud of his efforts.

"I can see that," said the captain. It wasn't empty flattery. Despite the pain and his many, many reservations, he was tempted to get himself up onto his knees—if he could—and get to work worshipping his new friend with his mouth.

"I do not care to show you my true form, as I believe you would find it disturbing. Nonetheless, there was a time long ago when I was considered to be well formed. Prospective mates competed for the right to taste my body. And, like you, I enjoyed sex. In view of this commonality of interest, do you think that we should have some?"

"Generally speaking, I make a point of avoiding sex with people whose names I don't know."

"I see. Introductions, then. My name is Rux."

"Captain Amirmoez." He wasn't comfortable dispensing his first name to this stranger when he hadn't yet given it to Thomas, Rick, and Zachery.

As Rux crouched down in front of him, the captain noticed that his body had a strange, powerful scent, not unlike burning wood.

"Your body doesn't seem all that complicated," said the alien, its bone-rattling voice dropping an octave deeper. "I'm sure I can work it out, given my superior intellect."

"Did your species really die out, or did they find your bloated ego irritating and abandon you here?" inquired the captain.

"You're rather ill-mannered yourself, foreigner," said Rux, reaching for the bulge in the captain's suit.

The alien's skin was far hotter than a human's. Even through the Kevlar, it was as though his cock was being fondled by oven mitts that had recently clasped a hot coal. Most men would have found the sensation uncomfortable. The captain added it to a list of personal fetishes that would already have filled up ten of Antoine's notebooks.

"Forgive my haste, foreigner. I usually spend far more time seducing my lovers. I have been alone for so long..."

Pity blanketed the captain's heart. He understood loneliness. The four years he had spent without the companionship his new quintet afforded him had taught him to loathe it all the more.

Rux's tongue was human-shaped, but slightly too long, and its texture was rough and catlike as it dragged down the captain's neck.

"Wait," the captain said, before he forgot himself entirely. "We can do this later. I need to find my crew."

"Oh. Can't they wait? They've been without you for hours. I'm sure they'll last a while longer."

The captain set his jaw. Rux conceded defeat and drew back. "Very well, very well. I will help you return to your crew. Then, afterwards...?"

"Afterwards, I'll let you have me any way you like," said the captain, watching the alien's eyes flash with hunger.

"The entrance to my lair is concealed by a holograph. Unless they were to step on it, your men would not know it was there. If they were searching for you, they've probably moved on by now."

"Then let's hurry."

Without further hesitation, the alien scooped him up as though he weighed no more than the ship's cat.

"Some warning would be nice," the captain said, although he was entertaining ideas as to how such brute strength might be best put to use in the bedroom. Dear God—and to think he'd worried *Antoine* might bring home uncanny alien fauna.

CHAPTER SIX

Thomas sat with Moxie in his lap, stroking her mechanically. She was as upset as the rest of them and had spent the last ten minutes conveying her distress by biting the shit out of his hand whenever his strokes became uneven.

They'd activated the holographic map of the planet Antoine had spent the last two months constructing, and it hung in the middle of the bridge like a Christmas ornament, all blue and shiny.

"This is where we lost him," said Antoine, pointing at the map. "This circle represents the area we've inspected. This circle represents the maximum distance in any direction he could have walked under his own power if he started moving from the last moment any of us saw him up to the moment we started looking. This circle..."

The rest of them were slumped around the table, or against the walls, exhausted but concentrating on Antoine's every word. Zachery and Khali were pacing the room like restless lions. Echo was staring straight ahead, gaunt and ghostly. Thomas didn't want to know what was going on in his head.

"If we are to work from the position that this planet is host to an entity or entities who wish us harm, the most pressing question is to establish whether they pose a threat to the ship itself," Antoine continued. "In light of... Yes, Rick, what is it?"

Rick had stuck his hand in the air like a kid in a lecture hall. Glancing his way, Thomas couldn't help but notice that, of all of them, Rick looked the worst. His eyes were bloodshot, and he'd bitten his nails so far down that two of them had started to bleed.

"Sorry for interrupting, Ant—sir, but I was wondering if we should get the other guns out? We do have more guns, right?"

"We have a few spare laser rifles. And at least two of us are proficient in their use," said Antoine, nodding at Thomas and Irene. "That said, we have no idea whether they will work on our enemies, as we know nothing *about* our enemies save for the fact that they're fast enough and strong enough to kidnap or devour a grown man."

Chewing at his lip, Rick said, "Okay, so what if we used the ship's weapons to blow something up? Like, if we aimed the missiles at the mountain and took a big chunk out of it?"

"And what would that achieve, Rick?"

"Well, if they're watching us, it would show 'em that we mean business, and they shouldn't mess with us. Maybe even scare them into giving the captain back."

"Er," said Antoine, taken aback. "That's an...interesting idea, but..."

"Fuck me; how can you be this dense?" Zachery exploded, turning to Rick, his face red with anger. "I dismantled the weapons systems, remember? When we needed to fix the engines, because this stupid fucking crate should have been decommissioned decades ago? Christ, I know you're a pothead, but I didn't think you were that fucking oblivious."

Ah, hell, thought Thomas, wincing. He expected Rick to lose it right there, expected both of them to be rolling around on the floor trading blows in seconds.

What he didn't expect was for Rick to sit there, his lips parted, and... *Oh, no.* Fucking *tears* gathering in the corners of his eyes. Faltering, Zachery stepped back, clearing his throat. Before he could say another word, Rick stood up and walked quickly and silently out of the room, his shoulders hunched and his head down.

"Nice work, asshole," Thomas growled at Zachery. Dumping Moxie onto the floor, he stormed out after him.

He found him in the corridor outside, curled up against the wall, his knees drawn in and his face in his hands.

"Hey, little man," Thomas said, getting down next to him. "You all right? Don't pay attention to Zach. He's a jackass; everyone knows that."

Rick sniffed, wetly, and glared up at him. "No, he's not. Don't say that. He's worried about the captain, same as us. I'm not upset because of him."

"Oh. Well...good. That's good." Awkwardly, Thomas patted his shoulder, wondering what else he should do. He was a complete deadweight when it came to dealing with tears.

"Dude," Rick said, dragging the back of his hand across his nose. "I've had your dick in my mouth. I know you don't want to be boyfriends because you're emotionally dead inside, or whatever, but is a fucking hug too much to ask?"

"God, you are such a pain," Thomas muttered, wrapping both arms around him. "Don't get your snot on me."

Burying his face in Thomas's chest, Rick mumbled, "Do you think he's okay?"

"The captain? He's the biggest badass I've ever known. I mean, he's put up with *us* for four years. No way he gets eaten up by some alien just like that. And if he's not okay—and he is—we're going to survive. You've still got me, and we've still got Antoine, and he's a badass too. Even if he does act like a prissy bitch sometimes."

Rick gave the ghost of a smile.

"And even if he does look kind of like a giraffe," Thomas added.

At that, Rick hiccoughed a laugh. "He so does. That neck, man."

Thomas smiled and cupped his cheek. "Tell you what; when we've got the captain back, I'll teach you how to give a proper handjob. You're cute, but you hold a guy's dick like you're milking a cow."

"Fuck you," Rick retorted but accepted a nuzzle without complaint.

☆☆☆

When the captain emerged from Rux's lair, it was some hours past dawn. The sky was overcast and the plains blanketed with fog. There was no sign of the crew.

"As I predicted, your men have left you," said the alien. "A shame. Can we have sex now?"

"Antoine will have taken them back to the ship," said the captain. He looked to the horizon, but the fog was thicker in the distance, and he had difficulty making out *The Prayer*. Eventually, he spotted it several miles away from the landing zone, moving slowly and staying close to the ground.

"They'll be looking for me. Come on," he said, stepping forward. Then he shouted inarticulately, pain surging up from the base of his spine.

"Your affliction still troubles you," Rux noted, peering down at him.

Ignoring him, the captain ran his eyes over the grass. His pills were nowhere to be seen. Which meant that the crew had found them. *Damn. So much for privacy.*

"I myself have never experienced sickness, although my people were familiar with it," Rux went on.

Straightening up inch by inch, the captain said, "It's not sickness. It's age. Did your people know of that?"

Maybe they didn't, given Rux's apparent fitness and vigor at the age of... What had he said? Two thousand years? Presuming, of course, that he was telling the truth.

"Ah. Yes, we knew age, in our primitive days. We developed technology that allowed us to avoid physical deterioration."

"Extraordinary."

Extraordinary that a member of such an advanced, once-mighty species would live in a cave with only finger paintings to keep him occupied, mused the captain. He kept the thought to himself. There would be time to poke holes in Rux's story once he was back with the crew and his head didn't ache.

"Captain Amirmoez, I've a thought. If you can't walk, would you like to ride me?"

"I've told you, we're not having sex until..." The captain trailed off as he became aware of the fact that his companion no longer stood next to him, having been replaced by a large, four-legged creature with six lidless eyes and a thick green pelt.

"That was not what I meant," said the animal, in Rux's voice. It sounded a trifle smug.

"Very funny," muttered the captain, climbing onto his back.

☆☆☆

"Can't believe you're messing around with your science experiments at a time like this."

100

"As I have explained at least three times now, I am trying to learn more about the local flora and fauna, so as to get a better idea of what might have taken the captain."

"You're looking at *grass*. Whatever did take him, it wasn't the goddamn grass."

"Mister Halberstam, you're not a scientist. If you feel the need to be useful, why don't you go do something you're good at? Breaking rocks with your head, for example."

Such was the discourse to which Echo had been an unwilling audience for the past half an hour. Zachery had volunteered to assist Antoine in his research—probably, Echo thought, because he felt guilty for bullying Rick. Every single contribution he had made so far had been derisive; although Antoine wasn't helping matters by addressing him the way an eighteenth-century French aristocrat would a disobedient footman. The fact was that if Antoine tended to bring out the captain's inner Bligh, then Zachery tended to bring out Antoine's inner Napoleon.

When Antoine made a sharp noise of surprise, Echo assumed it was because Zachery had finally lost his patience and punched him. He was surprised to turn around and find both of them leaning over one of the screens displaying the surrounding terrain.

"What the fuck is that green thing?" Zachery asked.

"Thomas!" shouted Antoine. "Get the guns."

CHAPTER SEVEN

"A fine vessel," said Rux as they approached *The Prayer*. "Not able to rival those marvels which my people constructed in our glorious Golden Age. Nonetheless, it will do."

"I can't wait to introduce you to Antoine," the captain said to himself. "The energy created by your colliding egos might well tear a hole in the fabric of space-time and allow my crew to return home."

His heart lurched at the sight of his first officer emerging from *The Prayer*, flanked by Thomas and Irene.

"Captain?" Antoine called through the fog. "Is that you?"

"Who else would it be?" he shouted back.

"Are you injured?"

"Yes, and hungry and tired. Why are you armed? If this is a mutiny, I should tell you that I'm not in the mood."

"Captain, is the life form you're riding hostile?"

The captain realized he'd completely forgotten about Rux.

"Has it taken you captive?" Antoine continued.

"No, you idiot. He's a friend." The captain gingerly eased himself off Rux's back and listened to his men shout in surprise as the alien turned back into his humanoid form. He stood there naked and nonchalant as Antoine approached, lowering his weapon and looking from the alien to his captain.

Then Antoine growled and said in disgust, "I should have known, you ancient letch. Do you have any idea how much I...how much you've upset the crew? We were looking for you all night! Rick wanted to incinerate a mountain! I electrocuted Zachery, for Christ's sake! And all this time you were busy getting acquainted with this planet's *one fuckable inhabitant*?"

In confusion, Rux asked the captain, "Is this one also your mate?

Does he always shout so much?"

"It talks?" Antoine yelped, jumping back.

Thomas, meanwhile, had lowered his weapon and approached them, while Irene signaled those inside the ship to say that all was well.

"Hi, captain," he said. "Glad to see you're in one piece."

"Thank you, Thomas," said the captain and pulled him in for a kiss and a grope. When they parted, Thomas's lips were glossy and his pale cheeks stained pink. Ruffling his hair, the captain asked, "Is everyone all right?"

"They're rattled, but they'll be okay. Where'd you find the big green slab of eye candy?"

"We haven't had intercourse yet," Rux was saying to Antoine. "Does that help?"

Antoine was still spitting French oaths as they returned to the ship. When no one was looking, he slipped two red pills into the captain's palm and squeezed his hand.

☆☆☆

The captain's room wasn't big enough for Rux. To accommodate his new lover, the captain folded away his bunk and spread his blanket on the floor.

"My people mated in mid-air, or else hanging suspended from a stalactite," Rux imparted, lying down on it.

Fascinating as that was to envisage, it wasn't doing anything to aid the captain's burgeoning erection. Trying to get matters back on track, he finished undoing the buttons on his shirt, neatly folded it over the back of a chair, and pushed Rux down onto the blanket. Once there, he took a moment to admire him. It had been ages since he'd made love to someone so much larger than he was. All those muscles...

"What do you want, Captain?" Rux asked.

"I don't know. I've never had a shapeshifter at my disposal before. Tell me, can you grow..."

"Tentacles?"

"How did you know?"

"Our two species are more alike than I had reckoned," Rux smirked.

104

"They all wanted tentacles too. That, or extra genitals. Or tentacles shaped like extra genitals."

Then he examined the captain's face. "Your eyes have glazed over. Is your head injury troubling you again?"

Actually, after a few hours in the med pod, his injury had more or less vanished. That hadn't deterred Antoine from subjecting him to an unnecessarily rigorous examination. ("For all we know, the creature might have impregnated you when you weren't paying attention. Did you consider *that*, Khurshed?") Rux's trials had been yet more arduous; Antoine had all but dissected him in the quest to ensure he carried no devastating alien viruses, and then he had advocated implanting a bomb in his head, in case he turned on them.

Visions of prehensile phalli dancing through his head, the captain shook himself. "No, no. I'm fine. I think, however, we should stick to the basics for now. Tentacles can wait for next time."

Removing the rest of his clothes, he slid into position, straddling Rux's stomach while the alien lay on his back and watched him. Rubbing his hands to warm them, he retrieved the jar of lubricant from where it sat on the edge of his desk. He'd taken care to get everything ready beforehand; much as he loved the spontaneous encounters that characterized his relations with his men, he thought that Rux would value preparedness, and he wanted to make a good impression. He was, after all, representing the human race.

"These marks," said Rux, touching the old keloid scar on his thigh. "How did you get them?"

"Now, now, you can't just ask me that," he chided. "That's one of my many dark secrets. If I told people how I came by them, I wouldn't be dashingly mysterious anymore, would I?"

When erect, Rux's cock was intimidating, the largest he'd ever taken. The sight of it gave him a shiver of glee.

Dirty old size-queen. You should be ashamed of yourself, said Antoine's voice in his head.

It was, in fact, Antoine who he had to thank for this evening's entertainment. He was able to delight in Rux's glorious body without concerns for his own health and safety largely because his first officer

105

had sprayed the alien down with every disinfectant they had available before allowing him onto the ship. Regarding the risk posed by Rux's semen, Antoine's lab had established that every other fluid he produced was identical to that which might be produced by a human, save for being greener.

Rux shifted in place as the captain applied lubricant to his cock in firm, rhythmic strokes.

"Given that I've no idea how your body works, it would be helpful if you'd let me know when I'm making a mistake," the captain said. "Does this feel good?"

"Yes. Should I make some sort of noise to let you know?"

"If you feel inclined."

Rux threw back his head and produced an eerily accurate imitation of Rick's breathless moan.

"That was the noise the youth made when the largest member of your crew took him behind a tree," Rux imparted. "I watched."

Did you, indeed? The captain was no stranger to the joys of spectatorship; for him, watching two or more of his partners enjoy one another was every bit as agreeable as taking part himself. What made him uncomfortable was the thought that his men had been observed without their knowledge. If Rux was to remain with them, he would need to ascertain how clearly the alien understood the concept of consent.

The captain gave Rux's cock one more stroke before tending to himself. Although he'd never needed much preparation before, and he didn't object to pain, he spent several minutes stretching himself and savoring the sensation of his own fingers. It had been too long since he'd last pleasured himself properly.

"I want to touch you now. Is that acceptable?" Rux asked.

"By all means."

The texture of Rux's skin was inhuman, a touch too smooth, as though he was made of butter. He wasn't hesitant, but he was unhurried, moving his hands over the captain's body with an investigative air. He took time to touch and pet his scrotum, which was pleasant, and in short order the captain felt they were ready to proceed.

Easing himself down onto Rux's cock was a laborious process, and he was glad that he'd swallowed both pills as soon as he'd stepped onboard. His back would leave him untroubled for the next few months at least. Just as well. If Rux became one of his regular bedmates, he'd be having more than enough trouble walking as it was.

"You really are very handsome," the alien told him, his hips beginning to thrust upwards incrementally. "Charismatic too. I suppose that's why your crew is so fond of you."

Smiling, and not just because Rux's thumb was playing with the crown of his cock, the captain recalled the way the men had stood and looked at him when he'd come aboard. Echo, of all people, had launched himself across the room and seized hold of him as though he were the last lifejacket on board the *Titanic*. It had been some time before anyone thought to ask who the enormous green humanoid he'd brought back with him was.

"It's a pity they lack for dignity," Rux continued, thrusting up again, harder this time.

The captain felt his ire pricked. "What do you mean?"

"Well, they are fairly...*coarse*, aren't they? Waving their weapons around, snapping at one another, letting their emotions get the better of them. I imagine they must embarrass you."

"I owe you my life, and I'm growing fond of you," said the captain, stroking his thigh. "If you insult my crew again, I'll break your neck and put you back where I found you. Are we clear?"

To cut off any further conversation, he rode him roughly, relishing the burn of being stretched without mercy. Rux's head fell back against the floor, and he made a variety of quiet humming noises that the captain guessed indicated gratification.

"Apologies, foreigner. I did not mean to cause offence to you or your pets."

In a conversational tone, the captain panted, "Do you...ah...want me to hit you? Is...*hng*...is that what this is about?"

"Yes, it is."

The captain sat forward and dealt the left side of Rux's face a resounding slap. At that, the alien's back arched, and he came with a shout. The captain growled in pleasure as Rux's fingernails dug into his thighs.

The alien collapsed boneless onto the blanket as soon as he was done, and the captain was forced to finish himself off with his own hand. It wasn't too great a disappointment. It wasn't every day he got to masturbate to the sight of a post-orgasmic extraterrestrial.

"Should I have helped you with that?" Rux inquired, as the captain was moaning his way through a satisfying climax. "I assume I should have. Oh, dear. That's twice I've offended you now."

"Don't worry. You'll have ample opportunity to make it up to me," said the captain, flopping down beside him. "That is, if you want to stay with us?"

Rux rubbed his own cheek, where the captain's slap had left a mark. "I would. Coarse as they are, your crew loves you. I've missed being surrounded by love. Your ship is, I fear, decidedly undersized, compared to the ships my people used to build. Are you certain there will be room for me?"

"Always room for one more," said the captain.

☆☆☆

"What are you up to?"

Echo glanced across the ship's kitchen to see Antoine standing in the doorway, his arms folded. He'd stripped off his suit and changed into a pair of white shorts and a T-shirt that showed off the dark skin stretched tight over his collarbone.

Echo stood back and made a *ta-da!* motion.

"Baking? Now? I'd have thought you'd like to come watch the sunset. It's spectacular," Antoine told him. Then the first officer's nose twitched, and his eyes were drawn to the tray at Echo's side, newly removed from the oven. "Are those..."

Echo was proud of himself. Cutting into the alien fruit's outer shell had been challenging, and he'd had to experiment with several recipes, but it was worth it to be able to bake with real food again. The steaming tarts were the first non-synthetic dessert he'd produced in years.

"I presume you performed a thorough chemical analysis to ascertain that they're edible?" Antoine asked, picking one up. As Echo nodded, Antoine bit into it, and made a noise that made Echo blush. While Antoine identified as asexual, Echo had never worked out what to call himself; he would go for weeks without feeling a trace of lust for anyone, and then the oddest thing would set his heart pounding. The unpredictability was aggravating.

Antoine finished the tart, licking his lips and his fingers clean. As always, Echo found himself fascinated by the man's white but uneven front teeth, made all the more apparent by the perfection of the face surrounding them. "Echo, that was the best thing I've had in my mouth since we left Earth. Of course, I suspect those members of the crew who have partaken of our mighty leader's...generosity of spirit would say otherwise."

His tone was light, but Echo detected in his expression a touch of gloom. Observant as he was, Echo couldn't fully characterize the relationship between their captain and his first officer, save for a deep suspicion that not all was as it seemed. He wasn't one to pry, though. He accepted the compliment and took a tart for himself.

"The captain's guest may prove to be a useful source of information," Antoine said, chewing thoughtfully. "He's promised to show us to the remains of his people's cities tomorrow. The reason we couldn't spot them from orbit is that they're concealed by the same holographic technology that hid his lair from view—or so he claims. Will you come?"

Echo made a gesture with his hands, which translated to: *If you'd like, but I doubt I'd be much use.*

"Don't be stupid," Antoine snapped. "If the last two days have proved anything, it's that you are one of the few members of this crew who can keep their head in a crisis. I need you."

Touched, Echo made another gesture: *We need you. All of us. Even Zachery.*

Antoine made a derisive snort but said nothing more. They devoured the rest of the tarts and then made a fresh batch for the others.

CHAPTER EIGHT

Thomas hadn't gotten to appreciate his first sunset on their new planet, what with being half convinced that the man he was in love with had been gobbled up by alien beasties. He was determined to relish his second and, to that end, now lay back on the grass with his head resting in his arms, a cup of not-coffee at his side and no inclination to move for the next hour. *The Prayer* was parked nearby, silhouetted in the grass like a huge cow. No one had decided what their next move was yet. Which was fine. Thomas was down with just staying put for a while. It was nice here.

"You busy?" came a gruff voice.

"Yeah, I am. I'm so busy that if you say one word to me I might die of exertion," said Thomas, keeping his gaze fixed on the sky, which was fading into lavender.

Zachery's fat, stupid head got in the way of Thomas's view.

"Wanted to apologize," the engineer said. "For earlier, I mean. I was a jackass."

Thomas shrugged. "It's not me you were a jackass to. Go apologize to Rick."

"I already did. We're cool."

"Really?" said Thomas, taken aback.

Scratching the back of his head, Zachery said, "Yeah. He wanted a *hug*, of all things."

Without waiting for an invitation, he flopped down on the grass beside Thomas, mimicking his pose. The sky went from lavender to mauve before Thomas said, "I know it's the way you are, but you're too rough with him, man."

"You coddle him too much," Zachery retorted. "He's tougher than you give him credit for. Hell of a lot tougher than I was at that age."

"And me. I was a fucking wimp."

"Not much's changed then."

Vengefully, Thomas pulled up a handful of grass and threw it at Zachery's face. "What're you here for, again?"

"I told you. To apologize."

"Right, fine, apology accepted. Was that it?" asked Thomas, rolling onto his stomach.

"No." Zachery was deliberately avoiding his gaze. "I wanted to ask if..."

"If?" Thomas prompted.

Zachery rubbed the bridge of his nose. "I'm fucking this up. See, I like you. You're dorky and kind of dumb, but I like you. And I liked being with you, the last time. Even if the captain and Rick hadn't been there, I'd have liked it. I want...I want all three of you, for me. But I also want you and me to do our own thing now and then. I'd like to...shit, Thomas, I'd like to get to know you better, all right? Do stuff together, eat together. And fuck, obviously. I think that would be cool. I think we'd be good together."

"If you can put up with me," he added, while Thomas mulled it over.

"You want to be boyfriends," Thomas concluded.

Zachery grimaced. "Ugh, don't say that word. I'm not a teenybopper asking you to the goddamn prom. Let's say 'lovers,' okay?"

"You know, Rick asked me the same thing."

"What'd you say to him?"

"That I'm not boyfriend material."

Zachery barked a laugh. "Come the fuck on. You? You'd be the best boyfriend in the history of the universe. You do birdwatching. You cuddle and make polite conversation. I'll bet my life you hold hands in public. What's the real reason? Is it 'cause he's younger? I told you; you need to give him more credit. He's not a delicate flower. And I already fucked his ass, if that helps."

"Talking about my ass behind my back? Man, you two suck."

They both looked up guiltily as Rick's shadow fell over them. He was tapping his foot like a put-out housewife who'd caught her husband dipping his dick in her homemade apple pie.

"Get lost, shrimp," said Zachery, lazily twining an arm around Thomas. "I seduced you yesterday, now it's this hot bitch's turn."

Smirking, Rick dropped down and straddled Thomas's lap, while Zachery drew Thomas back into his. "Oh? Is that so? Because what I remember is you *begging* for a shot at my adorable ass. Thomas, you know this sad loser couldn't wait until we got back to the ship? Had to do it up against a tree, like a dog who needs his nuts chopped."

Leaning over Thomas's shoulder, Rick exchanged a messy tongue-fuck with the aforementioned sad loser. Thomas felt Zachery's cock swelling against the curve of his ass.

"You realize we're outside, right?" Thomas said, putting both hands on Rick's hips and grinding their dicks together. "Anyone could see."

"Did that sound like a complaint to you, Rick?" asked Zachery.

"Nope," said Rick, unzipping Thomas's suit and peeling it off his shoulders. "Sounds as though he kinda likes the idea."

After tugging off his own suit, Zachery lay down in the grass, taking both of them down with him so that Thomas lay back on top of him and Rick straddled Thomas's waist. Working out what they had in mind, Thomas grinned and stole a kiss from Rick. Low and husky, he said, "Zach tells me he already had your ass to himself earlier. That right, cutie?"

Bashfully, Rick nodded. Thomas kissed him again. "Then I guess I'm going to have to show him up, aren't I? Get undressed."

Zachery, meanwhile, was pawing Thomas's ass, dragging his big fingers down his crack. No lube, only spit. Thomas could handle it. Zachery was brisk, but he wasn't brutal, and he took his time stretching Thomas open before pushing in.

"Oh, hell," Thomas moaned, seeing stars behind his closed eyelids.

Zachery laughed, the smug motherfucker. "You tell me you've had anyone bigger than me in you, and I'll call you a goddamn liar, twerp."

"Quit wriggling, Meléndez," Rick said. "Zach, can you hold his cock still for me?"

The feeling of Rick sinking down onto him while Zachery thrust up was every bit as awesome as Thomas might have hoped. He got a thrill out of the contrast between their bodies, Rick's narrow hips and

Zachery's broad, hairy chest, and the way both of them were as intent on pleasing each other as they were on pleasing him. Zachery reached around to jerk Rick off while he bounced up and down on Thomas's cock, and Rick kept leaning over Thomas's shoulder to swap messy kisses. They worked out a rhythm, and Thomas let them use him however they wanted.

I could do this with them forever, he thought. *I really could.*

He came first, staring up at the sky—dark blue, a few wisps of cloud, countless stars in the background. He didn't know who came second, but within a minute, all three of them had stopped moving, forming a disorderly heap of sweaty bodies on the grass.

"Hey, you guys?" Thomas said when his brain could be bothered with formulating speech. "You wanna be my boyfriends?"

"Guess so," said Zachery.

"Don't see why not," said Rick, and Thomas felt him smile against his heart.

THE CAPTAIN'S CALAMITY

CHAPTER ONE

The captain and his first officer were playing Monopoly.

Any member of the crew to have walked in on them would have been flummoxed. It was common knowledge aboard *The Prayer* that the two men didn't get on. No one understood why the captain had hired Antoine Mbaye given he so clearly disliked him. Why Antoine had ever agreed to work for Khurshed Amirmoez, a man whose decisions he criticized at every turn, was a deeper mystery still. The crew often speculated amongst themselves as to what might be the cause of such deep animosity; why it was that two otherwise level-headed individuals seemed to take such delight in quarrelling with one another. Now and then, someone would suggest that all they needed was a good hate-fuck to get it out of their systems.

Had either Antoine or the captain heard this suggestion they would have laughed themselves sick and then thrown whoever had made it into the brig.

"I want to buy the asteroid belt," said the captain. He lay on his side on his bed, with a tiny silver satellite dish held between forefinger and thumb. The Monopoly board was spread out before him, framed by Antoine's elbows.

"How many times must I explain this? You can't buy the asteroid belt. The asteroid belt was what they put in place of the jail," Antoine told him. Wearing only his socks, briefs, and an unbuttoned shirt, the smaller man was lying on his belly with his feet in the air and his hands folded under his jaw, looming over the left side of the board. It was home to Earth, Titan, and Europa; collectively, the most prime real estate in the solar system.

"That makes no sense at all. Interstellar space would have been a more fitting space-themed jail. Or...hmm...yes, or a black hole."

"You only ever quibble like this when you're losing."

"I'm not losing," the captain said, thinking to himself that he probably was. He knew himself to be the worst Monopoly player on board *The Prayer*. Antoine's extensive collection of board games was one of the ways they'd kept themselves entertained during their four years of aimless wandering. Echo and Yanmei could now play chess to a championship standard, and the Clue board was falling to pieces from overuse. The captain had played four hundred and sixty-eight games of Monopoly since last he had been anywhere near the real estate featured on the board. He never seemed to get any better at it.

He liked it, though. The dainty playing pieces amused him, and moreover, it was Antoine's favourite mindless pastime. Since he and his first officer had reconciled, they'd taken to playing a match whenever they could find the time.

"Oh, before I forget, *Bon anniversaire*, Captain. Your slow shamble towards senility continues unabated for another year. I'm sorry I didn't get you a cake."

"To the devil with your cake." The dice rolled, and the captain's satellite dish landed on Pluto.

Antoine smirked. "I'd advise you to be on your guard. Thomas might take it into his head to throw you a party. He seems the type."

"He doesn't know. None of them do."

There was a pause. "Oh. That's a shame. I imagine they'd like to know."

The captain grunted noncommittally, avoiding Antoine's gaze.

Antoine added, "You know all their birthdays, don't you?"

"If I tell them it's my birthday, they'll ask how old I am," the captain muttered.

"So? Tell them. And make sure I'm there when you do. I want to see their eyes pop out."

"Tell them *your* real age, that'll do the trick."

"They're not sleeping with me." Antoine removed his glasses and blew on them. "While we're on the subject; why haven't you told them your first name yet?"

"Oh, they probably couldn't pronounce it," said the captain, pretending to count his Monopoly money. Antoine's eyes were piercing, even when filtered through the lenses.

Rolling onto his side, Antoine shuffled around until his feet lay within reach of the captain's hands. Recognizing the implicit request, the captain pulled off Antoine's socks and started to massage his left foot.

"Your new companions... No, don't sigh like that. This isn't a lecture; it's a warning. I know you love them. However, the fact is that you know far, far more about all of them than they know about you. You let them have your body whenever they want it, but they won't be satisfied with that forever."

"Have you considered that the reason I haven't told them my name or my birthday is because they haven't asked?"

"Of course they haven't. You're their fearless leader. Even though they adore you, they're still a little in awe of you. You tend to have that effect on people."

"Not on you, if I recall."

"Don't try to change the subject. My point is, while you can be their lover and their leader at the same time, I think that attempting to maintain professional distance from four people with whom you are in love is a fool's errand."

"You think I'm trying to have my cake and eat it."

Withdrawing his feet from the captain's lap, Antoine crawled over until he could cup his jaw. "I think you're doing the best you can. I think there are few men who could have endured what you've endured for the last few years. You held the crew together when all hope seemed lost. You've done very, very well. I simply..."

"Want me to do better," the captain said, smiling and touching Antoine's cheek. "As ever, my talking cricket has dispensed sound advice."

It was an old joke, resulting from Antoine's having been reading Pinocchio in a café on the day they'd first met.

How much younger we were then.

The captain lost the game and stared out the porthole above his bed while Antoine put the board away. It was late afternoon—and how strange it felt to be able to tell that by looking outside, instead of checking the ship's clock. *The Prayer* was gliding over the great grass

119

plains that dominated this planet's terra firma, low enough for them to be able to make out fauna the size of a cow or larger—Rux insisted that there were some, albeit their numbers had been depleted in the multiple catastrophes that had wiped out his own people. Their destination was an abandoned city Rux had promised to show them, thus far concealed from their orbital surveillance by advanced camouflage technology. The captain had declined to remark upon the fact that said technology was still operational so long after the city had been abandoned. He didn't want Rux to launch into another of his orations on the brilliance and superiority of his long-dead species.

Standing, the captain said, "I should be on my way. I told Zachery I'd meet him in ten minutes. There's something he wants to discuss."

"I'm sure there is. No doubt some boring technical issue related to the maintenance of the ship," said Antoine, his voice rich with disbelief. "Have fun. How long until we arrive, by the way?"

"Another two hours or so."

Antoine stretched. "Then I think I'll go ask Thomas for a spot of tuition. I still can't get the hang of loading the damned thing."

Since their last excursion onto the planet's surface, it had been agreed that Thomas would teach every member of the crew the basics of how to handle a rifle. It had been his idea, and the captain hadn't liked it—guns revolted him—but he could see the practicality. Their knowledge of this planet and its environment was still dangerously limited. Best be prepared for anything.

Before the captain departed, Antoine stepped into his arms and held him for a moment. "Once again, happy birthday, Captain. I am rather glad you're not dead yet. Listen—let's celebrate when we get done with Rux's ruins. We could have dinner. Just the two of us, I mean."

With a pang, the captain realised it had been years since the two of them had had a private meal together—since they'd had anything he thought of as a real date. He also recognised the invitation as Antoine's signalling a need for reassurance there remained some part of the captain that belonged only to him.

He needn't have worried.

"What if we had dinner on top of the ship? We could lay out a picnic blanket and name some more constellations," the captain suggested.

"Ugh, how romantic. We really are getting old," said Antoine, pressing against his chest.

The captain lingered until the nearness of Antoine's body caused his own to start reacting. He withdrew, though not out of fear of Antoine's noticing—his first officer was already aware he found him desirable. Rather, the captain didn't want to arrive before Zachery with an erection that the engineer hadn't caused. It felt like bad manners.

"Off you go," said Antoine. "Don't let him maul you too badly this time."

☆☆☆

The stethoscope kept getting in the way.

When the captain had suggested he take it off, Zachery had insisted its presence was vital to maintaining the fantasy. The captain had refrained from pointing out that, as a proctologist, he wouldn't have any reason to wear a stethoscope. Although sex with Zachery was usually fuelled by just those sorts of pig-headed arguments—and all the more enjoyable for it—today was special. It was the first time Zachery was letting another man finger him.

So the captain put up with the stethoscope, even when an attempt to alter their positions for comfort's sake resulted in its swinging forward and smacking Zachery's face. Instead of flinging the damned thing into a corner like it deserved, the captain had Zachery lie face down on the examination table, removing his handsome features from the danger zone.

"The door's locked, right?" Zachery asked for the third time.

"Yes, yes," said the captain, glancing once again over his shoulder to check that it hadn't miraculously unlocked itself. He understood Zachery's concern; God alone knew what Antoine would say if he saw the captain had stolen one of his lab coats to complete his costume.

Zachery himself was naked, spread out like a feast on the examination table. His dark hair was washed and combed, and his dreadful goatee had been shaved into some semblance of neatness. The captain hadn't asked for either concession and recognised them as gestures of good will.

"How are you finding it?" the captain asked.

"It's okay, I guess," Zachery said, which was probably the most lukewarm response the captain had ever received from a man whose arse had now taken three of his fingers. "I mean, it doesn't hurt like I thought it would. But it's not really doing anything for me."

Under the harsh light of the medical bay, his skin had taken on a golden shine. The sequence "3ZH66W2" stood out starkly on the small of his back, courtesy of the Martian justice system's gleeful propensity towards corporal punishment—one of the many reasons the planet had been on the receiving end of economy-breaking sanctions for decades. Running his fingertips over the brand, the captain reflected that there were many benefits to being lost far beyond the reach of civilization.

Even so, Zachery made a mouth-watering sight, with his gleaming muscles and tight buttocks. It was with regret that the captain withdrew his fingers. "Thank you for indulging me."

"Hey, hey, you don't have to stop! I mean... It might get better, right? We can keep going."

Such a sweet man. The captain leaned down and kissed him. "I don't believe that sex should be something you have to work to enjoy. It's fine. It was an experiment."

Zachery's expression was one of relief mingled with guilt. "Maybe we can try again sometime? Like, maybe it's one of those things where you need to be in the right mood, or something?"

"We can try as many times as you like," the captain murmured, distracted by the delicious smell of his sweat. Content, Zachery sat up and drew him closer, their tongues sliding against one another.

When the captain started to pull off Antoine's coat, Zachery said in a voice that had regained its habitual growl, "Wait a sec. We're not done with that yet. I still want my sexy proctologist fantasy. You promised."

"Very well," the captain conceded. "Given that penetration isn't working out, perhaps we could try something different."

"Like what?"

With a grin that felt feral, the captain sat down on the edge of the examination table and set about arranging Zachery over his lap.

"Congratulations, Mister Halberstam," he said in what he thought sounded like an authoritative doctor's voice—it might, in fact, simply have been his "captain on the bridge" voice. "It is my considered medical opinion that you are in peak physical condition. Your arse in particular is one of the finest I've seen. That said, I regret to inform you that you appear to have contracted a mild case of what we professionals call 'wilful recalcitrance syndrome'."

"Fuck, sounds scary," Zachery said, straight-faced. "There a cure, doc?"

The captain nodded. "It's a common illness and easily treatable."

He pulled off the white plastic gloves Zachery had insisted on earlier. Zachery, being far more intelligent than most people gave him credit for, had shifted so that his cock rested against the captain's thigh and his backside curved upwards like a ripe apple.

Gorgeous. The captain licked his lips. "Please remain still while I operate, Mister Halberstam."

The first smack was experimental, barely hard enough to sting. He measured Zachery's reaction and modulated the force of the next one.

Zachery cried out, rocking forward. "Jesus! Do you practice by bitch-slapping Antoine? Ow."

There was a faint handprint visible on his rear, and his cock had stiffened in the captain's lap. The captain, for his part, had been hard from the moment Zachery had removed his clothes and, given that he wasn't wearing anything underneath Antoine's lab coat, had now stained it with precome. He reminded himself to clean it before putting it back.

Twenty smacks later and Zachery's backside had turned an attractive shade of pink. Even so, he was doing a manful job of keeping still, although whimpers and groans fell from his lips unabated. The captain's left hand rubbed soothing circles on his back, while his right hand left irregular gaps between each strike. The trick was not to let one's partner predict exactly when the pain would come next.

"Oh, Daddy, fuck," Zachery whined, as the captain's hand drew back again.

"Really?" said the captain, pausing and arching an eyebrow.

Zachery blushed. "Screw you."

"Now, what sort of sense does that make?" the captain said, palming his reddened arse. "You don't mind asking me to pretend to give you a sexy proctology exam, but you're too shy to ask if you can call me 'Daddy'? You're a confusing man, Zachery."

"I'm not 'shy', asshole. It's just that you're so old I thought I should probably be calling you 'Granddaddy' instead."

Crack went the captain's hand as it connected with Zachery's rear for the twenty-first time. Zachery bit on his hand to stifle a howl, his cock grinding against the captain's thigh.

"Apologise," the captain ordered. "Unless you want me to flog you with the stethoscope. And that will hurt."

Zachery murmured something he couldn't quite hear and then said, "S-sorry, Daddy."

His blood surged in his veins. "Apology accepted. Now, Zachery, if you can be good and not climax for another ten strokes, Daddy will give you a treat."

And he *was* good, very good, even with his cock rock-hard and rubbing against the captain's own erection. In between groans and flinches, the captain saw his lips move as he counted off the strokes.

"Well done, darling boy," he purred as he delivered an unexpected eleventh blow and then hoisted Zachery up into a sitting position in his lap. The engineer's pupils were blown wide, and his lower lip had been bitten so hard it had split, leaving a thin trail of blood to trickle down his chin. "Daddy's very pleased with you."

To his surprise, Zachery threw both meaty arms around his shoulders and pressed his face against his neck. The captain returned the hug, saying, "Do you want your treat now?"

Sniffing, Zachery nodded. "Whassit?"

"Up to you. Would you like a blowjob or would you like to fuck me?"

Zachery pondered his options, before asking, "Can we stay like this for a while? And...maybe you can get me off with your hand? Oh, and quit calling me 'Zachery' when we're screwing. Call me 'Zach'."

The captain kissed his forehead. "Certainly. Call me Khurshed."

How startled he looked to hear that, how honoured. *Antoine was right*, the captain thought with a pang. *I've been careless.*

Keeping one arm wrapped around him, the captain reached down and took hold of both their cocks, squeezing them together.

"You look so fucking sexy in that coat," Zachery sighed, rocking forward into his grip. "Can we ditch the stethoscope, though? It's kind of digging into my ribs."

Away it flew, landing in a corner.

Neither of them lasted much longer. Zachery's hand slipped down to fondle the base of the captain's shaft, his touch light and teasing—he was so good at rough play Khurshed tended to forget he was capable of subtlety. Shuddering, he felt himself start to come and retained enough presence of mind to ensure that most of it ended up in Zachery's chest hair.

"Y-you mean little bitch," Zachery panted as the older man collapsed against him. "I should... Oh, Jesus..."

Moaning, he followed suit, crushing the captain to his chest so hard he could barely breathe.

They reclined together on the examination table, enjoying the afterglow, until the captain's back began to send him quiet warnings against lying too long on a hard, uncomfortable surface. Mouthing the hollow of Zachery's throat, he said, "We should shower. We'll be arriving soon."

"Whatever you say, Cap. Hey, are you sure about this alien of yours?"

"His name is Rux."

"Yeah, yeah. How do we know he isn't leading us into his...I dunno...his hive or something, so he can feed us to his ten million alien babies?"

"The thought had occurred to me," the captain said, putting the coat into a laundry bag. "Given there is a chance we might find tools or technology we can use to improve our chances of survival on this planet in Rux's city, I think it is worth the risk. Besides, we will be armed."

"Don't get me wrong; I like the guy. I just don't know if we should be so quick to trust him, that's all. I mean, he's hot, but..."

"Why Zach, surely that isn't jealousy I detect in your tone?"

"Ah, fuck off," Zachery returned, biting his shoulder. "Can't blame me. I'd got used to being the only one on board who's bigger than you."

"Irene's bigger than both of us."

"Fine, the only person you're sleeping with who's bigger than you."

The captain squeezed his limp cock. "Only in some respects, Zach."

Zachery erupted in protest at that, so they had to measure in the shower. Echo was waiting with two cups of coffee when they came out.

"Exactly what I need," declared the captain, taking his mug. "Thank you."

The blond man accepted his gratitude with a familiar gesture. The captain leaned down to kiss him, aware of Zachery watching them in confusion—maybe fascination. The captain knew the other members of his quintet didn't understand Echo's place in his life. Their silent crewmate never joined them in bed, despite multiple invitations from the captain himself, and although he'd become less reticent around them in recent months, he still reserved his kisses for the captain's lips alone. Privately, Echo had imparted to the captain that while he was open to the possibility of future intimacy with Zachery, Thomas, or Rick, he'd approach them in his own time.

The captain wasn't in any hurry; he was content with their arrangement as it stood. Echo's touch was gentle, almost genteel after Zachery's aggressive style of lovemaking, and his fingers brushed over the captain's soft cock as he departed.

"No kiss for me?" Zachery asked in mock disappointment that the captain knew concealed an edge of the real thing.

He ruffled his hair. "You haven't earned one yet, Zachery. Echo's far less of a slut than—"

He was cut off by the deafening roar of an explosion, and both men were thrown to the floor as the whole ship shook. Alarms began blaring while automated voices recited instructions as to how to evacuate the ship in an orderly manner in English, Arabic, and French.

His ears ringing, the captain sat up. "What on earth...?"

"The engines. *Fuck*." Zachery got to his feet and charged out of the medbay with a damp towel still wrapped around his waist.

"Wait!" the captain shouted and set off after him.

126

CHAPTER TWO

He could smell smoke. By the time they reached G deck, he could see it, a black cloud filling up the corridor. The door to the engine room was open, although it didn't seem to have been damaged by whatever had taken place beyond it. Inside, red lights were flashing, and the smoke was so dense the captain couldn't see where it was coming from, much less how bad the damage was.

Zachery, knowing the engine room like the back of his hand, found his way to his station despite the smoke and started barking questions at the ship's audio interface program. As he did, the captain heard a voice coming from somewhere in the surrounding miasma.

"Zach? That you, man?"

"Rick?" shouted the captain, making his way towards the voice. "Where are you?"

"Over here. On the floor. Shit, I think I'm bleeding," Rick called out and coughed.

"Keep talking. I'm coming towards you now," said the captain. His eyes and throat were stinging. "Where are you bleeding?"

"My hand and...I think, my face? I can't tell. My head fucking hurts."

The smoke was so thick in this section of the room the captain ended up almost stepping on him. He was lying against the wall, evidently having been thrown back against it, his right hand cradled in his lap and his clothes singed.

"Hi, Captain," he said, smiling weakly. The left side of his face was covered in blood, most of which issued from a cut on his scalp—although, to the captain's disquiet, some seemed to be leaking from the vicinity of his left eye, which was squeezed shut. "How's it going?"

"All the better for seeing you." The captain knelt down and checked him for serious injuries before picking him up.

By the time they reached Zachery, the alarms had stopped blaring, and the smoke seemed to be dissipating. The engineer took one look at Rick and went several shades paler.

"Jesus, kid, what happened to you?"

"I got blown up," Rick croaked.

"Yeah, I see that. What were you doing down here, dummy?"

"Looking for you, asshole. Wanted to let you know I've got a new batch of w... of fresh, healthy vegetables," Rick amended, glancing up at the captain.

"What seems to be the problem, Mister Halberstam?"

Zachery shook his head, patting the control panel as though *The Prayer* were a sickly pet. "Can't tell you that until I shut her down and get up inside her. She's stable for now. The antimatter generator's working fine, so there's no danger of us all being oblit..."

"Captain!" came Antoine's voice over the comm. "Where are you? Something's happened to the ship. We've started descending."

Rubbing his chin, Zachery said, "Seriously? Huh. That's weird. The anti-grav systems are still operating, and there's nothing wrong with..."

"Zachery," the captain interrupted, "my ship appears to be losing altitude. It is logical to conclude that if this state of affairs continues, it will crash-land. Regardless of the root of this crisis, do you have a solution to the immediate problem?"

Zachery blew out his cheeks. "Not really, Captain. Her emergency systems were one of the things I shut down to make sure she doesn't explode again. It's not safe to turn them back on until know what caused the first blast."

"Right. Crash-land it is, then. Come with me."

Rick tugged on the captain's lapels as they left the engine room. "Are we all going to die?"

"Nah," said Zachery. "Even without any power, the ship's designed to glide for one hundred kilometres before hitting the ground. We'll be fine, so long as we don't land on anything hard."

That was a *very* optimistic take on the situation, which the captain decided not to correct.

The elevator wouldn't work, so they ran up the stairs to reach the medbay on C deck, where the captain left Zachery to tend to Rick. This wasn't *The Prayer*'s first forced landing, and he knew from personal experience that the medbay was one of the safest places to be. Sprinting, he made his way to the bridge and found the rest of the crew were already present, talking over one another from their stations while Antoine tried to maintain order.

"Quiet!" the captain roared. "Someone tell me how long we've got until we touch down."

"At this rate, twelve minutes," said Antoine. "We're currently over marshes, but there's solid ground coming up ahead. More good news; the autopilot's not working. For some reason, Khali is happy about this."

"It's nice to feel useful for once," said Khali from her pilot's seat, her gaze fixed on the screen in front of her.

"Corporal Bansal, can you get us down in one piece?" the captain asked, sliding into his beloved chair.

"Hope so!" she said. "You should all strap in. It'll be bumpy."

It was. If they'd been any higher or going any faster, and if the grassy plain they landed on hadn't been smooth and devoid of obstacles, it might have been calamitous. The landing gear gave a tortured squeal as it connected with the ground. They bounced, once, twice, and the bridge shuddered beneath them. Anything that wasn't strapped down—Thomas's mug, Antoine's clipboard, Moxie's chew toy—was thrown across the room. After what felt like hours, they stopped moving.

"Is anyone hurt?" asked the captain.

"I think I lost a filling," said Irene, her hand over her mouth. Across the room, Thomas and Mehtab were both retching.

"Get to the medbay," the captain told her. "Take those two with you, and check up on Rick and Zachery while you're there. Antoine, damage report. Echo, more coffee, please."

☆☆☆

The damage to *The Prayer*'s exterior was negligible. Nothing that couldn't be repaired over the course of a few weeks with the tools they had to hand.

Her engines were a different matter.

129

"The good news is that I can keep the life support systems operational," Zachery told them. He stood at the front of the room, having concluded a comprehensive rundown of the sequence of mechanical errors that had led to the explosion, which the captain suspected few of his crew had been able to follow. "The bad news is that I can't get her spaceworthy. Not with the tools I've got."

"We're stuck here? Forever?" said Irene, her face taut with dismay. She had been born in space and had spent most of her life on one ship or another. The thought of being permanently marooned planetside must have been bone chilling.

"Not necessarily," said Rux.

The captain looked towards the latest addition to his crew: a handsome, green-skinned man standing quietly at the back of the room. While the ship had been going down, he'd apparently been dozing in one of his many feline shapes, and had only woken up when their harsh landing had thrown him into the ceiling. He looked no worse for the wear, any injuries he had sustained having healed already.

A remarkable body indeed, thought the captain, his gaze lingering on it.

"What're you talking about, freak?" Zachery demanded.

Rux pointed to the hologram Zachery had activated: a minutely detailed depiction of the ship's engines and all their components. "That part—the small one in the shape of an octagon. What did you call it?"

"The DG ring," said Zachery.

"And—if I have followed you—that is the part that broke, yes?"

"A lot of parts broke," Zachery said, impatiently. "Or snapped, or melted. The DG ring just happens to be one of the most important, and also the only one I absolutely cannot fix. I couldn't even fix it if we were on Earth. We need a new one."

"I believe I know where you might find one," announced Rux, turning to address the room at large. "As I have mentioned before in passing, my people's technological capabilities far outstripped your own. Despite our tragic decline, much was left behind. Many of our cities are home to warehouses and laboratories full of marvels still in perfect working order, thanks to the foresight and unparalleled skill of..."

Cutting him off, the captain said, "You believe that there might be something on this planet that could help us? Something that could save my...our ship?"

"Yes. In fact, I know exactly where one such 'DG ring' might be. There is a research centre in..."

Rux uttered a string of clicks and hisses the captain recognised as the name of the abandoned city which had been their original destination.

"It was one of our main industrial hubs, and its factories assembled our spacecraft," Rux continued. "Walking there would take you several hours, but the terrain is not challenging. I would be glad to show you the way."

After a moment's internal deliberation, the captain addressed the crew: "*The Prayer* is our chief asset. We need her for our food, our water, our transport, and our safety. Returning her to full functionality must be our top priority. In pursuit of this goal, half of us will remain here to implement what repairs they can with the tools we have available. The other half, including Zachery and Rux, will accompany me to the city, where we will scavenge whatever parts we can and return with them as soon as possible."

Thomas had his hand in the air. "I want to come with you, Captain."

"Very well. Any other volunteers?" he asked, knowing which hands would go up.

In addition to Zachery, Rux, and Thomas, his team ended up including Antoine, Echo, and Irene. Doubtless, Rick would have volunteered himself had he not still been recovering in the medbay.

☆☆☆

"No fair," Rick whined when the captain visited and told him of their plans.

He lay in one of their two medical pods, a transparent cylinder that allowed the captain to see the full extent of his injuries. His hand had sustained second-degree burns, with first-degree burns up to his elbow. Ugly as it looked, it wouldn't take the pod much more than a day to heal, if all went well. His cracked ribs and the welt on his scalp would both mend within twenty-four hours. What worried the captain was Rick's left eye. It had been punctured, and all he could see out of it were murky shadows. Although *The Prayer*'s medical pods were well maintained, like most of the ship, they were old and second-hand. While military vessels were equipped with Class 1 pods, able to perform any and all operations less complex than brain surgery, merchant vessels were only legally required to fit Class 4 pods, best suited to repairing cleanly broken bones and closing flesh wounds. Working with a limited budget, the captain had opted for a Class 3, which could handle burns as well. He didn't know how well it would work on an eye.

"Can't I come with you? I won't slow you down, Captain. I promise," Rick pleaded.

The captain lay a hand on the glass separating them, wishing he could touch his face. "That's not the point. Rick, has it occurred to you that you and Zachery are the only members of this crew who aren't expendable? No one else can fix our engines, and no one else can grow our food. It would be irresponsible for me to put you in harm's way unnecessarily."

"Zach's going with you," Rick pointed out.

"He has to. We'll be scavenging parts; he'll know best what to look for."

Pouting, Rick subsided. "How long before you're back?"

"If all goes well, less than two days. If we're delayed for any reason, I'll contact the ship and let you know."

Zachery stomped into the medical bay, already suited up and ready to go. He leaned against the pod and grunted, "Hey, shrimp. Thought I'd check in on you before we left."

"Aw. I'm touched. Gimme a kiss, you asshole."

Zachery's lips left an imprint on the glass. "You get better quick, all right?"

"Yeah, yeah. Wouldn't want you to have to fuck a one-eyed freak."

"My first boyfriend was a one-eyed freak, I'll have you know," Zachery retorted.

"Not as pretty as me, though, right?"

"No. Not half as pretty."

Rick waved through the glass as they left.

The captain studied his engineer's face.

"Mister Halberstam, I'm sure the thought hasn't crossed your mind that you are in any way responsible for Ricardo's current condition?"

Zachery snorted. "Captain, I've got one job on this crate, and that's to keep her from blowing up in our faces. I fucked up."

"Actually, the job for which I hired you was to keep *The Prayer* running for the duration of a one-and-a-half-year journey to Pluto, with regular access to repair stations at which you might be supplied with whatever tools and spare parts you required. I didn't hire you to keep the ship running for almost five years single-handed, and the fact that you have managed to do that is..."

"Cap, I get that you're being nice. Could you knock it off? S'only making me feel worse," said Zachery. Then he pulled him into a tight bear hug. "You want to be nice, tell me that I can fix this."

"You can fix this," said the captain, stroking his hair.

The others were waiting for them outside. Rux had transformed into a muscular, ox-sized quadruped, and acquiesced to their strapping various supplies and pieces of equipment to his back.

"Good luck, Captain," said Khali, who would remain in charge while he and Antoine were gone. "Don't get kidnapped by aliens again."

"I'll do my best," he assured her, and the seven of them set off towards the city.

CHAPTER THREE

"Oh, fuck no," said Thomas.

"Language," snapped the captain.

But he commiserated. The ruins looming before them resembled nothing so much as the skeletal remains of a lion's jaw, sharp tooth-shaped structures rising up out of dry, lifeless soil. The aura of menace the city gave off was not helped by the barrenness of the surrounding landscape or the iron-grey sky that seemed a permanent feature of this region of the planet.

"This was once one of the crowning jewels of our civilisation," said Rux as Zachery and Echo unloaded their gear.

"You say it was abandoned two thousand years ago?" Antoine asked. The captain knew he didn't like Rux or the smug superiority that coloured every word he spoke. That said, Antoine was a scientist. Ever since Rux had joined the crew, he had pumped him for information about this world and its late inhabitants.

"After the plague, yes. Most of the city's population was already dead by that point. Knowing the disease had spread to all regions of the planet, the few who were still uninfected decided to try to escape to our nearest inhabitable neighbour. They boarded an experimental ship—a last resort, cobbled together in a hurry. I don't know what became of them."

"Why didn't you go with them?" Antoine asked.

After a short pause, Rux said, "There was limited space on the ship. I was strong and healthy. I decided to stay behind and take my chances so those weaker than me might survive."

Thomas looked touched. Antoine looked sceptical. The captain reserved judgement and asked, "Rux, I'd like a better idea of what we're walking into. What are the chances that wild animals will have made

ADRIFT: THE COLLECTION | T.J. LAND

their homes in the ruins?"

Rux assumed his human form, green-skinned and gloriously naked. Thomas had evidently planned for this, thoughtful soul that he was, as he took a pair of clean, folded briefs out of his suit's pocket and gave them to him. Putting them on, Rux replied, "I wouldn't concern yourself, Captain. There are a mere handful of carnivorous species in this hemisphere and none that would not be deterred with a warning shot."

"Is it safe to fire?" asked Thomas, who had also brought his laser rifle at the captain's behest. "I mean is there anything lying around that'll explode if we hit it by accident?"

In mildly offended tones, Rux answered, "No. As I have told you, my people were wise and prudent. Even in our last days, we didn't leave dangerous materials scattered about."

Raising his voice, the captain said, "One last time, has everyone checked that their equipment is in working order? Your comms in particular?"

"Yes, sir!"

As he led them into the city, Antoine walked at his side. In French, he said, "I have bad news, Captain."

"Oh?"

"You know how whenever we leave the ship and you're wearing that suit, half the crew can't stop staring at your rear? Well, I'm afraid to have to tell you that their attention is now divided between your good self and our newest recruit."

Glancing back, the captain ascertained that both Zachery and Thomas were sneaking peaks at Rux's briefs.

"Good for morale," he said briskly.

A sidelong glance allowed him to observe that rarest of wonders— his first officer's dimples. "Very good, I'm sure."

Ahead of them lay the largest of the surrounding buildings. Like the rest, it was grey and featureless, though its roof was more rounded that those of its peers. On the side facing them, there was a black circle, in the centre of which were a series of black squares of varying sizes.

"It is our language," Rux said. "It demarcates this building as the foremost scientific research facility in the city and warns away

136

trespassers."

"So are we going to get vaporized the second we walk through the front door?" Zachery said.

Rux frowned at him. "Is it instinctive to your kind to assume the worst? It will be fine. I will show you."

The closer they got to the building, the more apparent its decrepitude became. Its greyish colour was the result of an inch-deep coating of some moss-like substance. It had several dozen round windows dotting its exterior, many of them cracked or broken, and all so filthy as to be impenetrable. Tall grass pressed up against what seemed to be the main entrance. A single featureless panel sealed it off and on the left were a series of black markings; although their placement suggested they served some functional purpose, they had a curiously organic look, as though they'd been scratched into the building by large claws.

Rux stepped up to them and stood there unmoving.

"He does know what he's doing, I presume?" Antoine whispered to the captain.

Glancing his way, Rux frowned again and pressed one of his fingers against the markings. With a low rumble, the wide panel slid away, revealing the entrance. Peering in, the captain surveyed a lightless corridor stretching deep into the abandoned building's heart.

"I have disabled the security systems," Rux said. "You see? There is no need to worry. I lived in this city for many years. In fact, I worked in this very facility. I know how everything works."

Returning to his feline form, he stepped through the entrance. His green skin was bioluminescent and lit the whole corridor with an eerie emerald glow.

The captain looked back on the faces of his crew, now green-tinged. Irene—intrigued. Thomas—nervous. Zachery—impatient. Antoine—anticipatory. Echo—reflective, although only the captain could have known, as he wore his habitually blank expression like a shield.

My crew. My men.

"Let's go," he said and stepped inside.

☆☆☆

Zachery was disappointed. The facility had looked so cool and scary from the outside. Inside, it looked like nothing more interesting than an abandoned hospital. The walls were white, the floor was grey, and most of the rooms were either locked or empty. Now and then, he caught sight of a bug scuttling into one of the cracks in the ceiling tiles, but that was about as exciting as it got. There were no signs of violence; the previous occupants had apparently left the building in an orderly fashion, packing up all their valuables and switching the lights off behind them.

That didn't stop Antoine from going nuts every time they came across a sign or a room that wasn't completely empty. The words "What does this say?" and "What does this do?'" had been an omnipresent background noise for the last half hour, always followed by a polite, brief explanation from their alien tour guide.

Zachery, not a patient man by nature and anxious to get back to Rick, was getting peeved. Antoine had been having that effect on him more and more often of late.

Antoine Lionel Mbaye, he thought, watching him skip ahead like a schoolgirl on a field trip. *First Officer of The Prayer, first class pain in the ass. Earth-born, scientist, black, thirty-five or thereabouts, though he might have used rejuvenation tech, in which case who knows how old he is? What else do I know about him? Not much. He speaks French. He wears glasses. He mentioned once that his mom was a supermodel; I can believe it. Look at him, sashaying around like the world's his catwalk, like he can't imagine not being the centre of attention.*

Antoine and Zachery had never had a warm and fuzzy relationship. Things had become even chillier between them ever since Antoine had lost his temper and shot Zachery with his stun gun for being insubordinate. While Zachery was still smarting over that one, he didn't enjoy knowing he was on Antoine's bad side. If he'd had his way, they'd have settled matters between them with a punch-up and a manly handshake. But no matter how much Zachery provoked him, so far Antoine had refused to be drawn into a fight. He probably thought it was beneath him.

"Hey, Ant," Zachery said. "You think maybe we could quit stopping to see the sights every two minutes?"

Stiffening at the nickname, Antoine gave him a frosty look. "I beg your pardon, Mister Halberstam?"

Zachery gestured to the sign Rux had been translating for Antoine. "Not that it ain't all fucking fascinating, but I thought we were here to scavenge spare parts. At the rate we're going, we'll be wandering around this dump all day."

"Mister Halberstam, if you feel we are moving too slowly for your liking, you are welcome to proceed alone."

"No!" said the captain, coming to stand between them. "We will be remaining in one group. That is not up for debate."

"Sure thing, Captain," Zachery said, shrugging. "But, you know, maybe it wouldn't be such a bad idea if we left Ant and Rux here to get better acquainted while the rest of us do what we came here to do. They make a cute couple. I guess it figures that it would take an alien to get him going, seeing how no human being's ever managed to do it."

He gave Antoine the most provocative grin he could muster. It was no secret Antoine was one of the only people on board who hadn't once hooked up with a crewmate in the four years they'd been lost in space. No one knew why.

Not like he isn't hot enough, Zachery thought. *If I had to hazard a guess, I'd say his highness thinks he's just too good for the likes of us.*

"That's enough, Zachery!" the captain snarled, to Zachery's surprise. He'd thought Antoine would be the one to get angry. "One more word and you will return to the ship."

"Yes, sir," he muttered as Antoine shot him a smirk. *Little shit.*

As they started moving again, Thomas poked his ribs and teased, "Captain yelled at you, man."

"Shut up."

"Captain's gonna send you back to the ship. Gonna cut off your allowance and make you go to bed with no supper."

"Shut up, twerp."

☆☆☆

139

Despite his annoyance at Zachery's troublemaking, the captain couldn't help but roll his eyes heavenward as Antoine chirped "Ooh, what's that?" for the twentieth time that hour.

This time, however, the object Antoine was pointing at wasn't a sign or a light fixture or a smear on the wall. They had come upon a room with two translucent sliding doors, which parted as soon as Rux stepped in front of them. The room beyond was much bigger than any of the others they had entered. It was dominated by twenty opaque tubes, all twice as large as *The Prayer*'s med pod and connected to one another by thick, serpentine cables. To the left were a series of consoles, and on the floor a dark green stain stretched from one wall to the other. It seemed to begin at the tubes themselves, and was, presumably, the result of some fluid that had leaked out eons ago.

Rux touched one of the tubes with his fingertips, his manner pensive. "This is the facility's cloning laboratory."

Thomas gaped. "You made clones?"

"We did. Although 'clones' is somewhat misleading. Most of the people born in this room were amalgamations of four or five parents."

Ah, that's right, thought the captain. *He did say at one point that most of his species were poly, didn't he.*

"We also cloned pets and, when food was scarce, livestock. The wealthy could pay to splice together various animals for circuses and other trivial amusements. There were plans to use the technology to develop astronauts with bodies strong and adaptable enough to enable our colonisation of other planets. The plague derailed those plans before they could come to fruition."

He pointed to a door at the back of the room. "Through there is a storage room. I believe it might be a good place for Zachery to begin his search for his 'DG ring' and other bits and pieces."

"Finally," said Zachery, clapping his hands and heading towards it.

When left to their own devices, the captain and his first officer both had a tendency to wander in the other's direction and linger in their orbit. So it was without surprise that the captain noticed Antoine's arrival at his side.

"Captain, have you seen any roads?" he asked quietly. "Any train tracks? What sort of species develops cloning without first coming up with long-distance transport?"

Interesting point, the captain thought. Though he didn't want to give Antoine more reasons to distrust Rux, he himself had noticed a certain reticence on the alien's part when it came to explaining how his people had lived from day to day. He would ramble on for ages about their superior technology, but wouldn't elaborate as to what specifically they had done with it.

The captain replied, "Pure speculation, but whatever roads or tracks they built were taken up when they found more efficient means of transportation. Or they were made of a material that has since degraded naturally. Or maybe it had something to do with how their society was structured. They seem to have had a tiny population even at the height of their powers, and the planet's ecology is quite homogenous, so transporting resources from one region to the next might have been less of a pressing need. And their life spans ran to thousands of years, so saving time wouldn't have mattered as much to them as it does to us."

From the storage room, Zachery called in excitement, "Captain, I think I've got it! Hot damn. This might actually work. There's a ton of other useful stuff here—I'm gonna need something with wheels to get it all back to the ship."

"We'll go back outside and get our equipment when we've finished surveying the building," the captain said, thrilled at their luck. "Echo, mark this room on the map, please."

The translucent doors slid open again, and the captain completed his habitual headcount as his crew traipsed from the room.

Thomas, Irene, Echo, Rux... "Antoine! Hurry up! We're moving on."

"Yes, yes, I'm coming," said his first officer, who was still peering into the tubes.

"Now."

With a huff, Antoine obeyed, making his way towards the entrance. But just as he was about to step across the threshold, the doors slid shut so quickly they almost severed his foot.

"Whoa. How'd that happen?" said Irene.

Having jumped back, startled, Antoine shouted something the

captain couldn't hear through the closed doors.

"A malfunction, presumably," said Rux. He sounded, for once, less than utterly confident.

He helped the captain try to pry open the doors with his fingers, while on the other side Antoine did the same. Their efforts failed; there was nothing that could be gripped, no handles, no knobs.

"Zachery! You're the strongest. Come and help," the captain barked.

"Um, captain," said Thomas. "I think he's still in there with Antoine."

At that moment, through the translucent doors the captain saw Zachery emerge whistling from the storage room and stop, gaping at the sight of them. He joined Antoine in trying to slide the doors open, to no avail.

The captain stood back and said to Thomas, "I'm going to need you to shoot a hole in them, Mister Meléndez. Your rifle is fully charged, yes?"

Rux cleared his throat. "Captain, I do not believe that would be wise. If the facility perceives us to be a threat, it might activate its anti-burglary defences."

"You said that you disabled the security," said the captain, with mounting anger.

"I..." Rux faltered, avoiding the captain's gaze. "It is not outside the realm of possibility that I was mistaken."

"Oh, for fuck's sake," Antoine's voice erupted over the comms, making them all jump. His arms were folded and his expression sour. Beside him, Zachery was inspecting the doors' edges. "Answer truthfully, alien. Is there any way to open these doors that does not involve force?"

"I don't know."

"Is there any type of force we can use that will not activate the facility's security systems?"

"I don't know."

"You said you worked here!" the captain snarled.

Rux shrank back—literally shrank, losing a foot of height, and went a paler shade of green. "I... That is, I..."

"Okay, listen," said Zachery. "Everyone quit panicking. If shooting at the doors isn't safe, the next best option is to cut them open. We might have something that can do that back with all the equipment we left outside. Someone go get it, and we'll be out of here in no time."

The captain looked at Rux. "Can the doors be cut open?"

"I believe so," said Rux, his tone implying no degree of certainty whatsoever. "In order to make up for my error, I will go and retrieve Zachery's requested piece of equipment, if he will tell me what it looks like."

The captain shook his head. "No. No one goes off on their own. That was an ironclad rule even when we thought the environment was benign."

"I agree," said Antoine, to everyone's amazement. "There's no point in dividing ourselves up into digestible slices. Zachery and I are in no immediate danger. Captain, you should take everyone back outside and return with the necessary tools to cut the doors open as quickly as you can."

Zachery was nodding. "And you can also bring a dolly so we can get all these spare parts out of here and back to *The Prayer*."

It makes sense, the captain thought. Antoine was giving him that look, the one that meant "Come on now, don't make a scene."

"All right," he said.

CHAPTER FOUR

This is a fine kettle of fucks.

Zachery sat on the floor, leaning back against one of the clone tubes or whatever they were. For want of anything better to do until the captain and the others came back, he was checking out Antoine.

The ship's first officer was pacing back and forth in front of the doors like a caged lion, his hands clasped behind his back. He'd been all icy composure right up until the second the captain and the others had disappeared down the passageway, and then he'd kicked the shit out of the doors and cursed like a sailor for three minutes.

"You think Rux was telling the truth?" Zachery asked him.

Antoine stopped pacing and tilted his head to one side. "It's hard to say. He's inscrutable. If he knew the building's security was still active when we entered and decided not to tell us, then that has dire implications for..."

"No, no. I mean about these," said Zachery, rapping on the tube he was leaning against with his knuckles. "He said they used these to clone themselves instead of having kids the normal way. Does that sound likely to you?"

"What makes you think he was lying?"

Smirking, Zachery said, "Well, if I had a machine that could make clones, I know what I'd use it for, and it sure as hell wouldn't be churning out kiddies."

"What would you use it for, then?"

"First, I'd make thirty clones of me. Then I'd stick my dick in the first one's mouth. Then he'd stick his dick in the second one's mouth. We'd form a chain, yeah? Except the last one, clone number thirty, he wouldn't stick his dick in anyone's mouth. Instead, I get him to..."

Zachery spent several minutes elaborating on the details of his fantasy, watching as Antoine's face morphed from an expression of mild contempt to outright disgust. It was, he thought, a good look for him.

"Thank you for that, Zachery," Antoine said coldly. "I feel that I should point out a potential flaw in your otherwise brilliant plan. That many massive egos in close proximity would be more likely to end in a bloodbath than an orgy."

As Antoine returned to pacing, Zachery's gaze lingered on him. He was, Zachery admitted with no small amount of resentment, more than just a pretty face. Those collarbones were a work of art. Those legs— mmm. Yummy. And even though Antoine and the captain looked nothing alike, one thing they had in common was their gait—an economy of movement combined with a certain subtle slinkiness.

I'm checking him out, Zachery realized. *Huh. That's new.*

Actually, why was he surprised? Insofar as he had a type, Antoine was it—sexy, bitchy, too smart for his own good. Zachery hadn't ever hated the guy, at least, not until Antoine had zapped his balls, and in retrospect, that was partly his own fault. Getting on Antoine's nerves was so damn easy.

Zachery smiled wolfishly. Well, well, well. He had a crush on First Officer Prissyboots. Interesting. And with only each other for company... Might as well find out if the feeling was mutual.

☆☆☆

They made it back outside and found the equipment they needed. Then the captain said, "Only Rux and I will be going back in."

As Irene and Thomas erupted in protest and Echo frowned, he held up a hand for silence. "The decision is made. I don't imagine we'll need more than four pairs of hands to transport Zachery's spare parts. We'll stay in contact, and I doubt we'll be more than an hour."

"Sir," said Thomas, "with all due respect, earlier you said it was dangerous to split up."

"That was when we were all inside the facility. Now that we're out, it makes sense that some of us remain out here, out of danger, so that they can go back to *The Prayer* and get help if it becomes necessary. If anything goes wrong in there, Rux—who, I remind you, can turn into a large predatory animal—will protect me and the others at least as well as you can with your rifle, Thomas. Echo is in charge until I return. If you lose contact with us, you are to wait an hour and then return to the ship. Understood?"

Thomas and Irene gave gloomy murmurs of assent. Echo nodded.

As Rux and the captain walked back into the building, the alien said, "Echo is the mute, yes?"

"That word is vulgar, and you will not use it again," said the captain, wondering where he'd heard it in the first place. Every scrap of English Rux knew he'd learned from them.

"Very well. I must ask; why leave him in charge? He does not seem to possess the force of personality necessary to command men."

"My men don't need commands. They need leadership. Echo knows them and has earned their respect."

"Really? I have overheard young Rick refer to him as 'creepy'."

"A joke, nothing more."

"Ah. I see. Is Echo aware that it was a joke? From what I could deduce from his expression at the time he was distressed by the remark."

He was? The captain knew when his back was turned his crew would occasionally utter unnecessary remarks about Echo and his oddness. Though he worked to discourage it, he'd always thought Echo was unaffected by such things. It concerned him to hear otherwise. At the same time, he was impressed by Rux's assessment. Even the most empathetic human would find Echo difficult to read. That the alien could pick up on his unhappiness suggested that Rux had more depth than he had suspected.

The two of them made their way down the same passageways they'd come in by before. Rux pushed the dolly while the captain checked in with Antoine via the comms and ascertained that he and Zachery were still in one piece. They were still another five-minute's walk from the room where the two men were confined when the captain's com went dead. At the same moment, there came a siren, low-pitched and seeming to be coming from behind them and ahead of them at once.

"Rux?"

"I don't know."

The captain sighed. "When we're back at the ship we will have a conversation about the surprising number of things you don't know. Let's pick up the pace."

When they reached what the captain was certain was the right corridor, the doors weren't there.

"Have we come the wrong way?" he murmured, retracing their steps in his mind.

The squeaking of the dolly's wheels fell silent as Rux halted. "We must have. Perhaps if we turn..."

Cutting himself off, Rux looked upward. Shifting into a quadruped not unlike an emerald lion in appearance, he said, "Captain, I think you should climb on my back."

"Why?" said the captain, complying as he spoke.

"We are about to be attacked."

No sooner had Rux finished his sentence than a panel opened up in the ceiling, revealing a canon aimed directly at the captain's head.

☆☆☆

As soon as the captain and Rux entered the building, Echo turned to Thomas and made a series of movements with his hands.

That's new, Thomas thought. Even though all crewmembers had obtained basic fluency in sign language—willingness to learn it had been one of the captain's prerequisites when they'd first been hired—Echo didn't often "speak" to them directly. Usually, he kept his responses to nods or shrugs; if there was anything more complicated he wanted to convey he told the captain, who passed it on.

"You want me to shoot something?" Thomas said, doing his best.

"He wants us to set up some targets and for you to teach him how to shoot," said Irene, who'd known how to sign even before she'd joined the crew.

Thomas thought it was a smart idea. It would give them something to do besides stand around and worry. So they demarcated a danger zone and looked around for something to serve as a target. Not far from the facility, they found a pile of hollow crates, dragged them into position, and drew concentric circles on them. After that, Irene lay back on the grass and had a catnap; she was already a trained marksman.

First, Thomas showed Echo how to hold the rifle properly, putting a hole in the bullseye at six hundred yards. He'd have liked to put the crate further back and show off a little, but he was out of practice—*The Prayer* didn't have a shooting range—and he didn't want to make a fool of himself in front of Echo, who exuded an air of quiet competence with everything he did. From the day he'd met the man, Thomas hadn't seen him fuck up once.

"Your turn," he said, handing Echo the rifle.

Echo was a good student, a good listener. Though his aim was lousy, he paid attention to Thomas's instructions on how to improve his grip, and on his eleventh try, he hit one of the targets.

"That's great," said Thomas, clapping him on the shoulder. "Remember to keep your elbow steady. Try it again."

As Echo was lining up the next shot, he took one step backwards. Thomas thought it seemed less an absent-minded shuffle than a deliberate repositioning. It left Echo's back pressing against Thomas's front.

At first, Thomas didn't know what to do. Was it an invitation? Maybe. Echo hadn't made any effort to correct his stance, and he was leaning back on Thomas's chest in a way that sure felt intentional.

An invitation to do what?

Carefully, Thomas slid his arms around him until his hands enfolded Echo's hands, still clutching the rifle. He might have been correcting his grip. Or he might have been doing something else. *Ball's in his court.*

The next shot went wide. Thomas had a feeling that neither of them were concentrating on what they were supposed to be doing.

Wow, Echo's hair was soft, tickling his nose like duckling feathers. Come to that, he was soft all over, curving thighs, a bit of extra flesh at his stomach. Thomas liked it. The captain and Zachery both had hard, muscular bodies without an ounce of fat to spare, and while Rick wasn't at their level, he still worked out regularly and had a wiry strength in his limbs. Echo, so far as Thomas knew, didn't exercise at all.

"Your hair's nice," Thomas mumbled, feeling like a clumsy

adolescent. It wasn't a lie, however dumb it sounded.

Without turning round, Echo tilted his head up, giving Thomas what felt one hell of a lot like a nuzzle. Emboldened, Thomas pressed forward so there wasn't a millimetre of space between their bodies. Echo's hands, still enfolded within his own, were damp. Perhaps Thomas wasn't the only one out of his depth.

Just as Thomas was getting comfortable, Echo broke away, looking over his shoulder towards Irene. She was lying on the grass with her hands behind her head, and Thomas thought she might be asleep. Catching Thomas's gaze, Echo nodded in the direction of one of the nearest ruined buildings.

"What? Oh. Fuck, I...okay. Sure."

Bemused, Thomas let Echo lead him by the hand until they were shielded from the sun and scrutiny in the lee of a crumbling wall.

"This isn't going to fall over and squash us, is it?" Thomas said to the air, putting the rifle aside. He was nervous, halfway elated, unsure of why he'd been chosen instead of Zachery or Rick. He knew Echo had a thing going on with the captain, and that the captain thought Echo would join the rest of them at some point. Thomas had doubted it. If Echo had had an eye on any of them, he'd kept it to himself. No flirting, no smouldering looks, not even on the numerous occasions when he'd walked in on them mid-tryst to bring the captain his laundry. Thomas had begun to think he wasn't into sex at all. He'd never shown any interest in Rick's porn collection.

"We shouldn't be too long," Thomas said half to himself, as he fumbled with his suit. "Don't want captain to come out and wonder where we've gone."

Echo, meanwhile, had been removing his own suit. Now he turned and let Thomas get his first good look at him. Like Thomas had guessed, he was smooth and soft. No definition to his abs. Not much chest hair either. Maybe he shaved. The mastectomy scars were a surprise, mostly because of how visible they were; technology on Earth had long since advanced past the point of leaving marks perceptible to the naked eye. But then, hadn't Echo come from some or other backwater colony on the moon? Everyone knew those poor fuckers were a century behind the rest of the solar system. Figured that they'd still be using scalpels and stitches.

Do I act like I haven't noticed?

Echo was watching his face, Thomas realised. Recording his reaction, analysing it somewhere deep in that quiet mind of his. Ah. Maybe this was why he'd decided to do this now, miles from the ship and the rest of the crew. He hadn't known whether or not Thomas would make a scene. Out-of-date technology was far from the worst thing about living on the moon.

The tension was killing Thomas's erection, so to break it, he said, "That's nothing. Check this out."

He finished unzipping his suit and slid it off. The second Echo saw the stupid-ass cartoon hawk perched on Thomas's ribcage, he laughed. Enchanted—he'd never seen Echo smile before, much less laugh— Thomas struck a pose. "Classy as fuck, isn't he? You know, this piece of shit cost me two month's salary."

Biting his lip, his cheeks red, Echo came over and stroked its feathers like it was a real bird. Then his hand slid downwards and started stroking Thomas. Thomas moaned and dragged him in, bracketing his thighs with his own longer legs.

"C'mere, you," he said, burying a hand in Echo's hair.

Echo wasn't nearly as passive a lover as Thomas would have expected. He pushed him back against the crumbling wall with surprising strength and spent a moment just looking at him, his gaze intense and focused.

"You wanna have me? Right here?" Thomas whispered.

Echo nodded. Ingenious creature that he was, he produced a small bottle of lube from one of the pockets on his suit.

You planned this, you sneaky fucker, thought Thomas, thrilled.

When Echo also got out a pair of thin, translucent plastic gloves, he held them up for Thomas's inspection.

"Sure, that's cool," Thomas said, remembering the captain's once mentioning that Echo had a thing about germs.

He was, however, glad that Echo didn't put them on right away. When he turned around and braced himself against the wall, he liked the sensation of Echo's soft palms mapping out the muscles in his back.

Echo didn't rush things. He was damn near leisurely about it. Thomas, who had followed him into the shade of the wall in anticipation of a two-minute quickie, might have protested if the frustration hadn't been turning him on, working him up just as much as the teasing strokes and squeezes Echo kept giving his shaft. Even so, Thomas tried his best to keep his mouth shut. Apart from the possibility that Irene might wake up and hear them, he was also aware that Echo wasn't making any more noise than he normally did. Thomas thought he might prefer it if he followed suit.

His restraint wasn't limitless. When Echo's gloved fingers slid into him, then out, then in again, he whimpered, "Oh, Jesus, that's right."

Echo honoured him with another laugh, this one dark and velvety.

It didn't take long after that for Thomas to start giving the needy-bitch whines he normally reserved for the captain. He was first past the post, biting his lip as Echo milked him dry.

"You know, I thought surviving a spaceship crash was going to be the best thing that happened to me this week," he sighed, as Echo slowly withdrew his fingers.

He turned around on shaky legs, taking in Echo's flushed cheeks and bright eyes. *Fuck, he's so cute.* He was about to reach for his dick when he remembered that all he knew was that Echo *had* a dick. He had no idea where Echo had received his surgery. Of the two trans guys Thomas had been with before, one hadn't gone in for surgery and the other had lived on Earth all his life. If they were still leaving mastectomy scars on the moon, what were the chances Echo would have had access to the sort of technology that would enable Thomas to show off his legendary handjob skills?

"Can I jerk you off?" he asked.

Echo, who still hadn't stepped away from his body, shook his head.

Wait, does that mean that he doesn't want me to jerk him off or that I literally can't jerk him off?

Thomas leaned in close, getting another face full of soft baby duck hair as Echo kissed his neck. "What'll it be then, baby?"

Drawing back, Echo looked up at the sky, assessing the position of the sun, then looked pointedly in the direction they'd come from. No need for a translator: *We should get back before we're missed.*

Disappointed, Thomas deliberated with himself before saying, "So...does this mean we're friends?"

Suddenly Echo—so purposeful and collected up to this point—looked wrong-footed. He shrugged and nodded at the same time.

Thomas kissed him chastely, before saying, "Because I'd really like us to be friends. Or whatever it is you want us to be. I'm... I mean, you know about the captain and Zachery and Rick. I don't know what you think about that. I don't want you getting the idea that I want to add you to my...my collection, or whatever. It's not like that. I want you, I want to do this again, and... See, I'm not sure exactly what it is *you* want, but—"

Wow. For someone who didn't use his tongue much in day-to-day life, Echo sure knew how to use it when it counted. His eyes were dark and mischievous as he pulled away from the kiss. Before Thomas could start babbling again, Echo picked up the rifle—carefully, the way Thomas had shown him—and started to walk back to the facility.

"Huh," said Thomas, running his thumb over his lips. He wasn't one hundred percent sure what the fuck had just happened. But he thought he liked it.

CHAPTER FIVE

"They've been gone too long."

"Hmm?" said Zachery, startled from his reverie. He'd been working on his opening line—something incorporating *"Voulez-vous couchez avec moi?"* seeing as that was the only French he knew, and he wanted Antoine to understand that he was an educated man.

Antoine had quit pacing and was standing by the doors with his hands on his hips. "It's been an hour and a half. It took us less than an hour to get to this room in the first place. They should have been back by now."

His heart sinking, Zachery checked his suit's clock. First Officer Prissyboots had a point. "You think something's happened to 'em?"

"How should I know?" Antoine snapped. "I've been trying to get a response on the comms for the last five minutes. Nothing."

Zachery tried his own and received only ominous silence in reply. "Okay. That sucks. Listen, what if we..."

With a gentle hiss, the doors slid open.

"Captain!" said Zachery, a grin breaking out. But when he stared into the corridor, there was no one there.

"What made them open?" he murmured as they stepped out of the lab, half expecting the doors to slide closed on them before they'd crossed the threshold.

"A poltergeist, for all I know. Come on; let's get back to the ship."

The hallway was eerily quiet without the rest of the crew chattering in the background. Antoine strode ahead while Zachery dogged his heels, carrying the DG ring replacement and as many other spare parts as he could carry. Before they'd gone more than fifty metres, they heard a noise, a low siren coming from somewhere up ahead and somewhere behind them at the same time.

"Hell's that?" Zachery said.

"Why do you keep asking me things I have no way of knowing, Mister Halberstam? I can only conclude that you revere me as an omnicognisant deity."

The siren stopped. It came back after a seven-second break, then cut off again, and continued on like that, coming and going off every seven seconds. Zachery couldn't work out where the hell it was coming from; it didn't get any louder or softer as they made their way down the passage. To keep his mind from morbid speculation as to what it might mean, Zachery tried to make conversation. "So, Ant—you're not married?"

"What? No."

"No boyfriends or girlfriends back home?"

"No. Wait, are we going the right way? This passage looks different."

It did—cleaner, fewer cracks in the walls. Zachery's spine tingled. He was sure this was the way they'd come before. "We must have made a wrong turn. Let's go back to the lab and start over."

"By the way," Zachery added after a few moments of silent walking, "seeing as how we're crewmates... Well, I don't like to think that there should be any big secrets between us..."

He cleared his throat. "Ant, you know I'm sleeping with the captain, right?"

"I am aware."

"And also Thomas and Rick."

He'd hoped that that might provoke a flicker of surprise—that the three of them were the captain's boys was common knowledge aboard *The Prayer* by now, but Antoine was so wrapped up in himself he might not have heard. Nope, Prissyboots didn't bat an eyelid.

"I know that too. Is there a point to this?" asked Antoine, clearly only half listening as he scanned their surroundings.

Ignoring me. As usual. The irritation, the tightening across his chest—they were familiar feelings, for all that he'd never consciously registered them before. Hmm. How long, exactly, had he been harbouring a crush on Antoine?

Wanting nothing more than to provoke a reaction, Zachery said,

"Well, as you ask, I was wondering if you'd like to join in some time. The captain's bed's not that big, but you're a string bean; we could squeeze you in."

Antoine's high, piping laughter temporarily drowned out the siren.

"That...that is never going to happen," he said, gasping for breath. "No. Definitely not. Good grief."

Okay, that stung. Getting rejected was one thing, but did he have to be such a bitch about it?

"Right. Cool," said Zachery, staring at the floor.

Antoine's giggles slowly trickled away. "Mister Halberstam, I wasn't trying to be insulting."

"S'okay, you don't have to explain yourself. I'm a fucking adult."

Sighing, Antoine said, "No, I apologise. I wasn't laughing at you. The truth is that I don't have sex, ever."

He said it so casually, as though he was telling Zachery that he was a vegan or allergic to wheat.

"Like I said, you don't have to explain yourself," said Zachery. Then, still sore, he added, "You don't have to insult my intelligence, either. Even if I'm not a genius like you, I do know how basic biology works. Sex is like pissing. Everyone does it. Don't make up dumb excuses, man; if you're not into me, that's cool."

Antoine gave him a look then, like...like he was a cockroach, or something. He didn't say another word, though, and they kept walking in silence.

They looked for the room they'd been trapped in for another ten minutes and didn't find it. It was bizarre. They'd retraced their steps three times, even timed themselves. The damned thing wasn't there anymore.

"I'm spooked," said Zachery.

Antoine's suit came equipped with a portable first aid kit. Opening it, he took out a pair of scissors. "Bend down for me, Mister Halberstam."

He snipped off a thick lock of Zachery's dark hair, and then snipped a few strands off that and placed them on the floor. He did the same thing after five paces.

ADRIFT: THE COLLECTION | T.J. LAND

Bread crumbs. Smart, thought Zachery.

Had he been telling the truth about never having sex? No way. Antoine was in his mid-thirties. No normal, healthy man got to that age without dipping his dick in someone. Especially not when they were as sexy as First Officer Prissyboots. Unless... ah. Unless there was a problem. Unless he'd been in an accident or got a disease that had left his dick all messed up. That would explain why he was so uptight.

I bet that's it. He's too ashamed of his body to let anyone see him naked.

Geez, now Zachery felt sorry for him. It was a cruel fucking irony that a man with a face like Antoine's couldn't reap any benefits from it.

But hey, Zachery was an open-minded guy. He hadn't been lying to Rick; his first boyfriend had had one eye and two fingers missing, courtesy, in fact, of a knife fight with Zachery himself. Zachery could deal with whatever Antoine had down his pants. If he could only find a polite, tactful way of letting Antoine know that...

"Hey, Ant, listen. Even though we haven't always seen eye to eye, please be aware that I am totally down for giving your poor, mangled dick all the love and affection it deserves. Whatever it looks like, I'm sure the rest of you makes up for it."

Nah. This was Antoine he was dealing with. He needed to be classy.

"Putain!" Antoine yelled. He'd been leaving snippets of hair for the last ten minutes as they'd turned down corridor after corridor, and now, in front of them, were the very first few strands he'd dropped. "We're going in fucking circles! What is wrong with this building?"

"It's a mystery," said Zachery, his mind now firmly on other things. "Hey, Ant, I didn't mean to be a jerk earlier. It's just that, you know, I don't think you've explored all your options. There's this great quote I memorised in school; can't remember who said it. 'Sex is as important as eating or drinking, and we ought to allow the one appetite to be satisfied with as little restraint or false modesty as the other'."

"The Marquis de Sade. He wrote that."

"Yeah! That was the guy! Damn, you're brainy. Anyway, I always thought that was a fucking clever way of putting it. Sex is... I mean, sex is necessary, yeah? Not wanting to have sex with one particular person,

158

that's fine. Not wanting to have sex at all—that's not natural. It's like having anorexia in your balls."

Antoine had folded his arms and was staring up at the ceiling. "Mister Halberstam, there is not enough time left before the heat death of the universe for me to explain to you everything that is wrong in that statement, nor do I have the inclination. Let me say this; the Marquis de Sade was a rapist and a child molester. Less monstrous, but still worth noting, is the fact that his philosophy was intellectually bankrupt and his literary skills subpar. If you base your personal beliefs regarding sex on something that man wrote, I suppose it's not surprising that you're a criminal."

That did it. If you wanted to see Zachery blow his top, there was no faster way than to whip out that particular word. He knew his tendency to pummel the shit out of anyone who called him a criminal was, ultimately, only proving their point. He didn't give a shit. Right then, all he wanted was to teach First Officer Prissyboots a lesson he wouldn't forget.

He forgot all about the fucking stun gun. The fucking stun gun Antoine carried everywhere he went.

To give Antoine credit, string bean or not, his reflexes were impressive. Zachery was still drawing back the punch when he found the business end of Antoine's weapon of choice pointed right at his face.

"Do I have to make you behave again?" Antoine growled.

Oh. Hell. No.

In an instant, Zachery's rage was displaced by incredulity. He kept his eyes on Antoine's stun gun, while inwardly all he could focus on was his own dick. *What the fuck? What the fuck is wrong with you, you stupid piece of meat?*

What disturbed him even more than the way all his blood had started flowing towards his groin was the sudden memory of the captain smacking ass. The feeling that had evoked—he still couldn't name it— was uncannily similar to the feeling evoked by Antoine's playing the autocrat.

"Well, Mister Halberstam?"

Fuck, he even sounded like Khurshed when he called Zachery that.

159

Old man, you have seriously fucked me up.

Lowering his fist, Zachery managed to say, "Don't call me that. That's bellow the belt, even for you."

After a moment, the weapon was withdrawn. "Fine. On the condition that you vow not to vomit up your half-formed opinions on my sexuality in front of me ever again."

"Got it. I didn't mean any offence." Zachery winced. He sounded like such a pussy. It wasn't an act, though. He genuinely hadn't meant to be an asshole. And he wanted, more than anything, to get that expression of contempt off Antoine's face. "I just think it's a... It's a real shame someone who looks like you hasn't ever had sex. It's a waste, is what it is. Do you have any idea how many people would kill for a chance at you? You're fucking beautiful."

He cut himself off, blushing.

The contempt evaporated. "Thank you for the compliment. Now drop it."

They might have been about to have a moment when Zachery noticed something amiss. "Hey—the siren's stopped."

"So it has," agreed Antoine, cocking an ear. "Strange."

The sudden silence was unsettling, and Zachery picked up the DG ring and all the other stuff he'd dropped when drawing back his punch. "Maybe we should get go..."

Footsteps. Heavy, inhuman, coming from the end of the passage, barely thirty metres away. Zachery knew without turning around that it wasn't the captain. Judging by Antoine's horrified expression, he guessed he wasn't going to like what it was.

"Zachery," said Antoine, softly. "Don't make any sudden movements. It might not have noticed us. Ah—sorry, let me correct that. It has definitely noticed us."

Zachery looked, and fuck him sideways if it wasn't a robot. A real, literal, bona fide robot, humanoid and steel grey, with a big scary gun, heading right their way.

"Your orders, sir?" he asked Antoine.

Antoine never got a chance to issue any because that was when it started shooting at them, and they both ran like hell.

☆☆☆

"There you are," Irene said to Thomas. "Wondered where you'd gone off to."

"We heard a noise. Decided to check it out," said Thomas, who'd always been a lousy liar. "I think it was just the wind."

Echo took the rifle and continued target practice while Thomas sprawled back on the grass beside Irene. He was thinking ahead. As they'd been heading back to the facility, Echo had implied—in his inscrutable way—that he'd visit Thomas's quarters when they got back to the ship. That he'd maybe even spend the night. Thomas wanted to make him dinner. Nothing fancy—he wasn't much of a cook, nowhere near Echo's level. He'd learned how to make a passable broccoli soup a few years ago, out of necessity; it was the only way he could force down all the vegetables they had to live on.

The more he thought about it, the more excited he got. He was a sucker for romantic shit. On Earth, he'd have arranged flowers and wine, neither of which were an option at the moment.

I could play some music. Jazz. He'd like jazz. And...hmm...

"You think we've got any candles on board?" he asked Irene.

"Candles? What, for the captain's cake? He won't thank you for that, Thomas. Anyway, you'd need a hell of a lot of them. He's no spring chicken."

Thomas blinked. "Cake? What?"

"Oh shit. Ignore me. I didn't say anything."

"Oh my God. It's his birthday?"

"Don't tell him I told you, Thomas; he'll hate my guts. I promised I'd keep it a secret."

"Why?" asked Thomas, bewildered. "I'm sleeping with the guy, Irene."

She rubbed her eyes. "Yeah, I know. I don't get it either. He doesn't tell anyone. I only found out 'cause Antoine once told me by accident."

"Fucking Antoine?" Thomas squawked. "You're telling me Antoine, the guy most likely to commit mutiny on any day of the week, knows when the captain's birthday is? And I don't?"

"I am really fucking this up," Irene sighed.

"Echo!" Thomas shouted. "You knew about this?"

It turned out that Echo had not known about it, although on the whole he seemed less perturbed about it than Thomas was.

"Echo says 'Maybe he's embarrassed about his age. Or maybe he doesn't want a party. Not everyone does'," Irene translated.

"Why would he tell Antoine, though? Of all people? I don't get it."

Echo stared questioningly at Irene, who was scratching her knee and avoiding their eyes.

"Irene?" Thomas pleaded.

She grunted a stream of German curse words. "Okay, whatever. Antoine's my second cousin. That's how I got work on *The Prayer*; he recommended me to the captain. We're not close, but we talk now and then, and he once told me that he and the captain go back a long way. He never went into specifics. From what I could make out, I'd guess they hooked up for a while."

"I'll be damned," said Thomas. "That's why they're always fighting? A bad break-up?"

In his head, he made no bones about it. It hurt to learn that after half a year of sleeping together, the man he was in love with hadn't deemed him worthy of a level of intimacy he'd apparently had with fucking Antoine. Thomas thought he deserved better than that.

"You'd think he'd have said something," he grumbled.

"Hey, don't take it so hard, Thomas. Antoine might have asked him to keep it a secret. They both like their privacy."

Echo squeezed Thomas's shoulder in agreement.

"Yeah, well, I'm still going to give him a fucking talking-to when he gets out of there," said Thomas. He looked at the sun. "Speaking of which, haven't they been gone a long time?"

"Good point," said Irene. "Lemme get in touch."

When she tried to contact the captain on the comm, there was no response. She tried again with Antoine and Zachery; same deal.

"Shit," Irene hissed. "What do we do?"

They both looked at Echo.

"Your orders, sir?" said Thomas.

☆☆☆

"God, this is such a stupid way to die," Antoine said as they cowered behind a chunk of fallen masonry.

It was a godsend. Outrunning the robot had worked like a charm, at first; it didn't move above a walking pace. But then the building had started playing tricks with them again. They'd run into random dead ends and found that all the doors they'd passed before were suddenly either closed or gone. As they'd struggled to orientate themselves, their pursuer had kept coming, slow and relentless. Its gleaming bulk filled the corridor, so they couldn't run past it. Though its aim was erratic, one of its lasers had clipped the edge of Zachery's suit and burned a hole through it.

Then, like a miracle, they'd reached a section of the facility so run down that it was in the process of falling apart. Big chunks of the ceiling were scattered all over the floor for them to hide behind. Just in time, because they were both out of breath. In the distance, Zachery could see a hole in the wall that led outside. It was wide enough for them to squeeze through.

A pity they didn't have a hope in hell of reaching it, given that now the robot had them pinned down, firing relentlessly at the masonry they were crouched behind. Neither the rocks Zachery was throwing at it nor Antoine's brave little stun gun seemed to be doing jack shit, and it was less than fifty yards away.

"A robot. What next? Will we find out the facility's built on top of a fucking sarlacc?" Antoine ground out. "What are you doing? Get down!"

"Got a plan," said Zachery, making ready to stand up. "I'm a fast runner; I'll get its attention and draw it off down that way, while you try to get outside through that hole. I'll lead it in circles for a while, and then I'll follow you out."

"Don't be an imbecile. You'll get yourself killed," Antoine snapped, grabbing a handful of his hair and forcing him back down.

Oh God. How fucked up was he that having his scalp almost ripped off by Antoine's skinny girl fingers was a turn-on?

"You got a better plan?" Zachery asked to cover his embarrassment.

"Hey, look down there. You see that?"

From where they crouched, they could see straight down three corridors: the one down which the robot was steadily advancing, the one that led to the hole, and a third, down which...something was coming towards them. The only source of illumination they had were the lasers being fired at them and a few beams of sunlight coming in through the hole, and it took a moment for Zachery to realise that the object coming their way was green.

"I think it's Rux," he said. "The captain's on his back."

"That is the usual state of affairs."

"No, I mean the captain's riding him."

"That, too, is..."

"Antoine!" came the captain's hoarse voice.

The robot took that as its cue to divert its efforts away from the two of them and towards the green lion bearing down on it. It fired twice, thrice, and three more times, and Rux dodged every one, lunging this way and that while the captain clung to his mane for dear life.

Super agile, super strong, ageless, and a shapeshifter, thought Zachery. What else was he capable of? If there'd once been a whole species of Ruxes, what had their wars looked like? *Maybe it's no wonder they went extinct.*

Rux sped up, and when he was less than ten metres from the robot, he jumped into the air and came down right on top of it. As he did, one of its shots hit home, and Zachery saw a wide swath of green fur burned clean off. It didn't seem to bother him. Raising one massive paw, he took off the robot's head with a swipe and then used his teeth to tear off its flailing limbs.

"Nice," commented Zachery.

While Rux mauled the twitching remains, the captain waved the two of them over.

"Get on, quickly," he said. "Have you got the parts? The DG ring?"

"Dropped them a way back when the robot showed up," said Zachery. "It's not too far."

Big as Rux was, fitting all three of them onto his back was a squeeze. Antoine, to Zachery's disappointment, chose to sit up front, in the captain's lap. The extra weight didn't slow Rux down at all. As he charged down the corridor towards where Zachery had left their prizes, Antoine rapped on his feline skull. "Alien, I trust you have an explanation for this absolute pig's ear of a situation?"

"The facility has registered us as intruders and is attempting to expel us," said Rux.

"I grasped that much. Didn't you give us your assurance that wouldn't happen? Because you 'know how everything works'?"

"I will explain as soon as we are out of danger."

The DG ring and the other parts were lying where Zachery had dropped them. Zachery, who by this point was thoroughly creeped out by the whole fucking building, had half expected to find that the floor had eaten them.

Less fortuitous was the fact that as soon as they had picked them up and made ready to leave, a panel opened in the ceiling, and three more robots dropped down to land in front of them, guns at the ready.

"Well, shit," said Zachery, and he did the only thing he could think of; he charged the one closest to him.

To his surprise, he landed a solid punch on its jaw without being vaporised. Not that it did much good; the robot didn't flinch, and he heard something crack in his hand, but it didn't hurt. Back in the days when he'd beaten up other guys for money, he'd never felt his injuries until the match was over. He tried punching its chest with his unbroken hand instead, looking for a weak point, only for it to push him back as though he weighed as much as a pillow. He was thrown into the captain, sending them both to the floor.

Rux was busy tearing one of them apart, but the other two paid no attention to him or to their unlucky friend. They took one step forward, raising their weapons while Zachery scrabbled to position his body in front of the captain's and the captain tried to push him aside, presumably so that he could do the same thing. Antoine, meanwhile, had taken out his stun gun and was waving it at them, screaming invective. It was pathetic and also so badass Zachery's balls ached.

First Officer Prissypants, I am one hundred percent gone on you. This is going to be such a fucking problem.

"Antoine, get back!" the captain shouted.

Then the unmistakable crack of a laser rifle split the air, and the leftmost robot's head exploded. Before it had even hit the floor, the second one followed suit, crumpling while sparks flew from the new gaping hole in its metallic skull.

"Hi there, losers," said Thomas from behind his victims, lowering the rifle. Echo stood at his shoulder, regarding them all with his habitual air of detachment.

"Twerp!" Zachery cried, rushing forward to seize Thomas in a bear hug.

"Well timed, Mister Meléndez," said the captain as Antoine helped him to his feet. "Echo, congratulations. Your first ever failure to obey a direct order came at the best possible moment."

Rux, bits of robot dangling from his jaws, said, "If your engineer now has the parts he requires, I believe we should all leave this place at once."

CHAPTER SIX

By the time they were far enough away from the facility for Thomas not to keep looking over his shoulder for advancing robot hordes, it was nightfall. They made camp beneath two trees, and the captain contacted *The Prayer* to let the others know they were all right. Now that they were out, their comms were working again.

As the temperature dropped, they sat around a fire, chewing on protein strips.

"What a fucking day. Sure could use some fresh, healthy vegetables right now," said Zachery, rubbing his neck.

"Explanation time," said Antoine, addressing Rux. "Alien, you said you deactivated the facility's security. You lied, and as a result of your lie, we were almost killed."

Rux had turned back into his humanoid form and sat cross-legged beside Zachery, his hands in his lap. "There is something I must confess. You remember I told you that I worked in the facility, and that was how I understood its inner workings?"

"Let me guess; you lied about that too?"

"No. I was truthful. To a certain degree. I did work there."

"Wait, I know," said Zachery. "You were a janitor, right? Or the guy who made the coffee while everyone else did the real work?"

"I was an experiment. I was born in one of the tubes as part of their programme to create highly adaptable, resilient servants who could help them colonise other planets."

"'Them'?" said Antoine. "So when you refer to 'your people', you are in fact referring to the beings who made you?"

Rux nodded. "In truth, I had as much in common with them as your ship's cat has with you. I did consider myself one of them for a while, though I eventually learned that the feeling was not mutual. When they were forced to divert all their energies towards finding a cure for the plague, they lost interest in creating more of me. I was used as a test subject, then a security guard, then a low-level assistant. That is why my understanding of their technology is incomplete. I don't know what they would have done with me if they hadn't gone extinct. I suspect they would have been horrified at the thought that I would outlive them."

For the first time since Thomas had met the guy, he looked meek and ashamed of himself. "I didn't intend to put you in harm's way. I thought I remembered how to gain access to the facility without triggering the alarm. Clearly, I was mistaken."

"I suppose that goes some way to absolving you," said Antoine. "Nonetheless..."

"Aw, lay off him, Ant. He's sorry," Zachery interjected.

"'Sorry' doesn't quite cut it, Mister Halberstam."

"Enough," said the captain, who was lying with his head in Thomas's lap. "Rux, your deception endangered the lives of my crew, and it will be some time before I forgive you for it. That said, I am sympathetic to your situation. We all have our secrets."

"Yeah, we do," agreed Thomas. "All sorts of secrets. Like when our birthdays are. That's one hell of a secret to keep, isn't it, Captain?"

The captain cleared his throat. "Er...yes. Indeed."

"One hell of a secret to keep from people you're sleeping with," Thomas continued, glaring at him. "Kind of a shitty thing to do, keeping a secret like that. You could really hurt someone's feelings."

He kept the glare going until the captain sighed and reached up to touch his face. "I'm sorry."

"Hmph. How come you didn't say anything? I told you when it was my birthday. Hell, I've told you everything there is to know about me."

"I was afraid you would want to celebrate."

"Oh. Well, that's dumb. If you didn't want me to bake you a cake and stuff, you could've asked me not to. I'd have understood."

To show that he accepted the captain's apology, Thomas leaned down and kissed his forehead. Drawing back, he added, "Of course, now I'm going to have to bake you a cake to get back at you, you duplicitous motherfucker. Oh yeah. I'm going to bake you a spite cake. And I'm going to sing the world's most obnoxious birthday song while you eat it."

"How old're you, anyway?" asked Zachery.

The captain sighed and said a number. Thomas's jaw sagged.

"That... Damn," he said. "You look a lot younger than that, Captain."

"Khurshed. Call me Khurshed."

"Khurshed," said Thomas, suspecting he was mispronouncing it.

Zachery squinted at the captain's face. "Even on Mars, there were a lot of guys who went in for those anti-ageing treatments. Gotta say, Captain, never seen them work that well."

"He supplements the pills with the blood of virgins," said Antoine, glancing at his comm. "Speaking of which, we just received a message from Rick. He's out of the med pod and doing well."

On the other side of the campfire, Echo was stargazing. Seen through the floating sparks, Thomas thought he looked ethereal, far more alien than the actual alien in their midst. Much as Thomas wanted to call him over or catch his eye and wink at him, he wouldn't have dreamed of doing either. One thing Thomas understood was that Echo preferred being alone most of the time. Whatever they were to each other now—and Thomas still hadn't figured that out—Echo was never going to be as demonstrative as Rick or Zachery or even the captain.

I can live with that.

That night, they all slept in a loose ring, Thomas on the captain's left, Zachery on his right. When the camp was quiet, Thomas felt a warm body cuddle up against his back. Rolling over, he spread his arms and let Echo into them.

☆☆☆

Four days later, Zachery staggered out of *The Prayer*'s engine room, filthy and victorious, and found Antoine waiting for him.

"Oh," he said. "Hey."

They hadn't spoken to one another since returning to the ship. Instead, Zachery had spoken to the captain, telling him all about what had happened, what he'd said and what Antoine had said. Without understanding how, Zachery felt as though he'd fucked up, and the captain was the closest thing they had to a confessional. He was also

Antoine's ex, if Thomas had been telling the truth.

The captain had listened to the whole story, looking now and then as though he wanted to laugh his ass off and, now and then, as though he wanted to hang Zachery upside down over a bucket of radioactive waste. When Zachery had finished, he hadn't done either of those things. He'd explained, schoolteacher style, what "asexual" meant, and wow, had Zachery felt like a chump when he was done. He'd known without being told that he owed Antoine an apology. Not that he'd relished the prospect. The challenge posed by installing their new DG ring and getting the ship back on her feet had been a handy excuse.

"Mister Halberstam," Antoine greeted him. "How go the repairs?"

"I think I've got her up and running. Going to run some tests after lunch."

"The captain will be pleased to hear it."

Zachery had been hoping for a compliment. The grudging satisfaction in Antoine's tone was a palatable consolation prize. He was coming to understand that, where First Officer Prissyboots was concerned, he'd have to take what he was given and like it.

"Hope there aren't any hard feelings, Ant," he said.

"Whatever are you talking about, Zachery?"

Bastard. Always got to do it the hard way. "On account of my being a jackass. I said a few stupid things. I didn't mean nothing by 'em. I didn't... I didn't have much of an education, so there's times when I get my facts wrong and shoot my mouth off about things I don't get. Might have made myself look like an idiot. 'Course, you've got so much education that we probably all look like idiots to you. Anyway, I hope I didn't piss you off past the point where we can...get along in the future. We're crewmates, after all. Be a shame if we couldn't get along."

Fuck, Antoine could be harder to read than Echo when he wanted to be. Zachery couldn't get a damned thing out of his expression.

"Yes, it would," said Antoine, taking a step towards him, then another. Zachery was half-afraid he was going to whip out Mister Sparky. "We are going to be stuck with one another for the rest of our lives."

He was really close now. Zachery didn't know if he should move back or not; he felt rooted to the floor.

Then Antoine took hold of a handful of his hair and gave it a sharp tug. "More to the point, someone needs to teach you to behave. I can't very well do that if we're not on speaking terms, hmm?"

Right at that moment, Zachery thought he would have spat on his mother's grave if it had meant that Antoine would let him drop to his knees and suck his dick. He hadn't ever sucked dick before, had never wanted to. Not that he didn't like dick. Dick was awesome. Putting one in his mouth, though? Nah. That shit was for girls. Except apparently he was a girl, because all he could think about was how much more gorgeous Antoine would look glistening and erect, thrusting into his mouth, using him like a cheap...

Antoine let go of his hair. "And you aren't without admirable qualities. Attacking that robot was very brave of you."

What's the matter with you? Zachery asked himself angrily. *You shouldn't be getting off on this. He's not flirting; he's not getting turned on himself. That doesn't happen for him.*

Then he looked into Antoine's eyes and thought: *He's not getting off on this, but he's getting something from this. What is it? Does he just like making me feel weird? Is he a fucking sadist?*

"You were brave too, Ant," he managed, his voice raw. "Got some things in common, I guess."

"We do. Maybe more than you think." Antoine rolled up his shirt, putting paid to all Zachery's higher brain functions, until he saw what he was supposed to see. Letters whose shape and size were hauntingly familiar to him, stretched over Antoine's lower left ribcage, easily discernible even on his dark skin: 9AM33X9.

Covering himself up again, Antoine said, "I'll go tell the captain that we're ready for a test flight. Good luck, Mister Halberstam."

☆☆☆

Echo sat under a tree, an unattended book in his lap, watching *The Prayer* soar overhead as Khali put her through her paces. Above him, looped around a branch, hung a long, green serpent. Rux had assumed the form shortly after his confession, and had yet to shift out of it. Echo assumed it was a gesture of penance.

Echo himself wasn't angry with Rux, which surprised him. Generally speaking, anyone besides Antoine who so much as inconvenienced the captain, much less put his life in danger, earned Echo's eternal hatred. He thought that his lack of any real anger might be due to the fact that the captain himself didn't seem to blame Rux for his deceit. Or perhaps it was simply that Echo had always felt a sense of kinship with shape-shifters.

Setting aside his book, he reached up and took hold of one of Rux's coils, tugging on it. The alien remained inert for a moment and then released his hold on the branch, allowing Echo to draw him down, loop by scaly loop.

"Hello, mute one," said Rux. "Ah...forgive me. The captain said I was not supposed to call you that."

Echo shrugged. He'd been called worse.

Now with the bulk of his body in a pile in Echo's lap, Rux began to twine around his arm. "I find it difficult to understand your species' moods. Although perhaps that is less your failing than mine; I also found it difficult to understand the moods of those who created me. Tell me, Echo; do your crewmates despise me?"

Echo shook his head and squirmed as Rux slithered by his armpit. He was ticklish.

"Are you sure? The one with the shrill voice...his attitude towards me was hostile."

Antoine's always like that, Echo signed.

Rux was now draping himself across his shoulders, like a stole. It was, Echo reflected, the sort of behaviour that the others would have found intensely "creepy". Yet another trait he and the alien shared.

"Thank you. The reassurance is appreciated," said Rux, flicking his forked tongue at him.

Echo petted his head and settled back against the tree using Rux's serpentine bulk as a neck rest to watch *The Prayer* descend gently to earth.

☆☆☆

The captain sat in his study, listening to the contented hum of his ship's engines. A knock made him glance up. "Enter."

Rick poked his head around the door. "Captain? You busy?"

Their gardener's ribs had been repaired. His hand had been salvaged, save for a touch of scarring and a pinkie that wouldn't unfold all the way. As for his eye... The med pod had done its best. Its best hadn't been good enough. Rick was currently wearing an eyepatch over the empty socket and had tried to make his captain feel better by saying that "now when we role-play that I'm a pirate and you're my cabin boy it'll feel more believable, Cap."

Levity aside, the captain knew it could have been much, much worse. That knowledge did nothing whatsoever to curb the guilt that swelled up in his throat as Rick's remaining eye settled on him.

"How can I help you, Rick?"

"There's... It's kind of hard to explain, sir. There's something you've gotta come and see. It's important."

"Is it, indeed?" said the captain, thinking he had a fairly good idea of what it was. *I deserve it, I suppose.*

Rick nodded fervently. "Oh, yeah. Super important. Urgent, even. If you don't come right now, the ship'll blow up and everybody'll die."

Sighing, the captain placed his hands on Rick's shoulders. Injecting a note of pleading into his voice, he said, "I suppose there's nothing else we can find to do that's equally 'important'?"

As usual, he derived an illicit thrill from how far he had to lean down to kiss Rick's mouth.

"Um..." said Rick, swallowing.

"If we were to adjourn to my quarters, I'm sure I could muster up a cabin boy costume," the captain whispered, kissing him again.

Rick stayed the course. *Brave lad.* "Nope. Sorry, Captain. You've got to come and see this first."

Seeing no way out, the captain acquiesced. Rick took his hand, as though expecting him to try to make a run for it, and led him out of his office and in the direction of the kitchen.

The captain had not addressed God in many years and was ashamed to do so now, under such embarrassing circumstances. *Please, let there not being any singing. Let Thomas be merciful enough to spare me that. If there must be singing, please send Antoine a stroke so that he doesn't tease me for the next decade.*

The kitchen was dark and ominously silent. Rick shut the door behind them, locked it, and turned on the lights while the captain braced himself for the perdition of candles and cake.

There was no singing. There was only Zachery, holding what looked like one of Echo's treasured baking tools—the one for making icing patterns on cupcakes—and Thomas. Thomas, who was naked. Thomas, who had the words "Happy Birthday Kurshid!!!" written across his chest and stomach in icing, along with a sloppily etched party balloon whose string ended at his groin.

"Wasn't my idea," said Zachery. "I was gonna draw one balloon on him for every year of your life, except it turned out that there wasn't enough icing. In all the universe, I mean."

"The joke is that you're old, sir," said Thomas, solemnly.

"As God is my witness, I'm going to flog you insolent brats to within an inch of your lives," the captain hissed, half his clothing already on the floor.

By the time he'd finished giving Zachery the spanking of his life and wringing every last drop out of Thomas, they'd made a horrible mess of Echo's kitchen. Worse, Rick started to hum "For He's A Jolly Good Fellow" while clenching around his cock. Even so, lying on his back afterwards, licking icing off Thomas's torso, the captain was hard pressed to recall a birthday he'd enjoyed more.

THE CAPTAIN'S PROMISE

CHAPTER ONE

Dirty, panting, and sweating like a pig, Rick stood back and surveyed his greatest achievement. Ten rows of newly sown green beans, ten rows of spinach, and ten rows of zucchini; the first crops he'd planted outside the rigorously controlled and monitored confines of *The Prayer*'s oxygen garden in four years. The first Earth crops that had ever been planted on this planet. In this galaxy, even.

"Bitchin'," he said to himself.

"Don't curse in front of the baby vegetables," said Thomas, slinking up behind him and draping his lanky arms over Rick's shoulders. "You don't want 'em growing up as warped and perverted as you, do you?"

"Fuck off, Meléndez," Rick drawled, tilting his head up to accept a kiss.

"How come our first crops are fucking greens? I haven't had a donut in close on five years. Why can't you plant some...bread seeds?"

"Wheat, you ignorant loser. We don't have any grain."

When they'd first set out from Earth, they'd been equipped with everything they needed for the duration of the one-and-a-half-year journey to Pluto, including a cargo hold full of supplies for the dwarf planet's fledgling colony. They'd had nutrient shakes, chewable protein bars, enough canned food to feed one hundred people for four years, the reliable bounty of Rick's vegetable garden, and flour. When they were set adrift by the enemy, they'd comforted themselves with the knowledge that they'd die of boredom and cabin fever long before they starved. Even so, Rick recalled vividly the bleak looks on everyone's faces three years ago when Echo had informed them that the last of the flour was finished.

"Besides, donuts? That shit's bad for you. Echo's fruity desserts aren't doing it for you anymore?"

Thomas made his *meh* face. "He's been using that weird melon-shaped thing we found a lot lately. I can't get used to the aftertaste. It always feels like someone coated the back of my tongue in cement."

"Don't let Echo hear you say that. He'll be whatever his equivalent of upset is. And he might poison your dinner."

Their new vegetable garden had been planted in the lee of the rocky hill next to which *The Prayer* currently squatted, her landing gear obscured by the long grass. Being situated in the planet's temperate zone, they wouldn't have to worry about the periodic decades-long draughts that assailed the southern regions. Because Antoine's current fascination was the local marine life, they were within walking distance of the beach. There was another ancient abandoned town a few miles east, though Rick wasn't all that eager to go exploring again just yet. Not after what had almost happened to Zachery and the captain.

Khurshed, Rick reminded himself. *That's what he asked you to call him.*

Thomas was resting his chin on Rick's head, a habit he'd picked up since Rick had started shaving his scalp. The explosion that had taken his eye had also burned off a good chunk of his hair, and Zachery had said it was as good a time as any to try a new haircut. Rick had agreed. Then, stupidly, he'd given Zachery free reign to experiment on him. The result was so arrestingly hideous that he'd had no choice but to go bald. Thankfully, it turned out that all three of his boyfriends thought his new look was sexy as hell. Rick wasn't so sure, but he couldn't deny that having his bare scalp stroked and fondled made it feel as though someone had pumped kerosene into his dick.

"Comfortable up there, asshole?" he inquired of Thomas.

"Sorry," he said, not sounding the least bit sorry. "It's the price you pay for being my shortest boyfriend."

"Okay, I'm gonna bite your nipples off for that," said Rick, peeling off his gloves and turning around so he could get at them.

When Rick had first met Thomas, he hadn't thought much of him. He'd come off as a bland everyday nice guy, maybe a bit of a worrywart, with unassuming good looks. Nothing special. As they'd gotten to know one another better over the course of the four years they'd been lost in space, they'd become amicable acquaintances, though not quite friends. Rick had liked him while never being one hundred percent comfortable in his presence, his feelings towards the ship's security officer muddled by what he now recognized as a huge, unacknowledged crush. Then the captain had come along and dragged them all into bed with him, and after that, everything had worked out.

Rick wasn't the type to rate his boyfriends; he felt as drunkenly, giddily in love with the captain and Zachery as he was with Thomas. That said, they were all vastly different people, and they each had their own place in Rick's life. Thomas was the one Rick went to when all he wanted was someone to make him smile. When he'd emerged from the medical pod, Thomas had been the first to be allowed to see his empty eye socket, and in the weeks that followed, Rick had turned to him whenever he started thinking dark thoughts. No matter what else was going on, Thomas always made him feel good.

"Oh yeah," Thomas said, his breath hitching as Rick settled a hand over his dick.

Rick smirked. One of the reasons Thomas always made him feel good was that making Thomas feel good was so, so damn easy.

"You're such a whore," he told him, rubbing the spot behind his left ear like he was a cat. As Thomas sagged against him, mumbling incoherently, Rick kissed him hard, grinding their dicks together while he moved his hand from Thomas's ear to massage the back of his neck. As soon as Rick had learned where Thomas's soft spots were, he'd realized that he could do pretty much anything with him.

"You like that?" he asked. Not because he had any doubt that Thomas did. It was just nice to see Thomas try and fail to make his tongue work, because sweet gentleman Thomas never ignored a question.

"Y-yeah," he husked. "'S nice."

Rick smirked. *I have so got your number, pretty boy.*

"How about we go inside?" Rick said. "Wouldn't want to traumatize the baby beans, would we?"

They didn't make it to the bedroom. They barely made it into the ship. The oxygen garden was closer than Rick's bedroom, and as its manager, Rick knew for certain it would be empty. He ended up dragging Thomas into the small side room where he kept his gardening tools, a pillow, a spare blanket, and lube because this wasn't the first time he'd brought one of his boyfriends back here. Wasn't even the third.

Despite how well he knew his way around by now, he stubbed his toe on the doorframe as they went in. He was doing that a lot lately; since losing his eye, the left side of his body kept knocking into shit. He'd picked up three new bruises in the last day alone.

"You okay?" Thomas asked.

"It's nothing," he said, limping in and rolling out the blanket. "Down you go."

In ten seconds, Thomas had shed his clothing and slid gracefully onto his stomach.

"Comfortable up there, shrimp?" he said as Rick manhandled him up onto all fours. That was something else being with Thomas gave him: the chance to play the big man, the guy in charge. Even though he was short as hell and naturally slender, he was more muscular than Thomas, who'd lost a lot of weight during their four years adrift—and he hadn't exactly been bulky when Rick had first met him. Rick spent enough time in the ship's gym to make himself look positively ripped by contrast, even though he no longer had aspirations of building himself up into a brick shithouse like Zachery.

"You got any lube stashed away here?" Thomas asked. Of course he'd worked out what Rick was hoping for. Rick didn't even have to ask if he was up for it. Thomas was always up for it.

Such an awesome boyfriend, thought Rick. But he was playing the big man, so he said, "You think you deserve lube? Lube's for people who're nice to me, Meléndez."

"Oh, is that so?"

While Rick was tugging his own shirt off, Thomas reached back with his beautiful pianist fingers and gave Rick's cock a few delicate caresses, followed by a good, workmanlike squeeze.

"Is that nice enough for you?" he asked, smirking.

Rick was sorely tempted to beg him to keep going; Thomas gave the best hand jobs in the universe. But Rick's mother had always told him the people who never amounted to anything in life were the people who couldn't focus on a goal. To be an achiever, you had to keep your eyes on the prize, she'd said. And, as evidenced by the sexy man currently jerking him off, Rick was an achiever.

"Quit it," he growled, forcing Thomas back into position and draping himself over his back so he could bite his earlobe. "Or I'll oil you up with that bottle of pesticide over there."

Anal, he thought as he stretched Thomas open, *is definitely my favourite kind of sex.*

Weird, that. For most of his life, anal had been one of those things he just didn't get, like basketball and marmite. When he saw it in porn it didn't do anything for him—sometimes it even grossed him out. He hadn't ever felt the urge to try it himself, and the only girlfriend he'd ever had hadn't been down for anything more than a blowjob before marriage. Then the captain had given him his first taste of what it was like to screw a guy and ruined him for anything else. Looking back on his performance, in hindsight, Rick was amazed that Khurshed had let him do it. He was also embarrassed as hell by how bad he'd been about preparation. When Rick had let another guy fuck him for the first time, it had been Zachery, and they hadn't used any lube other than spit; while he'd loved every minute of it, the soreness afterwards had taught him a lasting lesson.

In Rick's opinion, the best thing about anal was...well, obviously the *best* thing was the noise Thomas made when Rick thrust into his cute, pale ass, bringing their bodies as close together as Rick had ever been with another living thing. The other best thing was the view it gave him of Thomas's shoulder blades growing slick with sweat, and of every muscle in Thomas's back tensing up and relaxing again and again. And the third best thing was how tight it felt. And how hot. And how...

Okay, there were a lot of things Rick liked best about anal. The one and only thing he didn't like about it was that the most effective way to do it—and *yes*, Rick was confident that he knew which way was most effective, he'd been doing this for *months* now so he was practically an expert—was from a position that prevented him from seeing his boyfriend's handsome mug. That was kind of a pain.

"Hey, are you crying?" Rick asked, seeing Thomas's shoulders tremble.

"No," Thomas gasped and then giggled. "No, God, no, I..."

He gulped as Rick thrust forward again, keeping their momentum going, and continued, "I thought of this...this stupid sex pun."

"Let me guess; it was about the seeds. And ploughing. Right?"

"Y-yeah. Sorry, man."

"Next time Khurshed lets us at his toy box, I'm going to put the cock ring on you and leave it there for a whole day."

It worked like a charm. Even though Thomas wasn't all that into pain, he got off on thinking about it, imagining what it would be like. Threatening to use the ring did more for him than using the ring ever would have. He took one more thrust and then came, moaning and shaking. Rick didn't take much longer.

One other thing Rick had learned about his preferences in the last few months was that he really liked the way men smelled after sex. He wondered if it was something the other three ever noticed; they'd all been doing this much longer than he had. Maybe they were used to it by now.

"Quit sniffing me, you freak," grumbled Thomas. "Feels like you're about to bite a chunk out of my side."

Rick smiled against his skin. That was the third time he'd heard that exact complaint from Thomas in the last week.

The four of them—Rick, Thomas, Zachery, and Khurshed—had been sleeping together more and more often recently. Not just fucking, actually sleeping together. And not just sleeping together *after* fucking either. A few weeks ago, after a day spent helping Antoine collect samples on the beach, Rick had staggered back to his room exhausted and crawled into bed fully dressed, without turning the lights on. When the door had opened about an hour later, and he heard Khurshed's throaty chuckle, he'd blearily opened his eyes and noticed for the first time that he was, in fact, in Khurshed's room, lying in Khurshed's bed. As he'd slurred his apologies, Khurshed had undressed him and crawled in alongside him, the bristles on his chin tickling Rick's scalp. When Rick had woken up the next morning, he'd found the captain sitting up in bed reading one of his poetry books, and he'd thought: *Yes. This, I like.* Then he'd looked to his left and seen Zachery and Thomas, both asleep and drooling on one another.

It hadn't been long after that that they'd all decided Khurshed's bed needed to be bigger. To do that, they needed to expand his room. After arguing the matter back and forth for a few days, they'd agreed that the most practical approach would be to take down the wall dividing Khurshed's quarters from the empty neighbouring room. Its function, when Khurshed had first bought the ship, had been as a space for the captain to eat meals away from the rest of the crew. As the captain never used it, taking all his meals either in the mess hall with them or in his office, it was now where Antoine stored his growing collection of specimens. Persuading him to start moving them into the cargo hold had been the biggest challenge so far.

Removing the wall had finally put an end to any pretensions towards secrecy regarding the captain's relationship with them. Khali had been making cracks about "the honeymoon suite" for days, while privately she'd patted Rick's back and congratulated him as though he'd achieved some important adult milestone.

"So, how long until your baby veggies are big enough to eat?" Thomas asked as they basked in the afterglow.

Before Rick could answer, the captain's voice rumbled from the nearest com.

"*Everyone to the bridge, now.*"

CHAPTER TWO

The first thing Thomas noticed upon walking onto the bridge was that Antoine and Khurshed were arguing. No surprises there. What *did* surprise him was what they were arguing about. Having known them both for years, he'd come to recognize a certain pattern. Whenever a polarizing issue arose, the captain would be the one advocating caution, restraint, and safety, while Antoine would come down on the side of action, exploration, and investigation. The arguments they put forward wouldn't always reflect their true feelings towards the matter; Khurshed wasn't a fretful mother hen and Antoine wasn't a reckless hothead. In trying to win the debate, they pushed one another to extremes that they wouldn't have contemplated otherwise.

Today, the pattern had been disrupted.

"It's too dangerous," Antoine said, his arms folded. "I can't believe you're even considering it, Captain."

"How can you be content to sit there and do nothing?" Khurshed demanded. "We have a responsibility. To ignore it would be indefensible."

"What flavour of crap's on the menu today?" Thomas whispered to Zachery, who was watching the two of them with obvious amusement.

The engineer pointed to the nearest console. "We've got mail."

"We've *what*?"

"Is everyone here?" called Khurshed, breaking off his argument with his first officer.

"Where's Rux?"

"Echo's got him," said Irene. Looking Echo's way, Thomas saw a big green bird of prey perched on his shoulder.

"Good. I have an announcement to make. As you are all aware, for the last four years we have been trying to make contact with any human ships that may also have been teleported into this galaxy by the enemy. We have been unsuccessful. An hour ago, however, we received a message—not from another ship, but from Yusra's neighbouring planet."

"Yusra" was the name they'd given their new home. Khurshed and Antoine had bickered about that too, the former insisting that it was presumptuous of them to assign a new name to a planet that had been formerly inhabited. Eventually, he'd accepted Antoine's argument that the planet's original name, given to them by Rux, was impossible for human vocal cords to pronounce. The crew had been invited to propose alternatives, and eventually they'd agreed upon the name of the captain's younger sister.

"Someone's talking to us?" Thomas said, his eyes wide. "Who is it?"

"We don't know. The message is short and fragmented. However, Rux says he recognizes the language as belonging to the species that created him—this planet's original inhabitants."

"Wait, I thought they were all extinct."

"You will recall Rux mentioning that a handful tried to escape the plague by departing for another planet. He believes this message has been sent by those survivors."

"What do they want?" asked Zachery.

"Our help. The message is a distress call. Whoever is currently on that planet is in trouble."

"Or is pretending to be," Antoine chimed in. "Perhaps to lure us there so they can steal our ship. Captain, Rux told us that the ship his people took was experimental—'cobbled together', he said. They may well have crash landed on the nearest planet and have been living there all this time with no way of getting off it. Who's to say they won't try to steal *The Prayer* if we get too close?"

While the argument booted up again, Rick turned to Thomas, beaming. "We're not alone. There's *other people* out there."

Thomas knew how he felt. The one disappointment Yusra had given them—and really, they had no right to complain because so far she'd been fucking great in all other respects—was that she only had one sentient inhabitant. From the moment they'd learned that the planet had the ability to sustain life, they'd all secretly hoped that they might find something that resembled civilization, even though they'd known how unlikely it was. It was pretty bleak to believe that they, the twelve men and women who crewed *The Prayer*, were the only community they were ever going to engage with again.

"We've *just* got here!" Antoine was saying. "We've *just* found a safe harbour. Now you want us to endanger our hard-won safety by launching ourselves into the abyss once more and flying into what may well be a trap? Captain, you're being unreasonable."

Rick held up a hand. "Wait, wait. Ant, back when you were researching this system, didn't you say that planet was an ice ball? How could anyone live there?"

"A very good question." Antoine pressed some buttons on the nearest console. In the centre of the room, a holographic image of the planet in question appeared. "Here's what we know. Its structure is similar to that of Europa. Smooth ice covers the entirety of its surface, underneath which lies a liquid ocean. It's about half the size of Earth. Sparsely cratered, geologically active, extremely thin oxygen atmosphere, maximum surface temperature of minus two hundred and sixty degrees Fahrenheit. On the whole it's far less welcoming than our new home."

"That said, given what Rux has told us about his people's astonishing physical resilience, it's within the realm of possibility that they've managed to survive there for the past two millennia," said Khurshed.

"So, when do we leave?" said Zachery.

Khurshed had settled into his chair and was staring at his hands. "This is not a decision I will make unilaterally. This isn't a military vessel. I'm your employer, not your commanding officer. And the fact is that we have one ship. If I took only a handful of volunteers to investigate the signal, whoever was left behind would have to camp out on Yusra for at least three weeks—possibly much longer depending on how much time we spend investigating—without access to the medical pod, any mode of transport besides walking, and the many basic comforts the ship affords us. That is simply too dangerous to countenance. So either all of us go, or none of us. I considered proposing a vote, but I don't want to engineer a situation in which even one of us is forced to abandon safe harbour unwillingly. If we're going, we need to all be in agreement. I'm going to give you twenty-four hours to think it over and communicate your decision to me—in private, if you prefer. If any of you are unwilling we won't go."

"Antoine's unwilling, isn't he?" said Irene.

"He thinks he can persuade me," said Antoine, snorting derisively.

After that, Antoine dragged Khurshed into his office so they could continue their argument in private. They kept it up for the rest of the day, pausing only once to join the crew for dinner before secluding themselves again. When Khurshed finally staggered into his quarters late that night, he looked dog-tired and barely acknowledged Rick, Thomas, and Zachery perched on his bed engaged in lively conversation.

"This is so cool," said Rick as Khurshed collapsed beside him, burying his face in the pillow. "All this time, they've been up there watching us."

"Freaks me out," said Zachery, hogging the blankets as per usual, his hand resting on Thomas's rear. "That's like... Tommy, what's that big word you like?"

"Voyeurism."

"That's the one," said Zachery, giving his left ass cheek a proud squeeze. "But hey, if they're all as tasty as Rux, I'm down for it."

"I don't know," said Thomas. "I mean...you remember those robots they built, right? Those fuckers were scary. And it wasn't even a military facility we found them in. What sort of people build shit like that to guard test tubes and empty rooms?"

"Quit being chicken," said Rick, tickling him.

"No, I'm serious. Maybe this is a risk we shouldn't take. You know, just because we've had a lot of lucky breaks doesn't mean we're invulnerable. We start pushing our luck, who knows what'll happen?"

He hadn't meant to glance at Rick's eyepatch but he did, and he knew right away that Rick had noticed.

"Oh, no," Rick muttered, rolling him over and moving to sit on his chest, the better to glare at him. "Don't do that. You don't want to go, fine, whatever. Don't use me as your excuse."

"Yeah, grow a pair," said Zachery. "Why do you get to be the overprotective one, anyway? I'm the guy who blew Rick up. You don't see me being a bitch about it. Now, in more interesting news... Did I see someone taking a second helping of dessert this evening, Meléndez? Or should I say being given a second helping of dessert *by Echo*?"

"Oooh," said Rick. "Now that's interesting. Because Echo's usually kind of stingy with dessert."

Zachery nodded. "The only other person I've ever seen him give a second helping to is the captain. I guess our boy here's found his way into Echo's creepy little heart."

"Halberstam, you call him creepy again and I'll spend the rest of my life treating your dick as though it's covered in anthrax," Thomas growled, elbowing him hard in the side.

"Sorry, shrimp. I didn't mean it. Your thing with Echo— I'll admit, it's kind of cute." Zachery kissed his elbow contritely.

"Say, you know what *I* noticed at dinner?" Rick interjected. "Zach spent a lot of time staring at Antoine."

"Holy shit, really?" said Thomas, staring at Zachery. "That is actually a bigger shock than the aliens. *Antoine*? Damn, you be careful, Zach. Antoine probably likes it preying-mantis style; as soon as you come, he bites off your head."

"I'm not fucking Antoine, and I'm not going to be fucking Antoine," Zachery told them both curtly. "I was looking; that's all."

"If you don't all stop talking, I'm going to have you neutered," growled the captain, who had been trying to sleep.

The three of them exchanged looks before pouncing on him.

"Aww, the captain's jealous," Zachery said, dragging Khurshed's inert body up to lie against his chest.

Thomas took hold of his cock while Rick cupped his balls, adding, "Yeah, he thinks he's not our favourite anymore."

"Right, come *here*," Khurshed snarled, seizing the nearest of them— Thomas—and kissing him hard.

Of all of them, Khurshed had the most stamina. When Rick and Zachery were lying prone, drained and barely conscious, he was still able to push Thomas onto his back and ride his cock so hard Thomas saw stars.

"Beautiful man," Khurshed rumbled. He was always sappy when he was tired. His hand found Thomas's, and he laced their fingers together.

"Love you too," Thomas said, closing his eyes.

CHAPTER THREE

The next morning Zachery woke up long before the others. He showered, shaved, checked himself over, and made a cup of coffee. Then he went looking for Antoine.

First Officer Prissypants wasn't in his quarters. He wasn't showering. He wasn't eating breakfast in the kitchen. Eventually, Zachery found him outside the ship, sitting in the damp grass watching the sun rise while scribbling in one of his notebooks. He was wearing a white T-shirt and shorts even though it was chilly, and Zachery was struck by the urge to bring him a blanket to cover up those scrawny limbs of his. He was getting used to weird urges where Antoine was concerned.

"Good morning, Mister Halberstam. What can I do for you?" Antoine said when he finally noticed him.

You can sit there forever and let me stare at you was Zachery's first thought. His second thought was *Jesus, I've turned into such a pussy.*

Antoine made an appreciative noise as Zachery handed him his coffee.

"I want you to tell the others that you're in favour of going," said Zachery, sitting down beside him—close, though not as close as he would have liked.

"Oh?"

"See, I know you *are* in favour of going. You love mysteries and exploring weird places. And I'm one hundred percent certain you don't give a shit about the risk to yourself. What you're worried about is the rest of us. You think we might decide to go because Khurshed thinks we should. What I need you to understand is that it's not like that. We're not a bunch of lovesick yes-men. And you should know that because if we *were* like that we wouldn't be here in the first place. I remember when you and the captain were first interviewing me for this job; you said one of the most important traits you were looking for was initiative and independent thought. That's why you hired us. So…yeah. Don't forget that."

After sipping his coffee, Antoine said, "That's a nice piece of pure speculation you've put together, Zachery. Let's say you're right. That still doesn't change the fact that I'm the ship's first officer, and it's my job to make decisions that I feel best benefit the crew. Frankly, I don't see what we get out of going to rescue Khurshed's aliens. Even if they aren't hostile, what can they do for us?"

"That's chickenfeed and you know it. You aren't that cold-blooded. And even if you are, there's plenty of things they might be able to do for us. They made Rux—you know, the immortal shape-shifting sex god? If they can do that, what can't they do? Maybe they can build us a better medical pod, one that could fix Rick's eye. Maybe they can cure Khurshed's arthritis."

Antoine looked up at him sharply. "He told you about that?"

"A few weeks ago." Zachery brushed away a ten-legged bug that had been crawling up his arm. "The captain's not thinking about what they can do for us; I'll tell you that. He's thinking about those four years we spent in space, waiting and waiting for someone to rescue us. He's thinking about how scared we were. He'll never be happy living here, knowing that we let the same thing happen to someone else when we could have helped."

He paused, wondering if he was going too far—not something he worried about when talking to anyone who wasn't Antoine—and continued, "Look, I know you don't give a shit about how Khurshed feels. Everyone knows you guys don't like each other. But *I* give a shit about how Khurshed feels, and so does everyone else on board."

"Mmm. Half of you are sleeping with him, so that's not terribly surprising."

"My point is that if he's unhappy, we're unhappy. Think about that when you're deciding 'what best benefits the crew'."

"Watch your tone, Mister Halberstam," Antoine snapped.

That *voice*. That snotty, icy, aristocratic voice tinged with Antoine's native Parisian accent. Zachery's breath caught, and his mouth went dry as he thought, *Fuck, not again.*

Even when he was a teenager, Zachery had never lusted after someone he knew wasn't into him. He drooled over people who he could imagine *might* be into him, one day, maybe, if the stars aligned. But if he knew for a cold hard fact that they weren't and wouldn't ever be? *Poof*—there went his erection, vanished in a puff of smoke. For him, part of the fun of having the hots for someone was indulging in fantasies of what might actually happen.

When it came to First Officer Prissypants, Zachery knew that nothing ever would or ever could happen between them. And still his erection persisted.

"Sorry, sir," he mumbled. *'Sir'? What the hell, Halberstam? You never even call the captain 'sir' unless you're being sarcastic.*

Antoine—goddamn him—was giving him one of those looks, like he could see inside Zachery's head. "That's fine. I'll take your advice on board. Go back to Khurshed. He'll be needing his morning kiss and handjob."

"Rick does the kissing," said Zachery, getting up. "Thomas does the handjobs. Fucking's pretty much all I'm good for."

"I'll bear that in mind."

What the hell does that mean? Zachery wondered as he went back inside.

☆☆☆

It was unanimous, much to Rick's surprise. He'd been sure Antoine would say no. He'd suspected that Yanmei and Mehtab might. But twenty-four hours after the captain's announcement they were preparing to leave, and Rick had to say goodbye to his vegetables. He felt awful, like he was abandoning a puppy at the roadside. With Zachery's help, he'd set up an automatic watering system and a lean-to to shield them from the wind. He hoped it would be enough.

Crouching down, he murmured, "See you, little guys. I won't be long. Hang in there, okay?"

"Quit talking to 'em," Zachery said. "'S weird. We're going to *eat* them."

Standing up, Rick bit his lip, embarrassed. Despite how excited he'd been yesterday at the thought of meeting more aliens, today he'd been feeling weirdly sad and sentimental. He thought it had something to do with his fuck-up at breakfast. He'd tried to pour himself his morning cup of liquid nutrients, missed, and ended up dribbling it on his shoes—another thing that had been happening a lot since he'd lost the eye. He'd stared at the mess and thought, *This is it. This is forever. This is your new life.* Then he'd thrown the cup on the floor and stomped on it.

Thankfully, the only person who'd seen him do it had been Echo, who'd helped him clean it up. Which had made Rick feel even worse; he remembered all those times he'd called Echo the c-word. *Never again,* he told himself. From now on, he was going to be on his best behaviour where Thomas's new boyfriend was concerned.

"Hey, Zach? Can I ask you something?"

"Sure."

"Do you ever think about...like, the future and stuff? What we're going to be doing in ten, twenty, thirty years?"

Zachery whistled. "Shit, kid, I don't even know if we're going to be alive in ten years. Until we landed on Yusra, I'd have laid even odds on us forming a mass suicide pact just for a change of scenery. And earlier, before I joined the crew, I thought I'd spend my whole life stuck on Mars. It's really hard to leave when you've got a criminal record, even if you've got a degree. These days, I've given up on thinking about the future. Never does any good as far as I can see."

He laid one of his big hands on Rick's bare scalp and gave it a rub. Rick nearly purred.

"What're you worried about, hmm?" Zachery murmured. "You think something bad's going to happen?"

"No. I was thinking about my mom. She always used to try to talk to me about the future—you know, when was I going to get serious about school, when was I going to meet a nice girl, all that stuff."

"You were a baby when the captain hired you, right? Sixteen or some shit?"

"Seventeen, asshole."

"I always wondered; why'd you leave home so young?"

"Aah, just...just regular boring teenager shit. Things weren't working out. I always wanted to be a horticulturalist like my dad, but I hated school. Never fit in. And all my brothers—I've got three, and a little sister—they did *everything* right. Scholarships, chess championships, captain of the football team, you name it. All I could ever figure out was how to grow plants. When I met the captain, my girlfriend had broken up with me, and I was looking for any way out. I didn't tell him how old I was—said I was twenty-two and got one of my cousins to put together a fake ID. Heh. He was *pissed* when he found out I lied. But by then, we were on our way to Pluto."

Thinking about his mom always turned him into a crybaby. He tried to blink the wetness away surreptitiously. "Anyway, that's why I'm thinking about the future. I'm never going to get a degree or cure cancer or do anything to make my mom proud of me. But I still want my life to matter. I want to achieve something."

The best thing about having Zachery as a boyfriend was that he never sugar-coated fucking *anything*. After thinking for a moment, he said, "Well, you're not going to matter to anyone back home, seeing as how we're never going home. And your mom's probably written you off for dead by now. So it's a good thing you've got those goody-two-shoes brothers to keep her company. Here's what I can tell you: there's only twelve human beings in this galaxy, and you matter like hell to all of us."

Shit, shit. Don't cry, you pussy, not in front of Zach.

"Thanks," Rick said, gruffly. "What about you? You ever think about your mom?"

"My mom's dead, and she never expected much of me anyway. As for achieving something...I guess I'd like to keep *The Prayer* running for as long as we need her. I'd like to write some more songs. Somewhere down the line I'd like to marry one of you assholes, or all of you. I always wanted to get married. Other than that, no big ambitions. What about you, Tommy?"

Rick hadn't noticed Thomas coming to stand behind them and squeaked as he received a cursory ass-pinch.

"I'd settle for tasting a donut one more time before I die," said Thomas, glaring at the zucchini patch.

"Come on, you guys! We're ready," Khali called from the ship.

"Off we go," said Zachery. He picked Rick up in both hands, hoisted him onto his shoulders and trotted back to *The Prayer*. Glancing back, Rick saw Thomas trailing behind, staring up at the sky with worried eyes.

☆☆☆

They worked out that it would take them one and a half weeks to reach Yusra's neighbouring planet. They hadn't agreed on a name for her yet, so in the meantime they were calling her Moxie 2, in honour of the ship's cat. Two days into their journey Echo was in the kitchen giving Moxie 1 her breakfast while Antoine sat on the table cross-legged and aired his grievances.

"I'm not happy about this, Echo."

You keep saying that, Echo signed after cleaning his hands and checking on the batch of tarts he had in the oven. Unlike the confectionary items he'd produced for the crew for the majority of the last four years, these were made with real fruit, a species native to Yusra that Echo had privately named the "painapple" because they tasted like pineapples and smelled a bit like paint. In the course of refining the recipe, Echo had learned that he could disguise that fact with a touch of vanilla extract. The smell emerging from the oven now was tantalising enough to soothe his omnipresent grief at being forced to bake with flour substitutes.

"Are *you* happy about it?"

The captain knows what he's doing.

Antoine rolled his eyes. "You would say that."

Echo nodded. He'd never been ashamed of his adulation of their captain. *What are you doodling?*

Antoine glanced down at his notebook. "I've been trying to put together some estimates regarding our remaining food supplies. I'm also making a list of other potential sources of protein once the chewable bars run out. Yusra has few large terrestrial animals, but an abundance of marine life. Most of which might be inedible—that fish Cecelia caught would have poisoned us if we'd swallowed so much as one mouthful.

That said, I might be able to develop a way of neutralizing the toxins and..."

We've enough supplies to last us the rest of our lives. You know that, Echo interjected. It had been one of the first things they'd checked when they'd been set adrift.

"Us, yes. But what if there were more of us?"

Bewildered, Echo said, *How could there be more of us? None of us are likely to have children.*

Smirking, Antoine leaned in, lowering his voice: "I've been thinking about that cloning equipment we found. I've spoken to Rux, and he says he might be able to get it working."

Echo kept his expression neutral. Apparently interpreting that as an invitation to continue, Antoine said, "If we're serious about making this planet our home, we need to start examining the question of how we can create a sustainable, lasting community. Now, if we are to consider what a minimum viable population number would be, we..."

Moxie jumped on the table and nudged Echo's hand. As Antoine prattled on, Echo stroked her, glad of the distraction. He was, he acknowledged, a touch sensitive to the idea of cloning. Most people who'd been born on the Moon in the last century were. One of the many reasons the lunar economy had been destroyed by sanctions was its government's enthusiasm for eugenics. A third of its population were clones. While Echo had never had anything against them per se, the fact remained that those who reproduced through conventional means and gave birth to children who didn't meet the Department of Health and Progress's exacting standards were heavily penalised. Echo had long suspected that was why his parents had chosen to give him up.

Not that Antoine knows any of that, Echo thought. Their first officer wasn't thinking of such things. He was thinking of their future, building a community, and saving them from the bleak fate of dying in this galaxy one by one, their pitiful numbers shrinking and shrinking until they were all gone, and there was nothing to show they'd ever been here. He was, as always, working with the best of intentions. That was what worried Echo. Good intentions, when coupled with Antoine's tendency towards a lack of foresight, tended to do more harm than bad ones, in his experience.

"...and then we'll need to start thinking about accommodation and what sort of electoral system we'll use, and..."

Everyone on board *The Prayer* knew Echo didn't talk. What only a few of them understood was that Echo's silences all had a different character; they might signal indifference, shyness, disdain, even lust. Those who had known Echo for a long time had learned to pick up on the tiny flashes of body language that indicated what sort of silence they were being subjected to.

While sensitivity to the feelings of others wasn't one of Antoine's greatest strengths, he had known Echo longer than anyone on board save for the captain. His excited ramblings trailed off while Echo rubbed Moxie's head and studied the table.

"I might be getting ahead of myself. Obviously, I wouldn't..." He stopped, cleared his throat, and continued: "I wouldn't go ahead with any of this unless we all agreed it was the right path for us to take."

The oven chimed and Echo retrieved a tray of tarts.

"Sorry," Antoine said as Echo put them to one side to cool. "I wasn't thinking."

Echo nodded in thanks. *It has occurred to me that if Rux's people are living on Moxie 2, they may not like us treating their planet like our own.*

"I agree," said Rux, making both of them jump. They hadn't noticed him asleep in his cat form underneath the table. "My people were not malevolent, but neither were they generous by nature. If we meet them on Moxie 2, I would advise you to keep your plans to yourself, First Officer. On an unrelated note, from this vantage point, I am able to discern that Echo has pleasingly shaped toes. I would like to suck upon them if that would not be discomforting to him."

Reaching down, Antoine picked Rux up by the scruff of his neck and flung him yowling out of the kitchen.

"Perhaps they'll take him back. Wouldn't that be nice?" he said to Echo and accepted a tart.

☆☆☆

Since the ship's near-catastrophic malfunction, Zachery divided his time between coddling her engines and training Thomas as his new assistant. He hadn't said as much, but Rick suspected he'd been thinking about what would have happened if he'd been killed in the explosion; without a replacement engineer, they'd all have been royally screwed. The end result was that sometimes whole days would go by without Rick seeing one or another of his boyfriends, which was all kinds of shitty. Rick was starting to realize that he was an attention-thirsty little whore.

That said, at least they were sharing the same quarters now. Every time the doors slid open Rick held his breath in anticipation of finding Thomas lying on the bed reading one of his old comic books, or Zachery practicing his guitar. Whenever his wish came true, they'd shuffle over so he could sit next to them, or drag him into their laps for a quick make-out session.

Eight days after leaving Yusra, Rick came home to find Thomas gazing out the porthole window brooding as Moxie 2 drew ever closer.

"All that ice," said Thomas, gesturing to the white world looming up ahead. "What happens if it cracks under the ship when we land on it?"

"The ship's engines freeze up, it sinks, and we all die," said Rick cheerfully.

"For fuck's sake, man."

"Cheer up, you wet blanket. It's pretty."

The door slid open again, and a green cat scampered in. As they watched, its body stretched and twisted until it had taken on the shape of a tall, naked man who looked a little bit like the two of them mashed together.

"You appear to be unoccupied," said Rux. "This is good. I am in need of fleshly comforts. My mute friend has spurned me, and the captain is busy with paperwork. I would therefore like to suggest that the three of us have sex. I realize that we are not well acquainted; thus far, I have confined myself to the captain's bed. To entice you, I offer any one of five hundred forms, many of which have tentacles."

While they were both processing that, Khali stuck her head in through the door and said, "Number one, Rux, you need to learn how to flirt better. Number two, Thomas is scared of squid, so I don't know about the tentacles. Number three, close the *fucking door* when you're talking about weird sex stuff. I didn't want to hear *any* of that. *Jesus.*"

"Sorry!" Rick called after her as she stormed off. "Rux, close the fucking door. Then turn into me."

Thomas, not one to look a gift horse in the mouth, was already taking his clothes off. "Into you? What, so you can have sex with yourself?"

"No, dummy, so I can watch myself having sex with you and jerk off to it."

Obligingly, Rux transformed into a perfect—if greener—simulation of Rick, right down to the missing eye.

"Nice!" said Rick, grinning. "Hmm...okay, bulk me up a little. Better abs. That's great. Maybe you could make me a few inches taller? Like, about ten inches? Yeah, perfect. Now give me cat ears. And wings, can you do those? Sexy demon wings, I mean, not angel wings. Wait, you don't know what a demon is. Lemme see if I can find you a picture..."

Ten minutes later, Rick declared his creation complete.

"How am I supposed to fuck that?" Thomas demanded. "I don't even know where his ass is!"

Stepping back, Rick acknowledged that the mermaid tail had been taking matters too far. Rux returned to his humanoid form, keeping the cat ears at Thomas's request. Then they set about climbing him like a tree.

"I wish you both to enjoy this experience," said Rux, wrapping his arms around them. "Tell me if there are specific preferences you have regarding the insertion of sex organs into orifices."

"Aww, he's gentlemanly *and* hot," said Thomas. "I wanna give him a blowjob. That okay with you, Rick?"

"Sure, it's his ass I want," said Rick, busy looking around for something to stand on. Another of the many, many downsides to being the shortest boyfriend was that fucking while standing up could be really awkward. "Rux, you know what a prostate is? You got one in there?"

"This form is biologically identical to yours, inside and out."

"Fantastic."

Rux's cat ears twitched when Thomas dropped to his knees and gave his cock a tentative lick. Drawing back, Thomas said, "Whoa—he's warm. Rick, feel him, he's like a hot water bottle."

Rick had found the small footstool that Khurshed liked to rest his heels on when Thomas was massaging his feet. Standing on it, he could align his cock with Rux's ass. Pawing said ass, he found that Thomas was right; Rux's whole body felt as though he had a fever.

"You're not sick, are you?" he asked him, genuinely concerned.

Rux smiled at him. Though the face it appeared on was less severe, it was Khurshed's smile; warm, secretive, a touch conspiratorial. Rick was glad to see it. He still didn't know Rux very well, and he was experiencing that same sense of mild discomfort he'd felt not so long ago when he was in bed with Thomas and Zachery for the first time. "No. I am always this temperature. Small one, are *you* afraid of squid?"

Catching on, Rick licked his lips. "Nope. I *love* squid."

As Thomas took Rux's cock into his mouth—or as much of it as would fit—Rick started sinking into him, one arm around his waist so he didn't lose his balance. When he was almost fully sheathed, he felt something tickling his shoulder. Glancing back, he saw three tentacles swaying back and forth behind him, each about the width of his dick. They were green, smooth, with no suckers—not really squid-like at all. Tracing them back, he saw that they were growing out of the skin on Rux's hips.

"Okay, I'm game," he said. "What're you gonna do with those?"

As he spoke, he felt a fourth and fifth tentacle twine around his legs. Weird feeling. Weirdly exciting. And they were even hotter than the rest of Rux's body. Rick started to sweat as though he was in a sauna. He closed his eyes, resting his forehead against Rux's spine as one of them slithered up his thigh and pressed against his ass.

Rux was vibrating, a deep, familiar sound rolling up from somewhere in his huge chest.

"I didn't know you purred," Rick said, reaching up to stroke his velvety ears.

Thomas must have been doing damn fine work, because Rux could only mumble, "I...*mhm*..."

Smirking, Rick gripped Rux's hips and thrust into him, making the purring louder. The tentacles wrapped around his legs clenched tight, and the one rubbing up against his ass started rubbing more insistently. Swallowing his nerves, he spread his feet further apart and let it at him.

Although Rick was now an *expert* on anal, he hadn't been on the receiving end all that much. Thomas and Khurshed both liked taking his cock, so that was what they usually did. Zachery categorically refused to bottom, but Rick had only let him fuck him a handful of times. He was two feet taller than Rick; his dick was a challenge. With lube and prep and, ideally, a little weed, Rick could take him. Otherwise, he'd still enjoy it, but he'd be hella sore afterwards. So when he and Zach were short on time—which was often—they fell back on handjobs and kisses. The upshot was that Rick hadn't yet developed the unflinching manliness that allowed the captain to take a dick the size of Rux's into him without a whimper.

The tentacles weren't quite as big as Rux's dick. But they were big. They were also hot; Rick's whole body was dripping with sweat now. As one pushed into him, he whimpered, pressing against Rux's back with his jaw slack.

"Small one? You seem to have gone limp. Is everything alright?" Rux inquired.

Rick tried to get hold of himself. Opening his mouth to formulate a reply, he instead gave a weak moan when the tentacle rubbed hard against his prostate.

He heard Thomas chuckle: "Oh, I know *that* sound. What're you doing to him back there, Rux?"

"Crewmate Thomas, I implore you to put my sex organ back in your mouth."

Rick had trouble following what they were saying. All his available brain space was currently occupied by listing all the ways getting fucked by a tentacle differed from getting fucked by a cock or fingers. Aim—that was one thing. The tentacle seemed to have a mind of its own. Even with Rux preoccupied with whatever Thomas was doing to him, its thrusts were pinpoint accurate.

Rick's own thrusts weren't half as impressive. Despite his being *a goddamn expert* at anal these days, he knew he was putting on a damn poor showing. In his defence, concentrating was difficult. On top of everything else, Rux was now purring so hard it was like being buried in a giant vibrator.

Get it together, he told himself.

Gritting his teeth, he tightened his grip on Rux's waist and started giving as good as he got. Barely ten seconds later, Rux came, and when he did, something weird happened. For an instant, the texture of his green skin changed, becoming harder—almost scaly. The tentacles became rougher, growing ridges as they thrust into Rick's body one last time, which was all Rick needed to push him over the edge.

His and Rux's moans were accompanied by a yelp from Thomas. "Ow! Christ, don't pull my hair so hard."

"Aah...ah...apologies," Rux gasped, swaying as though he might topple over. "Are you all right?"

"You got your green jizz in my fringe," Thomas said, in that adorably grumpy voice he used when someone had messed with his precious, precious hair.

"Poor baby," snickered Rick, basking in the warmth of Rux's back as the tentacle withdrew. "Rux, I think you need to make it up to him."

"I concur."

Rick hopped off the footstool and sprawled back on the bed to enjoy the sight of Rux dragging Thomas up from his knees and lavishing kisses on his mouth and neck. When Thomas was frotting against his leg, the alien picked him up, placed him on the bed next to Rick, then rolled him over, and fucked his brains out. Rick's cock wasn't ready for a second round yet, but he saved the image for later, along with a mental note to ask Rux if he could grow himself a cat tail to go with the ears.

They were lying back against the pillows, Rux in the middle, with the two of them on either side, when Rux said, "Are we friends now?"

Rick's blood ran cold. Apparently Thomas felt the same way, because he said, "Oh hell, this wasn't a trade-off, was it?"

"Rux, you know you didn't have to have sex with us to be our friend, right? You knew that?" Rick asked, sitting up to look him in the face. *Please say you knew that.*

"Yes, yes," said Rux. "I understand that physical intimacy is not a prerequisite for amicable relationships among your kind."

"Thank God," said Thomas, curling up again at Rux's side.

Rick wanted a touch more assurance. "So you came here because you're into us? No other reason?"

"I came for several reasons. Firstly, I was bored and wanted sex. Secondly, I know that the captain is 'into you', and I am 'into' him. I hoped to gain a more complete understanding of him by sharing intimacy with you. Thirdly, you are both attractive specimens and you interest me. The purpose of my visit was not to win your friendship. That said, if I have managed to do so, that would please me. I like having friends."

Rick's heart lurched as he remembered that before they'd come along, Rux had spent hundreds of years alone on Yusra. "Okay. We can be friends."

Rux beamed. "Splendid."

CHAPTER FOUR

"There's nothing there," said Antoine.

They'd arrived in Moxie 2's orbit forty-eight hours ago and, so far, had yet to encounter anything that looked like a trap. The distress signal was still coming through. The problem was that the place it was coming from—the equator—was as barren as every other inch of the planet.

"They might be using holograms to hide themselves. They might live under the ice. They might be very well camouflaged," said Khurshed.

Or very small, Echo contributed.

Antoine turned to Rux. "It occurs to me that you've not told us what your creators look like."

Lounging on the arm of the captain's chair in his cat form, Rux said, "They had a predilection for body modification, so I cannot say for certain what they might look like today. When last I saw them, they were bipedal. Most of them were slightly larger than me. The number of limbs they possessed on the upper halves of their bodies varied over the course of their lifetimes. They had mouths and ears and communicated through speech, as you do. While they were a hardier species than you, they were not invulnerable to the elements and built dwellings to shelter themselves. As we do not see any on the surface below, it may be supposed that they are still inhabiting their ship, the remains of which may have been concealed beneath the ice since their crash landing."

Antoine turned to Khurshed. "I assume you intend for us to go down there?"

"We won't land. As you have posited, it is entirely possible that they plan to steal our ship. A handful of us will descend to the planet's surface and see what there is to see. *The Prayer* will remain in flight."

"We have no detachable vessels. How will we get down without landing?"

Khurshed smirked. "I thought Rux might be of some assistance..."

☆☆☆

"You have lost your mind," Antoine told him two hours later, after they had entered the planet's atmosphere and come to hover half a mile above its surface.

"Do you have a better idea?

"Yes. We go home."

"I assure you, I am more than up to the task," said Rux, his razor-sharp beak clacking as he spoke. "Although, unfortunately, I can only carry a maximum of two passengers safely."

The captain turned to his crew, assembled in the cargo bay. They didn't have much room; the shape Rux had shifted into had a wingspan of twenty metres. More to the point, its horns and talons were all as long as Khurshed's arm. It didn't look the least bit aerodynamic, with its barrel chest and disproportionately large head, but Rux had assured them it could remain airborne for weeks on end.

"Captain, this is madness," Antoine insisted. "You can't even ride a horse, much less...whatever Rux is supposed to be."

"A species my people hunted to extinction. They called it 'the feathered death'," Rux said helpfully.

"Oh, did they? *Excellent*. Captain..."

"Rux can carry two people," Khurshed said to the crew. "One of them will be me. Who else?"

Every hand in the room went up.

"You're going hunting for aliens. I'm the only qualified astrobiologist here. If you're serious about this ludicrous stunt, I'm the obvious choice to accompany you," said Antoine.

Rick piped up, "Captain, I weigh the least. If I go with you, it'll be easier for Rux to get out of there in a hurry if something goes wrong."

"I worked on Europa for a few years in my twenties," said Irene. "I know what it's like to move around in that sort of environment."

"Captain, may I suggest taking Thomas? He is, after all, the best shot," said Rux.

"Good point," said Khurshed as Thomas punched the air and went to fetch his rifle. "Prepare the equipment. We leave in two hours."

When he and Thomas were sitting atop Rux's back, strapped to the makeshift saddle Zachery had cobbled together, Antoine's words returned to him. It was true; he couldn't ride a horse. The one time he'd tried, he'd fallen off and broken a rib.

"Good luck, Cap," said Rick as he and Echo checked their suits and their breathing equipment one more time.

"Rux, you bring them both back in good condition or I'll take a blowtorch to your balls," said Zachery.

"I am impervious to fire, both in this shape and all my others," said Rux. "I do find your threats charming, though. We should engage in coitus upon my return."

"Let's go," said Khurshed, putting on his helmet before the conversation could degenerate further.

The last face he looked at before the cargo bay doors slid shut was Antoine's. His first officer had his stoical expression on, the one he always wore when he thought Khurshed was being staggeringly stupid but knew there was no talking him out of it.

Am I doing this to show off? Khurshed wondered. There had been a time in his youth when he'd been in the habit of doing stupid things to win Antoine's admiration. He wasn't sure that time had ever actually ended.

His musings were cut short when the hatch opened and Rux reared up like a horse before lunging out into the open air.

☆☆☆

The less said about the journey downwards the better. They survived, didn't break anything, and landed roughly where they had planned to. That, Khurshed told himself, was what counted.

"Don't worry, Captain, I won't tell anyone," said Thomas, kneeling beside him and patting his back as the last of the dry heaves faded. Had his suit not been equipped for such eventualities, he would have drowned by now.

It was another ten minutes before Khurshed could get to his feet, leaning on Thomas's shoulder, by which point Rux had returned from his preliminary scouting mission. He had taken on his lion form and left huge paw prints in the snow.

"Captain, this area appears to be uninhabited," he said. "I should point out that though I cannot discern evidence of my people's presence, they may well be here. Their technology could be shielding them from our senses."

"Whoever sent out that distress signal wanted us to come here. Why would they hide themselves?"

"Maybe whoever sent it was the last one alive," said Thomas. "Maybe he died before we got here. Cap, what do we do if no one shows up? It's fucking freezing."

His arms were wrapped tight around his chest. Even though their suits protected them from the worst of the cold, it still felt as though they were in a meat locker.

Khurshed surveyed their surroundings. No wind, no clouds, only flat white ice and clear blue sky in all directions. He looked down, hoping in vain to see a shadow of the crashed space ship through the ice.

"Hey, what's that?" said Thomas. He was also looking downward— not at the ice, but at a thumbnail-sized black speck visible in a nearby clump of snow. Rux pushed the snow away while the two of them stepped back. Khurshed would have felt more guilty about using his newest crewmate as a bomb disposal unit had Rux not previously admitted to being nigh-invulnerable.

What he uncovered was a cylinder. Stood up straight, it was level with Rux's knee, and almost as wide as it was tall. It was black, shiny, seemingly made of some sort of metal, and had no markings on it whatsoever. The only thing marring its smooth surface was a white button.

"Intriguing," said Rux, and he pressed it before Khurshed could stop him.

To his relief, the cylinder didn't explode. With a soft hissing sound, its top section detached, revealing itself to be a lid. After a moment's hesitation, the three of them looked inside.

Then the captain spoke into his com. "Antoine? I need Rick to look at something."

He sent a picture of the cylinder's contents up to *The Prayer* and waited.

"Holy shit," came Rick's voice.

"Language," snapped Khurshed. "Can you identify these objects?"

"Captain, that's fucking grain."

☆☆☆

Antoine refused to allow the cylinder onto the ship without it first being scanned for explosive devices or dangerous toxins, so Khurshed sent Rux back up to retrieve the necessary tools with which to do so. Thomas and Khurshed had nothing to do but stand around shivering while they waited for him to return.

"Captain, this doesn't make sense," said Thomas.

"Thomas, there are a great many aspects of this situation that make no sense. You're going to need to be more specific."

"Okay, good point. Right now I'm focusing on the obvious one; how the hell does grain from Earth end up *here*? And how did Rux's alien buddies get their hands on it? And why are they giving it to us?"

"Let's not make any assumptions. We haven't encountered any of Rux's progenitors. We don't know what their motives are. We can't say for certain that they are giving us the grain. Maybe they just wanted us to see it."

"Why?"

"I've no idea."

"I don't like it. Not one bit."

"Look on the bright side. It now seems considerably less likely that they lured us here to kill us. If they wanted us dead, there are far less convoluted ways of going about it."

"Guess so." His rifle slung over one shoulder, Thomas circled the cylinder for the fourth time, trying to make out any marks that might indicate how long it had been there or how it had been made. "If..."

Something moved in his peripheral vision. He glanced towards it, and then he screamed louder than he ever had in his life and opened fire.

☆☆☆

Captain Khurshed Amirmoez was not a man accustomed to taking orders.

But he hadn't hired Thomas for his good looks. Even at the tender age of twenty-five, Mister Meléndez had an impressive CV. He'd won a dozen trophies in various shooting championships. He'd spent two years working as a police officer and two years working as a security guard on other merchant vessels. He'd received a medal for bravery after facing down three heavily armed smugglers, two of whom he'd shot dead.

So when he bellowed, *"Captain, get the fuck down!"* the captain got the fuck down. He ducked behind the cylinder; there wasn't any other cover available. He heard Thomas fire three times, and then silence.

Then Thomas said, "Captain, contact the ship. Tell them to send Rux back right now. We need to leave."

Khurshed did so, ignoring Antoine's demand for details. Barely a minute later, Rux descended to the ground, landing gracefully with the requested equipment held in his beak. Thomas kept his eye on the horizon and his rifle at the ready while Khurshed scanned the cylinder and found that it neither contained nor was comprised of hazardous materials.

As they strapped themselves and their cargo to Rux's back, Khurshed tried to spot what it was that Thomas had seen. But no matter which way he looked, the landscape seemed as empty and untrammelled as it had been when they'd arrived, save for their own footprints.

Flying back up to *The Prayer* was even worse than coming down had been. At least this time there was nothing left in his stomach to be thrown up. They arrived at the cargo bay to find it empty, save for one of the large sealable crates they used to transport dangerous goods.

Antoine's voice came over the coms. "Captain, the crew are on the bridge with me. For safety reasons, I'd advise you to put the cylinder in the crate and then proceed to the decontamination room."

Though Khurshed threw him many questioning looks, Thomas remained silent while they stored the cylinder and cleansed their bodies.

A round of applause greeted them upon entering the bridge. Zachery swooped down to hug Thomas and ruffle his hair, while Khurshed brushed off greetings and went to his chair.

"Antoine, take us into orbit at once," he said.

When they were clear of the planet's atmosphere, he turned to Thomas. "What did you see?"

Thomas sat at his station, his gaze fixed on the middle distance. He shook himself and took a deep breath. "I think I saw one of them. No— I know I did. Nothing else moves like that. I only saw it for a second, but I'm sure. It *was* one of them."

"'One of them'? You mean one of Rux's people?" said Antoine.

"I mean one of *them*."

"What are you..."

Antoine fell silent as realization dawned. Slowly, the others caught on. Mehtab made a whimpering sound while Cecelia clutched the crucifix she wore round her neck. The captain exhaled and sat back in his chair.

"Forgive me," said Rux. "I don't understand. Who is Thomas referring to?"

"An old acquaintance," said Khurshed. "I can't pronounce their name. You need mandibles for it. We called them 'the enemy'."

He ran a hand across the nearest console, bringing up a holographic image of one of the aliens responsible for *The Prayer*'s being teleported into a different galaxy four years ago. "They look like this."

Rux tilted his head as he scrutinized the image and then nodded. "Yes. Those are my people."

CHAPTER FIVE

In the ensuing shitstorm, Rick watched from the sidelines as Khurshed did his best to maintain order, Antoine shouted questions at Rux, Mehtab sobbed into Irene's chest, and Cecelia mumbled the Lord's Prayer. Rick probably would have joined her if he hadn't noticed Thomas wandering out of the room. After a moment's hesitation, he followed him.

He found him in the mess hall, having activated their hologram projector. The scene he'd chosen was of a leafy wood in early autumn. It was about midday, and the only noises were birdsong and the breeze. Rick walked over, his shoes crunching on red-gold leaves that weren't there, and crawled into Thomas's lap.

"Hey, loser. What's up?"

Thomas stared ahead as though he hadn't heard him.

Rick chewed his lower lip and then said, "I'm really scared."

At that, Thomas looked down at him, then nodded, and rested his head on his scalp. "Yeah, me too."

Heavy footsteps heralded Zachery's arrival. He sat down behind Thomas without a word and dragged them both back against his chest like a kid clutching his stuffed toys. After a long while, he rumbled, "You guys scared?"

"Yeah," they said together.

"Me too." He looked up at the surrounding trees as though noticing them for the first time. "Where's this?"

"Yellowstone," said Thomas. "My family used to come here on holiday when I was a kid. It's where I got into bird watching."

The door to the mess hall slid open again, and all three of them looked up to see Echo lingering at the threshold, as though he wasn't sure whether he had the right to intrude.

213

"Hey there," Thomas said, managing a weak smile.

While Rick couldn't completely understand what Echo signed, he picked up the word "scared". Thomas nodded, and Echo made his way over to sit cross-legged on a pile of autumn leaves beside them, managing to press one of his knees up against Thomas's side without any part of his body touching Rick or Zachery. Fascinated, Rick watched him reach out and press the tip of his index finger against Thomas's lips.

Thomas exhaled slowly. "Whatever happens, we're going to be together. Right?"

"Right," said Rick, reaching up to stroke his cheek.

☆☆☆

While the rest of the crew ate dinner that evening, an affair characterized by brief moments of excited speculation followed by long, anxious silences, Echo put four bowls on a tray and carried them to the captain's office.

Khurshed, Antoine, and Rux were there, talking in low voices. Echo placed their cabbage soup before them and then settled into a corner to eat his own dinner: a pile of white mush with steam rising off it. Although the crew had lived off of vegetables cooked by Echo's hand for four years, Echo himself could only occasionally stand to force down a mouthful of spinach or beetroot. He was a picky eater and despised most vegetables—a trait he shared with his newest lover. (He had a suspicion that might have been what first attracted him to Thomas.) It was little short of a miracle that among the many crates of supplies they'd been transporting in their cargo hold at the time of their encounter with the enemy, there had been one containing two thousand packets of dehydrated mashed potatoes.

"The facts as they stand are as follows," Khurshed was saying. "The enemy revealed themselves to humanity seventy years ago. Since that time, they have hovered at the outer edges of our solar system, resisting all attempts to make contact and opening fire on any ships that came too close. No one could ever work out what they wanted or what they were planning. When we ran into them, they teleported us to this galaxy for reasons unknown. We have now learned that the enemy are the same beings responsible for Rux's creation, the same beings who inhabited Yusra two thousand years ago. And now that we have settled on what used to be their world, they have provided us with what seems to be grain."

Antoine nodded. "I've finished examining the contents of the cylinder. Rick's initial assessment was correct. We now have the means to grow wheat, barley, and maize."

The captain rubbed his chin. "Is it a gesture of apology?"

"If they're sorry for what they did to us, why not simply teleport us home?" said Antoine.

"Do you have a more logical explanation?" Khurshed returned.

Rux, who still struggled to grasp the nuances of wielding a spoon, was lapping up the soup with his tongue. "I should mention that when I last knew my people, they were unable to teleport. More's the pity. Evacuating our home planet to escape the plague would have been much easier if they'd had such a skill."

Antoine stretched and rubbed the back of his neck. "All right, here's my best theory. Rux's progenitors are almost driven to extinction by a plague. A small number of them manage to escape Yusra in an experimental space craft. At some point after that, they develop the ability to teleport. They arrive in our solar system and observe that Earth is remarkably similar to their home world in terms of size, climate, and distance from its sun. After a period of time spent studying us from a distance, they decide to teleport a small number of humans to their home world to see if we thrive there. And since we arrived on Yusra they've been watching us—assessing our progress. They've given us the grain because they've seen us start to farm and want to supply us with some of Earth's staple crops to better our chances of survival and of repopulating their world."

After a long silence, Khurshed said, "I see two large question marks hanging over this theory. The first is why they haven't repopulated their world themselves. It's been two thousand years. The plague is no longer a factor. The second is why they didn't simply bring the grain to Yusra for us to find."

"Perhaps there's some cultural explanation," said Antoine, his left eyebrow twitching in annoyance as Rux noisily slurped down the last of his soup. "Rux has implied in the past that his people had a range of complex religious beliefs and practices. If their god or gods forbids their coming home... But we're into the realm of wild speculation. Returning to what we know, we have wheat, maize, and barley, and a planet to grow them on. We also have one sighting of a species we have always perceived to be hostile living in close proximity. So, do we leave?"

Aren't you afraid? Echo thought. *Must you all sound so collected? Honestly, they say* I *behave like a robot...*

"It would sadden me to leave my home world behind. But I do not want to be alone again. If you choose to leave, I will go with you," said Rux.

"We'll have to put it to a vote," said Antoine.

"First Officer, I confess to finding your voting system perplexing. Why should the majority be trusted with important decisions? This is the captain's vessel, is it not? Surely he should be the one to decide."

"We'll add 'democracy' to the ever-growing list of things your allegedly superior species didn't develop, along with roads and basic biomedical ethics."

"Antoine! That's unnecessary," Khurshed snapped. "Rux, you are correct in that the ship is legally my property. That doesn't give me the right to decide the fates of everyone on board. We'll communicate all the available facts as well as our theories to the crew, and then we will have a vote."

As Khurshed and Antoine went off to the mess hall to speak to the others, Rux lingered behind.

What's wrong? Echo asked, collecting up the bowls.

"I am ashamed to learn that my people are the ones responsible for your predicament. Those who left Yusra to escape the plague must know how painful it is to lose one's home. That they would inflict the same pain upon you... I would not have thought them capable of such cruelty."

Really? They used you as a test subject.

"Yes. But they had a right to treat me as they did. They made me."

Echo put the bowls aside and shook his head. *No. That isn't how it works. You're a person. No one should treat a person like a thing.*

Rux transformed into his feline form and rolled onto his back so that Echo could rub his belly. "I don't think the others realize it, but you're a very kind man. Tell me, Echo; how will you vote?"

The truth was that Echo had no idea himself. Unlike the rest of the crew, he had never suffered from the sensation of being trapped inside *The Prayer* during their four years adrift. He hated the outdoors. Spending his life within a spaceship suited him very well. That said, the captain's welfare was always Echo's first priority, and he knew Khurshed would be heartbroken if they voted to leave Yusra; he had begun to think of it as his home. Moreover, it had not escaped Echo's notice that now they had wheat, he might finally be able to bake *properly* again.

I don't know.

Rux rubbed his body against Echo's left leg. "I would like to restate my earlier comment regarding your toes. They are magnificent."

Leaning down, Echo scratched behind his ears and then went to do the dishes.

☆☆☆

As they left Moxie 2 behind, Zachery half expected to see hundreds of enemy ships rising up from the planet's surface in hot pursuit. The first few days of their journey back home were tense and quiet. When they were in orbit around Yusra and had yet to see any indication that the enemy would be coming after them to take their grain back, the tension eased a little.

The captain said they'd have another three days to make up their minds on whether to stay or not. Zachery thought that was a good idea. His initial instinct upon learning that *they* were literally one planet away had been to run screaming to the other side of the universe. He remembered being ten years old, back on Mars, and listening to his mom talking about *them* with her friends. What did they want? No one knew. Their language was impossible to translate—even listening to it made your ears hurt, apparently. Where had they come from? Conspiracy theories abounded. What would they do next? Zachery's mom and her friends had been convinced that any day now they'd start moving towards the inner solar system. Even when it had become clear they had no intention of doing so and were content to skulk around Pluto and harass the colonies, the thought of them had haunted Zachery's nightmares for years.

Now that the panic was wearing off, he was having second thoughts. It helped that now he could look down on Yusra and be reminded of how pretty she was, all green and blue and white.

To his surprise, Thomas was in favour of staying.

"How come?" Zachery asked him when the two of them were down in the engine room for Thomas's semi-regular engineering lesson. Zachery had just finished showing him one of the umpteen squillion basic maintenance tasks he had to perform, while Thomas made diligent notes. "I mean, you're terrified of them."

Thomas chewed the inside of his lip and said, "The thing is, it doesn't make any difference if we leave or not. They know we're here. If Antoine's right and they brought us here on purpose, then they'll just bring us back here if we try to run. Nothing we can do about it, not a damn thing. They've got technology we can't even wrap our minds around. I'm terrified of them, but it's like being terrified of black holes. They exist and there's fuck all you can do about it. Might as well get on with life."

"It's bullshit," Zachery growled. "Being their...their fucking experiment."

"Hey, look on the bright side," said Thomas, dropping a kiss onto Zachery's shoulder. "They can't be all bad. They gave us barley and wheat, even if we did have to go a long ass way to get it."

"Yeah, well, unlike you I don't have wet dreams about donuts."

"You know you can make beer from barley, right?"

Zachery's jaw dropped. "Holy shit, really?!"

A nearby com crackled to life. *"This is the captain. I'd like to see Mister Halberstam in my office."*

☆☆☆

"Antoine has asked me to find out if you might be interested in sharing a drink with us," said Khurshed, his expression blank and his voice without inflection.

A flurry of thoughts flew through Zachery's head:

'Us'? Antoine and the captain? In one room?

'A drink'? We haven't got any booze. Not yet, anyway.

Antoine asked if I 'might be interested'? Antoine doesn't ask politely for fucking anything.

Okay, maybe that was unfair. Antoine was bossy and demanding, not a bully. But he also wasn't the sort of person who extended invitations by proxy. *What the hell's going on?*

Despite his obvious attempts to appear as neutral as possible, Khurshed was fidgeting nervously. "I should tell you that I'm surprised he suggested it. Antoine's a private man. You must have impressed him."

"I don't know about that," said Zachery, scratching his head. "I think he... I think he's interested in me. For some reason."

Khurshed nodded. "And you're 'interested' in him?"

"Cap, what's this about?" Zachery sighed. "Yeah, I've got a crush on him. It's not going to go anywhere. I can't do relationships without sex; I don't even know how that would work."

"Speaking from experience, it can work very well. But I'm not talking about a relationship."

Zachery listened as Khurshed explained Antoine's idea. When he was finished, Zachery sat silently for a while before saying, "And this is something you've done with him before?"

"Yes. Not for a few years now, but we used to do it regularly in my twenties."

In his twenties? Zachery's eyes widened. When he'd learned from Thomas that Antoine was the captain's ex, he'd assumed they'd had one of those fierce, sex-fuelled hook-ups that burned out in a week, and that Antoine had come out as asexual afterwards. It hadn't occurred to him that the two of them might have sustained a stable relationship for any prolonged period of time. Moreover, if Khurshed had been telling the truth when he'd admitted his real age to them, then Antoine must have also used rejuvenation tech at some point. If his appearance—not a day older than thirty—was an accurate indicator of his age, then he hadn't even been born when Khurshed was in his twenties.

"Do you like the idea, Zach? I should add that Antoine insisted I tell you not to say yes to please me."

Zachery smirked. "He doesn't get how you and I work, does he? Captain, it sounds like fun. Let's try it."

That was how, three hours later, Zachery found himself cleaning and trimming his toenails for the first time in his life. Ordinarily, he kept them in shape with his teeth. He also showered for so long Khali growled threats through the bathroom door about cutting off his nuts because it was her turn. Lastly, he went to Cecelia and begged to borrow a touch of her last precious bottle of cologne.

Khurshed was waiting for him outside Antoine's quarters, his beard newly trimmed and his shirt and pants freshly ironed. "Zach, once again, if anything happens that makes you uncomfortable in any way, at any point, you may leave. You should leave. I'll understand and so will he."

Zachery gave his ass a smack. "Quit fussing, old man."

Zachery didn't often use the ship's holographic scene projector. It bothered him that he could never smell his surroundings. And most of the one hundred different locations it had been programmed to display were outdoorsy stuff: beaches, fields, quiet valleys, and majestic cloudscapes. There was only one rugby stadium, and he didn't like it. The sky was blue, not red, so he couldn't fool himself into thinking he was back in his home town for even a minute.

Upon entering Antoine's quarters, he was met with a location he hadn't seen before. It was a room with no roof, only the night sky overhead, showing constellations he hadn't known he'd missed until he saw them again. The room itself looked like a fancy hotel suite for ultra-rich people on honeymoon. There were pillars, a fireplace, paintings depicting sailing ships being tossed about on rough seas, and two chandeliers. There was a four-poster bed big enough to fit ten large men, with giant cream-coloured pillows and a wine-red duvet. There was also a grand piano, at which Antoine was seated.

"Good evening, gentlemen. Make yourselves comfortable," said Antoine, his fingers dancing gracefully along the keyboard. He was dressed as though he'd recently returned from the opera: pale silk shirt, dove-grey pants, dove-grey jacket slung over the back of his chair.

Looking closely, Zachery noticed that the tune he was hearing didn't match what Antoine's fingers were doing. The obvious fakery of it combined with the ridiculous opulence of the setting made him grin.

No, stop that. It's part of the game. You'll ruin it if you start giggling like a brat.

Zachery took off his shoes and socks, tucking them out of sight and sinking his toes into the soft, spotless carpet. Khurshed copied him before crossing the floor to stand beside the piano. His posture was oddly formal, like a soldier at parade rest.

After the recording finished playing, Antoine took a sip from the champagne glass at his side and then let Khurshed have one, holding the glass up to his lips for him.

"Zachery, won't you come and join us?" he said. It didn't sound like a request.

Khurshed had told him what to expect in broad terms. And he already knew damn well how Antoine's presence tended to affect him. So he wasn't surprised by the sudden gut-punch of lust. What did take him off guard was the dark little sparkle in Antoine's eye—amusement, he thought, and something else. It made his cheeks heat and set loose a wave of butterflies in his stomach, reminding him that when it came to Antoine his misbehaving dick was only half the problem.

"What d'you want me to do?" he asked, gruffly, remembering Khurshed's insistence that he ask questions any time he was confused.

Antoine tipped another mouthful of champagne into Khurshed's mouth. "It's up to you, of course. What I'd *like* you to do is help me tend to our captain. You could take off his shirt, to start with."

Zachery obeyed, noting Khurshed's burgeoning erection and uncharacteristic silence as he did.

"Thank you, Zachery," said Antoine, before saying something in French to the captain. Khurshed immediately went over to the fireplace and knelt down next to one of the armchairs.

In response to Zachery's quizzical look, Antoine said, "He feels more comfortable with the French in this setting. It wasn't an attempt to exclude you."

"Takes more than that to hurt my feelings. I'm not a sensitive buttercup," Zachery retorted.

"Good." Standing up and lowering the piano lid, Antoine rubbed his hands together. "Let's get down to business."

He sat down in the armchair next to which Khurshed was kneeling, beckoning Zachery to take the other chair. As Zachery complied, Antoine rested one slender hand in Khurshed's thick, dark hair, stroking it absently. "Have you ever tried anything like this before, Mister Halberstam?"

Not exactly sure what "like this" meant, he said, "Me and the cap have done a lot of stuff. Uh. He smacks my ass sometimes. One time he asked me to pull his hair. Oh, and I like getting him to dress up."

His eyes widening, Antoine said, "As what, might I ask?"

"Let's see, we've done a doctor, a pirate, a soldier, and a vampire. We tried a werewolf once but it didn't work out. The whiskers looked dumb."

Now it looked like Antoine was the one struggling not to giggle. "Ah...fascinating. And tell me, Mister Halberstam, have any of the costumes ever incorporated ropes?"

"Ropes? No, don't think so. We used a blindfold once..."

Antoine reached down the side of the chair and held up what looked like about thirty feet of coiled white rope and smelled a little like hemp.

"Oh," said Zachery stupidly.

Khurshed made a soft noise that might have been a hastily suppressed chuckle. Antoine gave one of his ears a sharp pinch, and he shut up again.

"Are you game?" Antoine asked Zachery, that same sparkle in his eye, with a conspiratorial grin to match it.

"Yeah. Oh, yeah."

Antoine spent the next hour teaching Zachery how to use the ropes. First, he tied Khurshed's wrists to the bed posts, then undid the knots and let Zachery try to copy him. It took Zachery several attempts to perfect his cat's paw, during which Antoine stroked Khurshed's hair and whispered to him in French. After that, he taught him three different ways of tying his hands together, and how to tie his arms behind his back with the ropes brushing his nipples as they went across his chest. By that point, Khurshed was fully engorged and biting his lower lip.

Then, for a grand finale, Antoine took out a thinner rope and tied it around his cock and balls.

"Fuck, look at you," Zachery breathed, gazing down at Khurshed. He didn't usually spend long ogling his lovers. Taking it slow wasn't his style. He liked his sex the way he liked his rugby: fast, dirty, and if he had a tooth missing at the end of it so much the better. Doing it like this, drawing it out... Yeah, he could see the appeal. It gave him a chance to get a proper look at Khurshed's body. He'd thought he knew it as well as his own by now; he'd spent enough time staring at his ass and muscles. Now, though, he was noticing all the things he'd missed before. Like the tiny marks on his upper ears where evidently he'd once had piercings; the pale liver spots on his shoulders and the base of his neck; the length of his eyelashes.

"He's beautiful, isn't he?" said Antoine. And there was something in his voice...

Zachery looked up from his attempts to replicate the masterpiece Antoine had made of Khurshed's cock. Antoine was lying down on his side at the top of the bed, still in his dove-grey suit with his sleeves rolled up. His fingertips were moving slowly over Khurshed's face, pressing against his lips, then his cheeks, then his chin. Khurshed was looking up at him with a shy smile that made him seem all of twenty years old.

The captain's ex'. Bullshit, Zachery thought. *You stupid asshole, Zachery. How did you miss it?*

"How are you getting on?" Antoine asked, glancing down at Zachery's efforts. "Oh, that's very good. You can make them a little tighter in future, if you like. Well, now that I've shown you the basics, what do you want to do next?"

"I thought you were running the show. Don't you decide what happens next?"

Antoine rolled his eyes, untying Khurshed's cock. "Zachery, we're both running the show. Why else would I have invited you?"

"Okay. So..."

"You have to guess what he wants. He's not allowed to ask for anything. That's part of the game."

Zachery nodded, all business now. "I'm going to fuck him. I want him standing, tied to that pillar, arms above his head."

"As you yourself said, it is what you're 'good for'. May I watch?"

"Whatever you want." Zachery snuck a peak at his crotch. No tent. No wet spot. *I don't get it. How can he be enjoying this if he's not getting off on it?*

"So," he said as they were tying Khurshed's arms to the pillar. "This is how you two make it work? The whole 'no sex' thing? You find some dumb stud like me and then let him fool around with Khurshed while you watch?"

"That isn't..." Khurshed began, before Antoine pinched his ear again, hard. He fell silent.

"No," said Antoine. "We've never tried this particular experiment before. We have other ways of 'making it work'. And please don't demean yourself in front of the captain. It distresses him, which is hardly fair when he's not allowed to speak."

Zachery checked the ropes the way Antoine had shown him; not too tight, not too slack. "How long have you two been together?"

Not 'how long *were* you'. He knew better now.

"Fifty-three years, on and off."

"Yikes." *So you do use rejuvenation tech.*

"We were young when we met."

"I had it in my head that he'd had lots of boyfriends and fuck buddies before we left Earth."

"Oh, he did. Hundreds. I just happened to be the first."

"And the one who stuck around. Yeah, I can see that. Persistent Officer Prissyboots, always lurking in the background."

"That makes it sound devious. It wasn't. All of them knew about me. The arrangements we came to were usually very cordial."

"Yeah, I'm sure. But I've got a hunch that you are one jealous bitch. Whether you told him or not, I bet you used to dream of guillotining every last one of them."

There was a pause. "Not *every* last one."

Zachery finished applying the lube and slowly slid into Khurshed's sweat-slick body. "Are you jealous of us? Of Thomas? Rick? Echo? Me?"

"A bit."

"Shit. Should I be scared?"

"I'd certainly prefer it if you were. I like the thought of people living in fear of me. However, so far as your relationship with Khurshed goes... I want him to be happy. You make him happy. More often than I do, I suspect."

Again, Khurshed began to speak: "That's not..."

This time, it was Zachery who pinched his ear. "Mouth shut, old man. Ant, you got a gag?"

Antoine brought him a ball-gag. Zachery had never seen one before. The few times when he'd gagged Khurshed—or, on one occasion, Rick— before, it had always been to enhance the role play, and he'd used whatever clean clothing was on hand. This was the real deal; a perfect sphere of black rubber, sliding past Khurshed's teeth and into place without a lick of fuss.

"Hey, wait a minute. He actually won't be able to speak at all through this thing. What if...?"

"He moves his head from side to side if he wants us to stop. Don't worry. He's used to this."

Antoine watched in the manner of an art connoisseur as Zachery did what he did best. Now and then, he'd make an admiring noise—not a moan, not a sigh, just a small, satisfied murmur. It made a nice accompaniment to Khurshed's deep-throated groans being half stifled by the gag.

Being watched by Antoine was a weirdly intense experience. Even though he wasn't touching him, and hadn't touched him since he'd arrived, his unblinking stare made it feel as though he was as close to Zachery as Khurshed. Assailed on both sides by Khurshed's hot, responsive body and Antoine's scrutiny, Zachery quickly felt himself start to lose control.

Then, a moment before he started to peak, Antoine whispered right into his ear, "Stop."

Zachery stopped. He was ready; he could feel it, right on the edge. Even without another thrust, he could have finished himself up with a thought. He didn't. He hung there, frozen, wanting more than anything to pass the test and show Antoine that he *was* good enough, that he could control himself.

The seconds stretched. His body eased back down, his heart rate decelerating as the fire in his belly banked.

"Well done," Antoine purred, his breath warm on his ear. "You can keep going now."

Like flipping a switch, he was on again, plunging back into Khurshed as hard as he could. Then, thirty seconds later, right at the worst moment, Antoine said, "Stop."

The sadistic bastard did it *three more times*. Zachery came to expect it. When at last he started to peak and Antoine didn't interrupt him, it caught him completely off guard. The closest thing he could compare it to was his first wet dream, the shock of waking up to incredible pleasure without any idea of what was happening.

"Oh God," he groaned, slumping against Khurshed's back.

Antoine stroked the back of his neck. "Nicely done, Mister Halberstam."

Zachery was relieved to find that Khurshed had gotten off too somewhere along the line and regretted that he hadn't noticed it happening. Untying the ropes, he kept an arm around his waist to keep him from falling over, then picked him up, and took him over to the bed.

"How could you be so rude to our guest?" Khurshed scolded Antoine, after Zachery had taken out the ball-gag. "Throwing him into the deep end like that? I thought you were planning to leave the ropes for next time."

Handing him a glass of water, Antoine replied, "Khurshed, you gave me two requests. 'Make sure he enjoys himself' and 'Surprise me'. I think I achieved both goals quite successfully, *non*? Zachery, what do you think?"

"I think you're both fucking crazy," Zachery slurred, exhausted, before passing out.

When he woke up, the lavish hotel suite had vanished. He was lying on Antoine's bed, with Khurshed and Antoine lying on either side of him, flirting in French.

"Don't like that," he said, stretching. "Feels like you're plotting against me. One of you has to teach me your cheese-flavoured frog-talk if we're going to do this again."

"And you were worried *I* would offend *him*?" Antoine said to the captain in English.

Antoine was as pristine as ever, but Zachery and Khurshed both stank. Before they headed off to get cleaned up, Antoine looked Zachery in the eye and said to him, "Thank you for participating, Zachery. You were wonderful."

Goddamnit, he saw your naked, hairy ass fucking Khurshed's. Why the hell are you getting bashful now? "Um...thanks, Ant. That means a lot. Anytime you guys want me back, I'm up for it."

Antoine's hand came up, and for a second, Zachery thought he was going to get a slap. Instead, Antoine tucked a lock of his hair behind his ear. "Might you at some point in the future be interested in experiencing the ropes for yourself? I have a feeling that you'd take to it like a duck to water. And I don't think fucking is 'all you're good for'. I think you might have many hidden talents."

Zachery swallowed, blushing furiously. "M...maybe. I'll think about it."

He watched as Khurshed gave Antoine a strangely grave kiss, before the two of them headed to the showers and Antoine went off in the direction of his office.

"What did you think?" Khurshed asked him as he scrubbed his back.

"Tell me the truth; do you pick favourites? Is *he* your favourite?" said Zachery. "It's okay if he is. I won't throw a tantrum. Just tell me the truth. I saw the way you were looking at him, and you don't look at us like that."

Zachery hated it when people sugar-coated hard truths, so he was grateful that Khurshed didn't immediately dish out some sappy reassurance. Instead, he thought for a bit and then said, "You're all my favourites. That said, you are right in that I don't feel the same way towards Antoine as I do towards you. That doesn't mean I love him any more or less than you. I...I know that he knows me. He knows things about me that I don't know. Whereas you and I are still learning one another. It makes things different."

Zachery rested his head on Khurshed's shoulder. "You promise you're not going to get bored of us and go back to him?"

Turning and drawing him close, Khurshed murmured, "You need to understand this; I've been in love with many, many people. Not one of those relationships ended because I wanted it to. I don't fall out of love. I can't. If you want me, I'm yours until *you* get bored of me."

"I won't. I want to marry you someday. And Rick, and Thomas. Would you be cool with that?"

"I believe that is an excellent idea," said Rux.

He hung over the towel rack in his snake form and flicked his forked tongue in reaction to their frozen stares. "Did I misspeak? I apologise. I only wanted to offer my support for the engineer's plan and to wish that your union be blessed with many fat children. To clarify, so that you do not think me ignorant: that is an expression, originating in the language of my creators, intended to convey optimistic congratulations. I am aware that the biological nature of your species would prevent your having children without..."

"Rux," Khurshed interrupted, his tone silken, "don't you think you should leave?"

The snake looked as disappointed as its reptilian features allowed. "Now? I was hoping to offer myself to Zachery. I have had good sport with your other two mates. They have permitted me to be their friend. Now I would like to be Zachery's friend too."

"Let's put a pin in that for now," muttered Zachery, reaching for a towel. "I need to go talk to Rick about making beer. Got a feeling I'm going to be needing some. Catch you later, Cap."

"Come here, you," Khurshed said to Rux, gathering up his coils and carrying him back into the shower.

☆☆☆

Ten hours later, the last votes were in. Zachery stood with one hand on Thomas's shoulder and one hand on Rick's as the captain counted them.

"I hope we don't screw this up," Thomas sighed. He'd been the last to make his decision, and he'd looked fretful ever since. Zachery rubbed the back of his neck.

Khurshed looked up from the ballots and opened his mouth to speak when Antoine said urgently, "Captain, we're receiving a new message. It's from *them*."

After inspecting it, Rux said, "It is hard to convey its exact meaning in your primitive tongue. The general gist is 'You are welcome' and 'Good luck'."

"Smug assholes," hissed Zachery.

They waited a day to see if any more messages came through. When none did, Khurshed told them that in light of this new indication of their enemy's motives—inconclusive as it was—he was going to ask everyone to cast their votes again.

"Unanimous," he said the following morning, setting down the ballots. "We're staying."

CHAPTER SIX

Five days later, Rick stood back and surveyed his new greatest achievement—ten rows of newly sown barley.

"Bitchin'," he said to himself and then tilted his face up to the sky. "If you're spying on us, I've got a message for you. Thanks, and go fuck yourselves."

"Well said," said Khurshed, pulling off his gloves.

While Rick and the captain had spent the morning planting their grain, the rest of the crew had declared themselves on strike and had a picnic. Most of them were either lying on the grass soaking up the sun or playing poker with Antoine under a tree. Thomas was way off in the distance with Echo, giving him another shooting lesson. Zachery had shown Rux a picture of a horse and was now sitting atop his back as the alien galloped over the surrounding hills.

"You look bothered," Khurshed noted.

Rick struggled to find the words. "Captain, you know that shitty feeling you get when someone does something really, really awful to you, but what they did changes stuff so that eventually you end up *happier* than you were before they did the awful thing? I've got that feeling."

Khurshed came to stand behind Rick and rested his chin on his bare scalp. *Mmm, stubble,* thought Rick, shivering happily.

"Did I ever tell you about my scars?" the captain asked him.

"The burns? Well, Thomas thinks you got them rescuing puppies from a burning house. Zach thinks you were in the army and someone dropped a bomb on you. I think Antoine tried to set you on fire after you broke up the first time."

"Good guesses all. I'm afraid the truth is far more mundane. I was in a car accident when I was eighteen. Because I was driving my father's car when it happened—his very expensive car—he took the opportunity to disown me. He'd been looking for an excuse ever since he found out about my first boyfriend. So while I was in the hospital, he informed me that as far as he was concerned I was no longer a member of the family. I couldn't live under his roof, and I couldn't attend family gatherings. To soften the blow, he gave me a considerable sum of money, enough to pay for my moving to Paris and studying at the Sorbonne. If he hadn't set me adrift like that, I wouldn't have met Antoine. If I hadn't met Antoine, I wouldn't have realized how unsuited I was to an academic life. If I hadn't realized that, I wouldn't have eventually purchased *The Prayer* or met any of you."

"Okay, I see where you're going with this. What they did to us was still evil even if we're okay now."

The captain nodded. "I used to be haunted by the feeling that I owed my father something whenever I was happy. Please don't make the same mistake. If we're happy, we're not happy because of them. We're happy despite them."

Rick touched his lips and was going to kiss him when they were interrupted by the approaching sound of clopping hoofs.

"Tally-ho, my fine bitches," said Zachery, grinning down at them from atop Rux's back. "I was gonna offer you a ride, but if you're busy..."

Rick's eyes lit up. "Rux! Can you grow a horn?"

"Certainly, my small friend."

When Rux obliged, Rick squealed like a six-year-old and clambered up to sit in front of Zachery. "I'm going to ride a fucking unicorn!"

"Have fun, you two," said Khurshed, slapping Rux's hindquarters. He reared up and set off at a gallop, while Rick clung to his mane and thought, *Yes. This, I like.*

☆☆☆

With his hands clasped behind his back, Khurshed gazed at the soil in which their grain was nestled. When he was sure no one remained in earshot, he looked up at the sky and said quietly, "On the off chance that you *are* watching us, I've got a message for you too. I don't know anything about your species or your technology. What I do know is that this planet holds some value for you. It must do, otherwise you wouldn't have brought us here. I also know that my ship has an antimatter generator, and it would not be all *that* difficult for me to convert her into a very, very large bomb. So bear this in mind; if you do anything to hurt my crew ever again, I will destroy this place."

Behind him, someone clapped slowly. "Very impressive, *mon capitaine*. I'm sure our god-like overseers are intimidated by your threats."

"It makes me feel better," Khurshed replied tartly, folding his arms.

Antoine's familiar body pressed against his back. "Out of interest, why is Rux a unicorn?"

"A very good question. Do you know, when I first hired this crew I honestly thought they were all quite sensible people. Well, except for you, obviously."

Delicious pain spread over his scalp as Antoine tugged his hair. "You really are remarkably insolent. It's a trait you share with Zachery. I suppose that explains why I'm so fond of you both."

Wrapping Antoine in his arms, Khurshed rumbled, "Only 'fond'?"

"No." Antoine's palms framed his face. "More than fond. Much more than fond."

Trying to keep his tone free of all traces of hopefulness, Khurshed said, "The last time I proposed, you said that the reason we shouldn't marry was because I'm not suited to monogamy, and you didn't want to spend your life sharing me. Is there any chance your newfound attachment to Zachery has led you to reconsider that opinion?"

"Mmm...perhaps. I'll think about it," said Antoine with a smile that made him look all of twenty years old.

About the Author

T.J. Land is a South African writer of erotic romance and sometimes other things. She reads a lot of early modern plays and watches a lot of cartoons. She's going to marry Mrs Lovett when she grows up, although she doesn't expect that to happen for a while.

Also by T.J. Land

Bad Fairies: The Collection

Bad Fairies Series
Midsummer Nights
Midsummer Sky
Midsummer Court

NineStar Press, LLC

www.ninestarpress.com